P9-DCE-198

The South Will Rise at Noon

Douglas Glover

VIKING

VIKING

Published by the Penguin Group
Penguin Books Canada Ltd, 2801 John Street, Markham, Ontario,
Canada L3R 1B4
Penguin Books Ltd, 27 Wrights Lane, London W8 5TZ
Viking Penguin Inc., 40 West 23rd Street, New York, New York 10010, U.S.A.
Penguin Books Australia Ltd, Ringwood, Victoria, Australia
Penguin Books(N.Z.)Ltd, 182-190 Wairau Road, Auckland 10, New Zealand
Penguin Books Ltd, Registered Offices: Harmondsworth, Middlesex, England

First published by Penguin Books Canada Limited, 1988

Copyright© Douglas Glover, 1988

All rights reserved. Without limiting the rights under copyright reserved
above, no part of this publication may be reproduced, stored in or
introduced into a retrieval system, or transmitted in any form or by any
means (electronic, mechanical, photocopying, recording or otherwise),
without the prior written permission of both the copyright owner and the
above publisher of this book.

Printed in Canada

Canadian Cataloguing in Publication Data

Glover, Douglas H.
    The south will rise at noon

ISBN   0-670-81892-5

I. Title.

PS8563.L64S68 1988   C813'.54   C87-094835-0
PR9199.3.S55S68 1988

The South Will Rise at Noon is a work of fiction. All the characters
herein are imaginary and any resemblance to actual people, living or
dead, is strictly unintended.

Portions of *The South Will Rise at Noon* appeared originally, in
somewhat different form, in *The Pottersfield Portfolio* and *Books
in Canada.*

For Peggy

Books by Douglas Glover

The Mad River
Precious
Dog Attempts to Drown Man in Saskatoon
The South Will Rise at Noon

I am on the loose.

- T. Stamper

1

Looking back, I should have realized something was up as soon as I opened the bedroom door and found my wife asleep on top of the sheets with a strange man curled up like a foetus beside her. Right away I could see she was naked. And there are few women who can stand comparison with Lydia, naked or clothed. Lust took me by the throat the instant I caught sight of those familiar tan lines. Then a pang of jealousy. I always became jealous at the thought of Lydia sunbathing. The whole set-up was indecent—my wife half-nude, prone, oiled and glistening under a hot sun, wearing sun glasses for anonymity, a well-thumbed paperback on the blanket beside her for inspiration. The moment we were married, I had bought her a shoulder-to-ankle caftan to wear on the beach. She had laughed. A lyric note of contempt. When I opened the bedroom door, I had not seen Lydia in five years.

Her body had assumed a typical Lydia pose, which I can perhaps best describe as a languorous sprawl. Those impossibly long thoroughbred legs were flung wide apart, one knee delicately cocked. One hand lay like a relic against her tiny extruded belly-button, the other was thrown over her head, tangled and hidden in a fluffy mass of golden hair. Her mouth was open; I glimpsed her caps like snow in the morning twilight. Her breasts rose and fell soundlessly; the right one firm and erect, pointing at the ceiling; the left one larger, more maternal, toppling somewhat to the side. As I watched, her hand moved slightly in a dream and I saw the silvery thread of her Caesarean scar, almost invisible along her bikini line.

My trouble is that I don't give myself enough time to think. Before I could remember who and where I was with the sort of clarity that breeds circumspection—the sight of Lydia having about the same effect on me as Proust's tea-cakes on him—I had stripped down to my jockey shorts and was sitting on the edge of the bed. The man beside her snored gracelessly. I was moving with confidence because I figured he was making enough noise to drown out everything up to an eight-piece country band playing "Orange-Blossom Special" in the same room. Besides, Lydia had always been a sound sleeper. I once told her it was what she did best, something she had in common, I could have added, with *naïfs* and saints. Not that she didn't do other things well: tennis, sunbathing, Szechwan cooking, decorating the house, making love.

The truth was I had just been released from the county jail, where I had spent a month locked in a cell the size of a clothes closet with a cheerful black bit actor named Cato French who did isometric exercises on the floor, sang light opera to keep his spirits up, and otherwise made life well-nigh insupportable for me with a thousand and one tales of Hollywood trade gossip. All that time, he had worn nothing but a pair of bikini briefs with the words "SMART ASS" embroidered across the buttocks. I hadn't seen a woman, much less a wife, in four weeks, and the shock of finding Lydia, legs asplay, veeing like runway lights in a fog, drove every other thought from my mind.

The man beside her looked familiar but not instantly recognizable. The fact that I took so little notice of him is an indication of my utter bewilderment. He had coils of hair like Slinky toys sprouting from his shoulders. That was all I could see because of the blankets he had wrapped like a cocoon around his body. His snore sounded like a death-rattle. As I snuggled next to Lydia, I almost felt sorry for him. A man with hair coming out of his shoulders and a snore like that could take an awful beating from my wife. The woman had a tongue on her.

Pulling my shorts to my ankles, I had a brief crisis of conscience. It was an old debate, one Lydia and I had had often enough in the course of our marriage: Did sex with a sleeping wife count as rape? In sour moods, Lydia was apt to say yes. But since she slept so much and was so difficult to stir once she had dozed off, I had opted for calling it one of the conjugal rights. Sometimes, when I was being slick and glib, I would say that this quarrel, along with the caftan, my habit of calling her Stilts whenever I caught her sitting on the toilet, and my involvement in the lamp-stand business, constituted the seeds of our divorce. But of course that wasn't the whole truth. Most of the time she just loved me and let me have my way with her, awake or otherwise.

I must have been a little crazy. As I say, it was the first time I'd seen her since before the divorce, and how she came to be in my bed, with or without the hairy-shouldered snorer, I hadn't any idea. But I was just out of jail, and I'd had to walk eighteen miles from Bronson overnight, not to mention rescuing the dog, which, as I knelt between Lydia's thighs, triangulating the target area, was sniffing the doorjambs, licking its forepaw and glancing up at me as if I were God the Father Almighty.

A month in jail can change your perspective on things; a hike through a Florida swamp at night can make you see worlds you've never seen before. I had hallucinated over the last few miles. I had seen a shadow man hanging from a tree. I had heard gunfire and the voices of men at war. Walking into town in the dark, I had tripped over a railway track that had been torn up a hundred years before and stumbled against earthworks and cannon mounts. I had even dreamed of Lydia, a sweet, brief dream, a requiem for our marriage. And then there she was, naked and waiting, looking not a day older than when we parted.

It was about 6:30 A.M. Through the window above the bedstead, I could see the Gulf of Mexico and the pelicans clapping their bills together to get their circulation going as the sun began to rise behind the mangroves and cabbage-palms. Only I didn't really see them. My mind had slipped back five years to Iowa, to our Governor Street duplex with the apple-green stucco siding, smack between the African Methodist Church where the Reverend Claude Penney smoked ribs every Saturday afternoon and the world's smallest religious grotto in Bert Kingsly's backyard. I was there with Lydia, who was asleep as usual, on a Sunday morning, with Mrs Penney's fine upright piano tinkling hymns next door while the congregation rocked in accompaniment, the odor of smoked pig still floating in the air, mixing with the tang of linseed, fresh paint, canvas and primer.

I had just rolled onto Lydia for a morning go, parched with hangover. She had moaned a little, and her hips went slack so I could spread her legs. And it was just then, just as old Peter-George began to squeeze and inch his way into his favorite place, she would mutter my name in her sleep, "Tully. . .Tully. . .Tully—"

"Tully!" she screamed.

I had three thoughts all at once. First, my mother was behind Lydia's turning up like this—asleep in her birthday suit when my guard was down. Second, Danger Babcox would hear about it and I would be back to square one with her. Third, my ex-wife's new boy-friend hadn't figured out how to get it while she was asleep.

"Tully Stamper," she hissed, her teeth clenched as she flattened her palms against my ribs and tried to squirm out from under me.

"Lydia!" I said, attempting to carry off the situation with a show of surprise.

"Get off me, you ape!" she said. This was one of her pet names for me. No reflection, mind you. Actually, many

women have found me irresistibly attractive. Old biddies
from Michigan used to ask me if I did those cigarette
commercials. Good bones was the way Lydia herself
described it. Seedy but sexy was what Danger used to say.
Like one of those French poets gone to hell on opium,
absinthe and TB. Sometimes my wife called me gorilla.
She called my cock Peter-George, but that's another story.

By this time the man beside her was stirring. I say he was
stirring, though, in fact, before I could turn my head, he
had already leaped out of bed. He was naked, too. He had
an erection the size of a large frozen-orange-juice can, and
it was pointed at my head. His right hand gripped a
revolver, by the looks of it a .38, big enough to do the trick.
He was about five-five and all muscle, built like a set of
encyclopedias from the hips up, with legs that looked as if
they'd been transplanted from a goat. Neanderthal face,
bushy eyebrows, kinky black hair pushed back from his
forehead. He was simultaneously pointing the pistol at
Lydia's left breast and trying to open the ear-pieces of a
pair of thick-lensed, horn-rimmed glasses.

"Walter Hebel!" I said. It was my turn to be astonished
again. "Don't shoot, you asshole!"

I had thrown my arm across Lydia's chest, not out of
any particularly heroic impulse, but because I couldn't
stand the idea of all that beauty ravaged.

"Get off!" yelled Lydia, who didn't seem to understand
that I was protecting her. "Otto," she added, "it's only
Tully. Don't shoot!"

Otto? I thought. Was there then someone else in the
bed with us? I was confused. My mind stretched to its
capacity by this bizarre turn of events. I was still kneeling
between Lydia's marbled thighs, but Peter-George had
lost his initial rigidity. My member lay like a white mouse
in the nest of her crotch. Walter had put his glasses on
and was eyeing me up and down to confirm Lydia's
intelligence.

"What are you doing with Walter Hebel?" I asked. "How could you?"

I turned to Walter.

"This is my wife, you asshole!"

Walter swung. The cold metal of the gun barrel caught my nose. I spouted blood all over Lydia's breasts. The pelicans were taking off toward the fish houses in Back Bayou, their sluggish bodies nicking the oily Gulf as they fought for air speed. The dog was cowering in a corner. Lydia shrieked. I had time to think, "Walter, I'll get you for this." And then I fell over unconscious.

2

Welcome to Gomez Gap, Florida, site of the famous Civil War battle, armpit of the Panhandle: a live-oak and palm-lined village with big frame houses down to the water, a tiny community beach with rusty cannon at either end, tourists living in former slave quarters turned into chi-chi condominiums and motel efficiencies, poor white trash in nigger shacks and mobile homes on the outskirts.

My name is Tully Stamper. I am six feet three inches tall, a tippler of corn juice, also pretty well hung. At the time of which I write I was twenty-nine, divorced, lover of the mysterious Danger Babcox, a fisherman, tourist guide, amateur archaeologist, bird-watcher, dog-trainer, curio-shop owner, the town's eighteenth largest employer, taxidermist and proprietor of the finest lamp-stand factory in Iowa. This last was disputed by almost everyone, but chiefly by Colonel Willis Armitage Parkhurst, swindler. My attorneys had the matter well in hand, however, and I was in daily expectation of an upper-court decision involving the ownership of said factory. Also I do not mention my earlier involvement in the arts. I do not mention it, but, of course, Lydia did. I told you she had a tongue on her.

"Have you been painting?" she asked through the door as I quietly heaved up my empty stomach in the adjoining bathroom. There was blood everywhere. It looked like the scene of some sadistic sex murder. The dog, a pit bull I had found by the roadside, mewing like a kitten, up to his chin in swamp water and mud, had crawled after me on his belly and was worshipfully licking the backs of my heels as I lurched from sink to toilet and back again.

"Sure, I've been painting," I said, lying.

Normally, I am that rarest of creatures, a fairly honest man, but Lydia knew where to slip in the hot nails. I hadn't set brush to canvas since the day she announced she was pregnant. To tell the truth I was completely blind to the disappointment and hurt this caused her. For the first couple of months I had gone around saying I had a block. After I started the lamp-stand business, I stopped thinking about it. Later, she said the words, "Sweetheart, I just don't think this is going to work out," and I fled.

We were in the University of Iowa Hospital birthing room. A doctor named Birdsong crouched between her legs mumbling ju-ju words, doing a little rain dance to induce delivery. I was lying under a gurney with a face mask over my eyes. *Sweetheart, I just don't think this is going to work out.* Eleven little words—my wife's judgment on all my frantic efforts to deserve her love, the climax of a long saga of defeat and lost opportunities, the slow declension of my hopes (as my hopes declined, her tummy ballooned): painting, lamps, marriage. Something curled up inside me and expired. Spirit turned to stone. In Gomez Gap, I had started to forget.

"I'd love to see some of your things," she said, in a cheerful, offhand way that concealed an inarguable imperative. "You know, I have my own gallery in Los Angeles now. That's where we live."

I flushed the toilet and stifled a howl of rage.

In the next room, I could hear Walter shouting into the telephone.

"I don't give a shit, Bernie. I don't give a flying fuck! I'm on a tight clock. I gotta be in New York next week to start cutting, and you want two masters, a close-up and reaction on every shot? If I start covering myself like that, I'll be here to collect Social Security. You need a dose of Vitamin V, Bernie. You need to take a week off, fly down to Guaymas with your receptionist. Bernie! Bernie! Watch my lips —"

This didn't make sense to me, didn't sound like the Walter Hebel I remembered from college, the Walter Hebel who lived, terminally stoned, in the lower half of our Iowa City duplex (Lydia nicknamed him "the Troll" because he was always lying in wait for her at the bottom of the stairs) and wrote arcane, minutely detailed film reviews for the campus newspaper. He had been pale and puny then, always blinking behind those glasses as though he spent too much time underground or in darkened theaters and screening rooms. His adoration for Lydia was pitiful; five times a day he would climb the stairs just to hear her say, "Get out, Walter-Troll. You make me sick." Finding them together like this put thought to flight.

"Are you all right, dear?" she asked when I failed to respond to her arty chit-chat.

I glanced in the mirror. Eyes like new potatoes. Cheeks the color of smoked mullet. Nose like a plum with little tails of toilet paper hanging from my nostrils. Tears catching like raindrops in a month's growth of beard. Lydia, first love of my life, my grandest failure, tossing her hair in the next room, bringing it all back. Walter hadn't said a word, but I was sure he knew everything. I was too humiliated to speak.

Turning on the shower to cover my exit, I slid open the pebble-glass window above the toilet and eased myself headfirst into the azalea bush at the side of the house.

Once on my feet I was immediately torn with a conflict of desires. There was a bottle of George Dickel in the kitchen, but I would have to risk running into Walter or Lydia to get it. Dressed as I was in my underwear, there was little chance of slipping unnoticed downtown to my store, or the Gap Hotel for a drink. Public nudity is frowned upon in Gomez Gap, as elsewhere. Sheriff Audie Driscoll had already put me in jail on what I considered less of a pretext (destruction of municipal property—I had cut down a live-oak tree on Nigger Hill after the

Gomez Gap Historical Society put up a plaque commem-
orating the town's eight recorded lynchings, a mad,
drunken act for which I have paid the price). That left my
mother, Ina Stamper.

I should explain that, owing to a financial embarrassment, I was living with my mother at the time. There was
plenty of room as she had earlier inherited a sizeable
estate from Bert "Tex" Baxter, her third or fourth
husband (I forget which). My own father, just to keep the
record straight, Husband Number One, had disappeared
shortly after I was born, suffering what Ina called "a
congenital inability to face responsibility." I have been
told he was a great wit and a bottle man and that drinking
may have had something to do with his leaving. Each year,
on my birthday, he would send me a postcard of some
place he had visited. No message. Just a postmark.
Niagara Falls, Elkhart, Bismarck, Saskatoon, Santa Fe.
Once he mailed us a check for $500 which bounced. Ina
cried. "He has such a good heart," she said.

Bert Baxter had bequeathed her a gaudy, ante-bellum
sea captain's house, a boathouse and two cinder-block
guest cottages which she rented out when she was sober,
though most of the time she wasn't. Together the four
buildings squatted like a family of shore birds at the
water's edge, staring toward the ship channel and the
outer islands. Mine was the nearest of the cottages. So
when I stepped out of the azaleas, I found myself within
easy reach of Ina's patio door.

Shivering a little, for there was a wintry nip in the early-
morning air, I skipped down the alley between the two
buildings and turned left on the bulkhead that kept
everything from washing into the Gulf. Tide out. Oyster
bars glistening like piles of rubbish in the mud.
Cormorant posing on the wreck of the *Sara P.* Down the
way, a woman was sitting cross-legged on a pile of gill-net,
writing in a Big Chief notebook, keeping an eye on things

through a pair of binoculars the size of anti-aircraft guns. She caught sight of me as I slid open the patio door. Frowned. I gave her a little wave and shut the door behind me.

Ina was asleep with her mouth open, arms outstretched in her crucifixion pose, in a high, canopied bed with a purple velveteen headboard that matched the curtains, broadloom and wallpaper. Somewhere a radio was tuned low to a local Bible rock station. A half-empty bottle of Beefeater gin and a kiddy-capped container of Darvon, Dr Coyle's latest wonder drug, kept her company on the nightstand.

Tiptoeing to the closet, I pulled from its hanger the first thing that came to hand, a silky, feathery something that fell to my knees, and slipped into it for decency's sake. Then I found the radio, switched it off and switched on a lamp. It was one of my own, a genuine Stamper lamp, a replica of Rodin's Balzac with the socket coming out of his forehead.

Ina sighed. She seemed so peaceful and pleased with herself that I didn't have the heart to wake her just yet. Instead, I tipped up her glass in a potted plant and poured myself a tall gin-and-nothing and took two Darvon for pain. The first sip made my eyes water. When I opened them again, I decided she didn't look half bad for a woman with cancer. Of course, it was in remission, that was what Dr Coyle said, though a lot he knew.

It was still there, lurking in her cells like the Spartan's fox, ready to eat her from the inside. They had removed her breasts the year before; but then, at her clamorous insistence, had reconstructed a new set with silicon implants, bigger than the originals. The first time I saw them she was holding up her shirt in the Gap Hotel bar so that Wade Fowler could admire her new bouncing beauties. (My mother is always doing things like that, things to embarrass me.)

I waved the gin bottle under her nose finally to bring her around. Nothing does it for Ina like gin. She thinks alcohol is one of the food groups. Her eyes snapped open, and began to search for the source of that delicious aroma. They found me.

"Tully" she said, her voice like air caught in the plumbing. "What happened to your nose? Why are you dressed like that?"

"Don't try to change the subject," I said, popping another Darvon into my mouth, like a peanut. "My wife, who hasn't so much as sent me a postcard in half a decade, is asleep not twenty feet from where we sit. Why is that?"

"Ex," said Ina.

"Ex-wife."

"I should have thought there wasn't any question," she said. "She's still in love with you."

"She's with a man."

Ina picked at her blankets, trying to get her bearings. "I thought you were in jail," she said.

"Thirty days. I was in jail for thirty days!"

"Are you sure, darling? I thought it was years."

Ina peered into the bedroom gloom with an air of perplexity. A well-known, incurable evader, she suddenly feigned loss of interest in our conversation.

"Have you seen Wade?" she asked. "He hasn't left, has he?"

Wade Fowler, a painter of the bank-lobby and medical-waiting-room school, was Ina's latest infatuation. He had recently moved into the house next door as the guest of some wealthy Baltimore widow who couldn't leave her life-support apparatus long enough to make the trip to Gomez Gap herself.

"He's not here," I said. "But Lydia is and I'd like an explanation. If it's not too much trouble."

"Don't be silly, darling. It's not too much trouble. Tully, why are you dressed like that? Why, it's my old peignoir."

There were cigarette burns in the rose sateen and some

of the feathers had pulled away from the hem. I pulled
the lapels closed across my chest.

"I left my clothes with Lydia."

Ina glanced up sharply, a tiny flame of curiosity kin-
dling in her eyes.

"I thought you wouldn't mind, darling. You being in jail
and all."

"But I'm not in jail."

"Yes, I can see that. It's obvious, isn't it? You're walking
around in my underclothes trying to get arrested again."

"Why did they come here?" I persisted. "I mean Gomez
Gap of all places?"

"Otto is making a movie about the battle. Lydia came
along because she wanted to see you. She thinks five years
will have made a difference, that you'll be more sensible.
I moved your things into the boathouse."

The boathouse, I recalled, was full of factory inventory
shipped to me by Colonel Parkhurst in lieu of cash payment for my share of our common enterprise in Iowa.
There wasn't even enough room for the boat, which I
kept moored in Back Bayou by Earl Albert's fish-company
landing.

"All right," I said, "then give me the key to the other cottage."

"Oh, I've rented that too," she said, sniffing virtuously.
"I rented it to a young woman from New Jersey."

Her lips twisted into a tiny triumphant smile; she began
hunting for split ends, tugging her flattened curls to her
nose.

I felt depressed; the room was full of the stale-sheet
smell of plots and treason. Briefly I entertained an
impulse to go for her throat with the lamp cord. Every
judge has a mother; how many years could I get for mat-
ricide with extenuating circumstances?

I gulped the last of the gin and dropped a handful of
Darvon capsules into a pocket of the peignoir. Gin went
up my nose and made me sneeze. Infuriated, I remem-

bered the woman sitting on the bulkhead, the one who had spotted me skipping between houses in my under-shorts. I went to the French doors and peeped out, but she had disappeared. A great blue heron stood on the bulkhead next to the oyster cookery staring at me, looking like a snake with wings.

3

There were several mysteries to clear up. What movie? Who was Otto? Where was I going to sleep? What was Lydia doing with Walter Hebel? And how was I going to explain her sudden appearance to Danger Babcox? I was also calculating my chances with Lydia if I could get her alone in that cottage.

I tried to ask myself if I was really that troubled about Lydia and Walter, if it really affected me that much, and got no clear answer. There was too much bruised masculine pride obscuring the view.

I wandered down the hall from Ina's bedroom to the can. While I was taking a leak, she said, "You were always a strange child, Tully. I was always finding you with your head almost buried in the sand."

I let myself out the front door. I didn't relish the thought of passing through town in a pink pajama coat but as far as I knew I wouldn't be breaking any laws. I was just coming down the step when the lady from New Jersey emerged from her front door with a knapsack on her back. She scowled when I waved, and pretended not to notice.

Just then I heard the dog yelping next door. I had forgotten about him in my anxiety to escape Lydia and confront Ina. I walked across the lawn, carefully keeping the front of my peignoir closed. The yelping increased in volume. I knocked politely on my own front door.

Lydia opened. She was naked.

"Tully, where did you get to?"

"Never mind," I said. "I just came to get my dog."

17

Lydia had the giggles so badly she could hardly speak. This despite my attempt to impress her with a stern facial expression and voice tone.

"Someone opened the bathroom window," she said finally. "The dog. . .the dog tried to get out." She stifled a guffaw. "He fell in the toilet."

I stared at her impassively. Walter Hebel stood behind her with the dog in his arms. He was wearing his glasses and a pair of Bermuda shorts that looked like a Jackson Pollock action painting. I took the dog without a word. It was wet and it licked my face excitedly in a sort of welcome.

"Here's something else you forgot," said Lydia, slipping an envelope into the pocket of my peignoir.

"What is it?"

"Pictures of your daugher," she said. "Pictures of Ariel Stamper. She turned five in February. You'll die."

I must have seemed confused. I didn't recall any daughter offhand, though I remembered Lydia being pregnant and the birth scar on her tummy. (Perhaps I did remember but didn't want to admit this to myself, a desperate condition of mind brought on by night swamp-walking and a desire to deny that I was anything less than a charming and lovable human being.) But she didn't belabor the point. She was too happy to see me to make a fight.

"Don't you want your pants, too?" she asked, her eyes dancing.

I didn't want to admit to anything. I didn't want her to think I cared. So I played it cool and said, "What pants?"

Lydia grabbed her ribs in agony.

"Tully" she said, between sobs of laughter, "you haven't changed a bit."

4

Hearing my wife's clear laughter, seeing her naked in the doorway with Walter's hairy hand crawling over her shoulder, I had an attack of queasiness. Call it a sign, a portent, an omen, a foreboding. This was one of those moments, I told myself, when the past and the future arrive together with a smash, and life begins to compress around you like an accordion bellows.

Yes, this was the beginning of something, I thought, feeling displaced and weary. I recalled the day of my arrest, when I had stood on the bulkhead, watching a sand shark some fishermen had nailed to a plank by its snout and used for target practice, lolling its tail sadly in a gently swell. I had had a similar sensation then, that things were going to get worse, and they did.

But if you believe the lies they have printed about me in the newspapers or the stories told after liquor has broken down the native obstinacy of speech in a Gomez Gap bar, then you are badly misinformed. I have it on good authority that Ted Maberly claims to know where my body rests and has offered to lead more than one curious band of tourists from the North to view my sunbleached bones. Let me say here, once and for all, that that is some other person. I *am* alive. Old Tomahawk Tully, old Nighttrain Stamper lives. I am on the loose.

At that moment, however, as I turned from the cottage and fled into the street—two rows of frowsy brick bungalows, the color of dried blood, with glassed-in Florida rooms, turkey cat and peach blossom at the sides, dog crap and bone holes dotting the mangy yards, road dust

coating parked cars, trees and palmettos—I felt contrast-
ing emotions stampede through my mind: hatred,
reluctant admiration, fear and embarrassment. I was
suddenly irritated beyond words with Lydia, adjusting
myself once more to the probability that she lacked
certain virtues which in blindness and early passion I had
formerly awarded her.

I hadn't gone far before I noticed how heavy the dog
was. It seemed pretty silly to be walking the oak-lined back
streets of Gomez Gap in a pink pajama coat with a bull-
dog in my arms, so I put the dog down. Immediately, his
rear legs gave out and he sat on the pavement.

"Walk," I said. "There's nothing wrong with you. You
can walk if you believe you can."

The dog whimpered and gave me a look. I had seen
that look before, my own sad face in a mirror just before I
lit out. I say "lit out" although Lydia swore before a judge
that I had suffered a nervous breakdown due to the per-
nicious influence of drugs and alcohol and my inability to
paint pictures. (In my opinion, I didn't take enough
drugs. And it wasn't because of the painting; I left
because I was terrified she was going to leave me.
Sweetheart, I just don't think this is going to work out.)

On the testimony of others, I know that I ended up in a
Cajun jail in the Mississippi Delta country, strung out on
chemicals and delirious. A local cop called Lydia. "Mrs.
Tully Stamper?" he asked in dialect. "Mizzz Staympuh?"
"Yes," she said, calm but fearing the worst. "The waf o'
one Tully Staympuh, Ioway Cita, Ioway?" "Yes," she said.
"Where is he? Is Tully all right?" "We got 'im, sho nuff.
He's in jayell." "Oh God! Is he hurt? Is he all right? What
has he done?" "Wayell, m'am, I don't rahtly know what he
done. But he's nakid and he thinks he's a bird."

To give Lydia her due, she came straight down to
Louisiana and rescued me. The only way she would spring
me was to have me bound over for observation at the

nearest loony-bin. So we spent a month together at a place called Elysium Inc. on the outskirts of Baton Rouge. A month was enough. At the end of a month, I escaped in the company of an ex-hooker who thought she was Teresa of Avila. I suppose that Lydia went back to Iowa. After that, the only news I had came via her attorney.

"Walk, damn it!" I said to the dog.

I could tell the neighbors were watching. A man has to preserve face in a Southern town; he doesn't let his dog get the better of him. So I gave him a kick, just a tap in the ribs really, for the sake of my image. But the dog fell over as though dead.

A car braked to a halt behind me, scattering gravel over my bare feet. It was Sheriff Audie Driscoll in her supercharged Plymouth. (Her real name was Audrey, but Audie looked better on arrest forms and official documents.) Audie was forty-eight years old and six feet if she was an inch. She had a nose like a beak and wore a patch over her left eye, which was blind and wandered and, so she thought, ruined her looks.

There were two shotguns on a rack behind her head, a .44 Magnum balanced on the dash, and handcuffs dangling from the rearview mirror. She was tapping a riot stick lightly against the chrome sidestrip through the open driver's window. In a cage in the back seat, a German shepherd named Vince, her constant companion, slavered in an unhealthy fashion against the glass.

The whole thing with the dog was turning into a major incident. I contemplated leaving it there in the road, pretending I had never seen it before. But I have always had a soft spot for the waifs and losers of this world. I am always seeing something of myself in their misery. And, as I say, I remembered that look. So I knelt, first tucking the peignoir carefully between my knees, and picked up the dog again.

Audie beckoned me closer with a flick of her riot stick.

Her good eye betrayed a malicious gleam.

"I might have known it was you," she said, with an air of triumph. "I had a call about an intruder."

"Who called?" I asked, glancing in the direction of my former home. Lydia had disappeared, but Walter still stood there in his shorts.

"You got a license for that canine?" Audie asked. "A pit dog, ain't it? I don't see no collar."

"Did that son of a bitch call you?" I asked, nodding at Walter.

In the opinion of most Gomez Gap taxpayers, an opinion I failed to share, Audie Driscoll was an ideal law-enforcement officer. She protected the town drug-smugglers and arrested only tourists, blacks and me. The previous sheriff had had the gall to pull a local boy for drunk driving one night only to find that the town council had met and fired him while he was transporting his prisoner to the county jail. Audie was a gun collector and a Christian. She also had a son named Bubba who had once been married to Danger Babcox, for a year and a half, about the time I came down from the North.

"I believe there was some mention of indecent exposure and possible lewd conduct if not attempted rape," said Audie, feigning a look of mild surprise.

Our conversation had not lasted more than two minutes, had indeed just reached the stage where I was beginning to look about for witnesses to police brutality, when Lydia came jogging toward us, clad, finally, in expensive running shoes, garish knee socks, shorts and a sailor shirt.

"It's all right, Sheriff," she said, with an expression of wide-eyed jocularity. Breathless, she was the picture of health, with those gleaming teeth and that agitated chest.

The truth is I have always been attracted to women who hold out the promise of what I would like best to find in myself. In Lydia I had discovered a particularly American grace and sang-froid, a coolness and cleanliness of both body and spirit, a certain order and self-control which, indeed, is the ideal toward which every toothpaste commercial aspires. Just as in Danger I had found an opposite virtue in her heat and passion and her willingness to throw herself willy-nilly into things, to abandon her self-possession.

"It was an honest mistake," Lydia continued, smiling at the sheriff. "Mr Stamper was unaware that his home had been rented out. He walked in on us thinking the place was empty."

"Mr Osterwalder called me himself," said Audie. "He seemed irate. We don't want anything to throw off his shooting schedule. We feel Gomez Gap would be an ideal location for other films and we would like to make a good impression."

"I believe Otto may have been having a little fun with you, Sheriff—at Mr Stamper's expense. I'm sure you understand," said Lydia, somewhat mocking Audie's drawl. Her eyes caught mine and held them an instant, sharing the joke.

"I understand, ma'am," said Audie in as courteous a tone as I had heard escape her lips.

"I believe Mr Osterwalder and I are of the same mind," she went on, not looking at anything in particular with her glassy good eye. "Tully has as good a sense of humor as the next fellow. Haven't you, Tully?"

She jabbed me in the ribs with her riot stick,

"Am I free to go?" I asked, recoiling from that stick and starting to turn.

"I'm sure the sheriff will be happy to give you a lift," said my former wife, smiling again. Audie looked like a snake; I gasped with alarm. "Your son looked wonderful in the rushes yesterday," Lydia added, incomprehensibly. "You must be very proud of him, Mrs Driscoll."

This time she winked at me, forming a conspiracy of

two as she had often done when we were falling in love. Often, as now, I hadn't the slightest idea what we were conspiring over.

"I'd be happy to," said the sheriff, flashing her gray teeth at me. "Why don't you hop in, Tully?"

"There, that's all set," said Lydia, jogging backward. "I have to be running. Otto stayed behind this morning to block a scene before we start shooting. Nice to see you, Sheriff. Say hello to Bubba."

"Get in," said Audie, shifting her stick.

"I'll walk," I said. "Am I free to go?"

"You'll see. Get in. Leave that outside," she snarled, as I attempted to enter through the passenger door while still holding the dog.

Vince was in the throes of a barking fit. His multiple lunges had caused a bulge in the wire mesh of his cage. Audie banged the cage with her riot stick.

"Shut up!" she yelled. "I can't stand that noise. Shut up, Vince!"

"I'll walk," I said, stepping back from the door and placing the dog on the ground so I'd be free to run if I had to.

"It was a mistake to come back, Stamper," said Audie, glancing over her shoulder to be sure Lydia was out of earshot. "I thought you'd be long gone."

She switched on her roof lights, hooted her siren for five seconds to give me a fright, and then screeched away down the street with a satisfied smile on her lips, leaving a quarter-inch of tire rubber on the pavement.

5

Walking through Gomez Gap in broad daylight proved more shocking than it had in the dark. The dog and I trudged past sandbagged redoubts, earth-filled wicker-work barricades, and palisades of sharpened stakes with neatly shoveled fire-steps, which earlier I had taken for the products of sleep deprivation and a youth spent abusing controlled substances. On Barksdale's Meadow (recently rezoned for condominiums) a dozen Sibley tents sprouted like rings of mushrooms around smoky cooking fires and tepees of antiquated rifles. Strings of mules cropped hay out in the open, swatting flies with their tails, patiently waiting for someone to harness them to a convoy of covered wagons that stood nearby.

My astonishment grew as I marched down Water Street. All the tea-cozy antique shops, art galleries, craft boutiques and real-estate agencies, which had once been captains' houses, ship chandlers, grog shops, gambling joints and bordellos, had been changed back into captains' houses, ship chandlers, grog shops, gambling joints and bordellos. A narrow-gauge railway ran out to the municipal pier where the fish restaurants had been disguised as warehouses. A steam-engine with a cow-catcher big enough to shift elephants leaked wisps of blue smoke in front of the Gap Hotel. Across the street the sign over Bethamae Hamsett's Island Art Co-op had been repainted to read: Hamsett & Co., Dealers in Slaves.

My store came in sight. Shingles off the roof. Cracked pane in the side window. Three planks missing at the front step like a hockey player's teeth. Paint peeling off the sign under the eaves:

TULLY'S FOLLY

Hardware, Stationery, Arts & Crafts
Toys, Gifts, Health Appliances
Pets, Taxidermy
Bicycles for Rent
Gomez Gap's Finest Selection
Imported Designer Lamp Stands

I knocked on the door and Oliver Kinch, my clerk, let me in.

"Hello, Kinch."

"Tully! Where'd you drop from?"

"Jail, Kinch," I said. "I've been in jail for a month. Not likely you noticed, is it? Get out of those pants."

"But, Tully—"

"They're only loaners, Kinch. I want them back. Emergency."

They were a nice pair of pants, too. Sailcloth with button flies. Cut off at the knees. A bit baggy in the seat. And Kinch had been using one of my trick ties for a belt. While he was taking them off, I walked over to the men's department and picked out a parrot-green bowling shirt and a pair of Korean-made black hightops. Somewhat toned down from my usual outfit, but dashing enough in a pinch.

I gave Kinch the peignoir.

"But, Tully—"

"I'm going to need the painting for a couple of days," I said, frowning as I glanced out the window and noticed the dog sniffing at the gap in the planks. "How's it coming along?"

Kinch's eyes teared up; he waved his hand as though brushing a fly away.

He was in his usual state of rack and ruin. Skin like wax paper. Nose like a sponge. All 243 hairs white as slush and driven down on his pink scalp like wheat after a summer storm. His hands shook so badly I could have hooked him up to a generator and made electricity.

He was an artist in transition, at least that was his excuse. As far as I could tell, he had been transiting modern art for years without completing so much as a sketch. No one knew where he came from. He had shown up one summer to enter a painting in the annual arts festival and never left. The painting (since lost) was called "Portrait of the Artist as a Young Chicken." I was on the run from Elysium when we met; Kinch was washing dishes at the Shrimp-Pot, a restaurant on the pier, and watering his brains with California sherry. He had welcomed me with the words, "Ah, a new Odysseus come to visit in the lands of the shades."

As time went on I had fixed him up with a bed at the back of the store, in a room which eventually doubled as my taxidermy shop, and borrowed a largish second-hand canvas from Bethamae Hamsett for him to work on. I say "borrowed" because we never got around to paying for it and "second-hand" because, when I first brought it into the store, it was covered with Bethamae's masterpiece, a panoramic view of Admiral Farragut's blue-uniformed marines storming ashore during the Battle of Gomez Gap, which we scraped off. Kinch kept it by his bed, dabbing away when he felt in the mood. Every couple of months he would paint it white and start over again.

Anxious to see if by chance I had become a millionaire in the past thirty days, I started totting up the figures in the ledger we kept on a shelf beneath the cash register. (Kinch's face turned suddenly wary and hunted.) But the accounts were a mess. My clerk had no head for figures. (He claimed to have been a math whiz.) Sometimes he forgot to make entries; sometimes he invented them

when he found he had too much or too little money at
the end of the day. He rarely charged the same amount
for an article twice running.

At the same time he was a sucker for all the retirees
who crocheted, built birdhouses or glued seashells on
tack board. He could not say no when they begged him to
take their stuff on consignment. Next thing you knew
they would be hanging around the store criticizing my
displays, harassing my customers, looking sad when
nothing sold. I would end up slipping them ten bucks to
make them feel useful and burning the merchandise in
the stove.

Still, I was glad to have the place. My trouble is that I
think big. I owned a boathouseful of lamps, and I had a
vision of a genuine Stamper lamp heading north in the
back seat of every car with a Michigan, Ontario or New
York license plate. Kinch's problem was snobbery; he just
didn't believe in the lamps. They insulted his abstract-
expressionist aesthetic. I was always finding them hidden
behind the seashell tack boards and birdhouses.

I was about to say something, for I could see from the
ledger that he had not sold a single lamp, when there
were a thump and a yelp outside. Kinch's eyes went up
like little birds. I ran to the door to see what was what and
found that the dog had fallen through the hole in the
planks and was sitting on the dirt with his head poking up
like a periscope.

"I see you've been burning up the porch again," I said,
giving my clerk a mean look. I hefted the dog by the
scruff of his neck and brought him inside where I could
keep an eye on him.

"I was c-c-c-cold, Tully," he said, wrapping the peignoir
closer about his chest, giving his imitation of a man going
down with hypothermia.

It was always the same story. He was an ideal employee
in that he couldn't keep track of his pay and lived on the

premises, only leaving now and then to spend an hour at the Gap Hotel, where Danger worked behind the bar and served him with a straw because of his shakes. But Kinch loved a fire. And when it got chilly in the store, as it often did in the winter, he would panic and throw anything he could lay his hands on into the wood stove and set it alight.

I don't doubt he harbored a streak of pyromania. If it didn't move, Kinch would burn it: packing crates, cardboard boxes, goods off the shelves, sticks of furniture. I had had to do a lot of patching to keep up with him. Over the years, I calculated, he must have burned a quarter of the original building.

"What's all this about a movie?" I asked, not wanting him to feel too badly about the porch. I already had a plan to take up the floorboards under his bed to fix the hole. As his landlord, after all, I did have a responsibility to keep him supplied with fuel.

"Movie?" he echoed, sounding like one of those trained birds. He wasn't paying attention to me; he was staring at the dog, which had seized the peignoir's feather trim in his teeth. "What kind of dog is this?"

"Pit bull."

"Is it vicious?"

"Never mind that. Gomez Gap's been turned upside down; I don't have a place to live; my wife and another man have taken over my bedroom; it's got something to do with some damn movie or other and you want to talk bloodlines!"

Kinch fingered his chin fuzz and said nothing. He was squinting out the window, his eyes like little blue wedges.

A troop of Confederate soldiers suddenly hove into view just outside my store, twenty of them, in red artillerymen's breeches and shoulder rolls, with two teams of horses hitched to Napoleon howitzers and caissons. They marched in neat columns led by a mounted officer in a long gray uniform coat, gauntlets and a Stetson with a feather in it. The officer was carrying a staff with a Florida flag flapping at the tip, not the current version, the Rebel one—white satin bound with blue fringe, with seven stripes of blue and red, a pale blue circle, three stars for South Carolina, Mississippi and Florida over twelve smaller stars, and the motto THE RIGHTS OF THE SOUTH AT ALL HAZARDS.

It was a tremendous sight in the morning sunlight. For a moment I was stunned, put under a spell of awe by the beauty and incongruity of it.

Before I could stop him, Kinch dashed to the door, screaming, "Racists! Slavers!" at the top of his lungs.

"Kinch!" I yelled.

He slammed the door shut, threw the deadbolt, then leaned against the panels, quaking, his shoulders hunched as if he expected lightning to strike. The column continued marching as though nothing had happened.

"What's got into you?" I snapped.

"It's that Kraut director," he breathed, suddenly indignant. "The fucking hypocrite."

"Otto?" I asked, a shot in the dark. Somehow, from the little Ina had told me, I knew I wouldn't like him.

"That's him. Otto Osterwalder, the director. He prances up and down ranting 'the South this' and 'the South that.' As soon as anybody says 'the South,' you know it's a pack of lies."

I had heard the name. You couldn't miss it if you read the entertainment pages, although his movies never showed outside the New York art houses. You know the sort of crap they write:

> Osterwalder's rigorous psychological realism is combined with a style that is baroque and operatic—naturalism and neo-realism have no attraction for this child of the cinema out of

Dada. In form, his films are invariably corrosive melodramas. But their pessimism is tempered by the delight Osterwalder takes in making them. They are technical funhouses, cinematic carnivals. In *Heroin Roulette*, the camera is the major character, an elegantly prying investigator that pins the cast to the Lucite walls.

He was the new Fassbinder, wunderkind of the eighties, the crest of a fresh wave of auteur filmmakers. A shadowy figure, he had won the Best Director award at Cannes the year before for a film set in New Guinea. Five head-hunters had been killed and the Australian army called in to quell a war he had started for the sake of realistic effect.

"Some wise ass in Hollywood signed Osterwalder to do a Civil War epic," said Kinch, his voice oozing scorn. "It's nothing but a lousy public-relations gimmick. They hired a Russian cameraman, Italian make-up people, and a Frenchman named Leotard, for Christ's sake, to play the dashing blockade runner—Tully, you can't imagine what a reproach this is to a real Southerner!"

"I'll bet everybody's just ready to eat their hands," I said. "Bethamae on the warpath, the Historical Society up in arms, the boys down at the Gap Hotel shouting 'Sacrilege!' between drinks."

Kinch gulped and blinked.

"That's the worst of it. Everybody's lapping it up. Everybody's a Johnny Reb. The drug-smugglers all think they're Rhett Butler. When somebody starts a fist fight outside the Gap, they call it a duel. The whole town is film crazy."

6

"What's this?" asked Kinch, seemingly innocent.

Twenty minutes had passed. I had just finished shaving and was rinsing my face in my taxidermy sink. Kinch had recovered from his fit of pique over movies, slavery, the Civil War, history and various failures of the American psyche.

Lydia's envelope dangled like a threat between his thumb and forefinger.

I had a moment of panic. Something struck, without preamble or warning, then disappeared into the murky depths of my unconscious, leaving me with the sudden conviction that some subjects by nature are too delicate to be approached in broad daylight, or any other time, without the comfort of heavy sedation.

Waving him off, I skipped out the door. Kinch had his moments of frightening lucidity and you could never tell when one might strike.

"Get yourself something fit to wear in public," I called over my shoulder. "And feed that dog."

The sun burned high above the rooftops, beating the pavement with knuckles of white. Palm trees nodded their fluffy heads like sleeping symphony conductors. I took a deep breath. The smell of freedom and rotting fish. Without a beard, I felt like a new man. Digging in Kinch's trouser pockets, I found a five-dollar bill folded in a neat, tight square. My heart gave a jump of joy.

As yet there were no tourists on the prowl and the Civil War had marched out of sight behind the old fiber factory at the edge of town. A half-dozen pick-up trucks nosed at the Shrimp-Pot like hogs at a trough as their owners guzzled Rita Braver's coffee inside and passed around the local gossip. Bubba Driscoll's Bronco was there, Audie's pride and joy no doubt amusing the boys with lies about my latest misadventures.

I was all aflutter with the thought of Lydia sleeping in my bed. I didn't understand it, but I believed in it. She was here all right. The sight of all that beauty had done wonders for my spirit. I felt tip-top. I was puzzled about Walter Hebel, but not jealous. I could see what had happened. After sticking by me through college, insanity and divorce, Lydia had been fed up with oddballs and malcontents. There is no doubt about it—a failed artist is the worst kind of family. Walter had been familiar, a convenient shoulder to cry on. He had a small trust fund left him by a dead aunt. Even before I lit out, that Troll-thing had gotten to be a joke between them. Many women prefer mute adoration to love on a roller-coaster.

Thinking about Lydia flushed hormones into my bloodstream, and Peter-George began to raise the sailcoth of my trousers like a jib in a wind. But thinking of Lydia also made me thing of Danger Babcox, chain-smoking those long black cigarettes called More, sipping Jose Cuervo behind the bar at the Gap Hotel, sweating and complaining about her fallen arches as she poured the booze and did her Southern-redneck routine for the tourists. I was in love with Danger; but I was still in love with my wife.

I was torn between doubling back to the cottage to talk with Lydia and heading out to Danger's house on Kiss-Me-Quick Creek by the Back Bayou. I also had it in mind to go up against the lady from New Jersey and evict her if sweet reason didn't convince her of the advisability of seeking accommodation elsewhere. Then I recalled that Danger had lately acquired the habit of joining the boys for their morning coffee at the Shrimp-Pot, the boys being what interested Danger most in Gomez Gap, or any other place for that matter.

In two minutes I was pushing through the screen door and climbing the stairs to the big tourist dining-room overlooking the Gulf and the outer keys. Up the steps I passed echelons of art pieces, mostly bas-reliefs carved out of native cedar, representing proud moments in the town's history: discovery by Juan Alpaca Gomez, the slaughter of the Indians, the internment of Southern slaves during the Civil War, a lynching, the burning of a crew of Greek spongers in the municipal jail, which had not yet been rebuilt. Rita's tables and chairs were still stacked; the coffee drinkers ranged along the counter on stools, exposing patches of white ass above their low-slung jeans as they bent over their cups.

They all had their backs to me, but right away I picked out Danger's suede jacket, the elbow cocked, and one of those cigarettes smoldering between her fingers, as she blew on her coffee. I was in luck, for there was a seat vacant just by her left hip. I sniffed my armpits and slid into the seat like a ghost, racking my brains for a snappy opening.

I nodded to our nearest neighbors, both Gomez Gap luminaries. On my left, sprouting a crop of stiff white hairs from his ears, lounged Roy Maberly, a Driscoll by marriage and the smartest and steadiest of the garbage-collecting Maberly brothers. Roy enjoyed a local reputation as a wit because of his joke: "How's business, Roy?" "Oh, picking up, Tully, picking up."

On Danger's right I recognized the corpulent nose and fingers of Wheezy Wentzel, a cousin of the Driscoll clan, the only man ever to survive being run over by a Sherman tank. This happened outside a Frankfurt *Gusthuus* during the Czech crisis of 1968. Wheezy had a Purple Heart and a pension, and, though he never spoke above a whisper, firmly believed that tank accident was the luckiest thing that ever happened to him.

"'Lo, Wheezy. 'Lo, Roy, 'Lo, Danger," I said agreeably, noting an atmosphere of crude antagonism apparently directed at yours truly. "Here we are again."

I cocked my hand at the coffee urn and winked at Rita for service.

"So you're out," said the love of my life. "I thought they'd throw away the key."

"Always the joker," I said. "You don't get life for a little pruning. That tree was a public menace. Dead branches ready to drop any time and strike innocent pedestrians. The judge was on my side. In my summation I was magnificent. I pleaded our common humanity."

"That's not what Audie said. She said you got down on your knees in front of the bench and said you had a sick mother to support instead of a sick mother supporting you."

"That's a lie," I said brusquely. "Need I mention that Sheriff Driscoll is hardly an objective witness?"

Smiling to herself, Danger swirled the dregs of her coffee in her cup. Underneath her jacket, she was clad in black with a slim gold chain at her throat. Her breasts, which she let run wild inside her shirt, had small, dark nipples like acorn caps that pushed against the cloth as she moved.

Crossing her lips at an oblique angle there was a tiny silver scar. We had talked about it. "How did you get that scar?" "Never mind." "It's no big deal. I'm not trying to pry. I merely wanted to know how you got that scar. Childhood accident?" "Never mind." "None of my business, right? I'll just step into the street and throw myself under the first car—" "Asshole." That sort of thing. She looked so good sitting next to me that only the presence of Rita Braver and ten other people in the room kept me from springing on her.

"I'm moving back with Bubba," she said, pointing her

breasts at me. A little voice against the grain, breaking a little at the edges in the manner of a country-and-western lament.

"You're a fine man, Tully, in your way. Why I want to live like a redneck without being one, I'll never know. But I don't want some flashy-dressing, tree-cutting, mother-fucking, lying-about-his-wife-and-kid son of a bitch messing up my life. I have to think about my two little girls."

Fair enough, I thought, blowing on my coffee, but how did she really feel?

"You don't love Bubba," I said. "He can't even read his name without moving his lips. How could you live with a man like that?"

She had told me all about his lava lamps, his shag-rug walls, tiki gods, photographs of Elvis at Graceland and the dish antenna for pulling in Christian TV stations; about the endless family picnics when they fed on fried mullet and gray, greasy boiled swamp cabbage, about his brother with the leg brace and several missing parts and his dropsical grandmother who was forever refusing to get out of the car because Bubba had driven too fast.

"You said your wife was dead—in a freak accident," said Danger, projecting her voice, playing to the gallery. I sensed our conversation had become the center of attention for the whole restaurant. She had a wicked glint in her eyes.

"You said she burned to death under a tanker truck in a Burger King parking-lot while she was still carrying your first child."

My heart leaped into my throat. I gave her a look that was positively Chinese and said, "I may have said something like that."

Danger's first husband, Willie Weber, a Vietnam vet who could quote the existentialists by the hour, had ridden an old warhorse DC-3 plugged full of Colombia Gold into the Gulf one night and disappeared forever. In my own mind, we had both come to Gomez Gap for the same reason—to escape the memory of disaster—though I had been somewhat vague in reporting what had happened to me.

"She's made a remarkable recovery," said Danger.

"Perhaps I meant it figuratively."

"Bullshit, Tully," she said, laughing aloud. "You tried to con me. You'd say anything once you got your tongue flapping. The truth ain't nothing to you but an excuse to make up another bizarre story."

Danger's laughter left me with a profound feeling of transiency. Each of her words was like a nail in the lid of a coffin of might-have-beens. I mentally cursed Lydia, Walter, Ina, Kinch: I felt a paranoiac's certainty of conspiracy, that a cunning reality was always running ahead of me laying ambushes.

I felt a nudge at my elbow. I brushed it aside. I had my mouth open, though I don't know what I was going to say, working more by likes and dislikes than by mere thoughts at that moment. Suddenly a hand reached over my shoulder and grasped the lapels of my bowling shirt. My eyes reluctantly left Danger and began to trace the arm to its source. Before I got past the elbow, I was on my ass on the floor, looking up as Audie Driscoll's son, Bubba, settled the twin soccer balls of his butt onto my stool.

He was about the size of a small hill, with wispy blond hair, red face, watery blue eyes, and a neck that was thicker than his head. He was wearing movie clothes, a Confederate uniform of butternut homespun, a Stetson, and a long cavalry pistol at his belt.

I had a chair in my fist before you could say West Palm Beach. I could have killed him with a blow, splitting his skull like a ripe peach. But everyone, except Danger and Bubba, had turned to stare, and I knew they would all plead against me in court. So I put the chair back and edged down the counter to a vacant seat by the window.

As I did so, I became aware of certain anomalies, clues and signs. Instead of rubber boots spattered with fish guts, sweat-stained tractor caps with bent-back visors and threadbare khaki pants with their underwear hanging out, the good old boys were wearing Foster Grants, pressed jeans and clean workshirts with string ties. Pig Morton's glasses still had their price-tag dangling by his ear. Wheezy, Roy and Bubba all exuded a cloud of cologne, an aura of recent bathing. Aspiring Paul Newmans and Robert Redfords, they were waiting to be discovered.

Bubba Driscoll shifted his buttocks in that uniform, too tight by the looks of it, the seams constricting his balls, tying knots around them.

Sean Connery had been an Edinburgh milkman before 007.

Give them half a chance, I thought, and they'd have eight-by-ten glossies, agents and answering services.

Kinch was right. The whole town was film crazy.

7

My new neighbor at the window-seat wore madras Bermuda shorts, knee socks, Puma court shoes and a Lacoste golf shirt. His head was bare as an egg except for three impossibly long strands of hair which he had trained to zigzag across the Gobi Desert of his baldness.

This was Julius Wachtel, Harvard graduate in social philosophy turned agent in the President's War on Drugs. Julius was a narc, a pigeon, a betrayer of his fellows, a man to be avoided at all costs. In Gomez Gap you didn't want to be seen holding forth with him. He was a Judas of a Julius.

"Hello, Tully," he said, showing a mouth full of teeth. Julius had the sort of smile that made babies wail for their mothers. His eyes shifted uneasily in their watery sockets. Out of habit, I ignored him, sipping my coffee like a man taking Communion wine.

I couldn't take my eyes off Danger at the other end of the counter. Blue smoke hung like ivy from her nostrils. She was a negative to Lydia's positive. Lydia was fair; Danger was dark. Lydia had never smoked; Danger's hands and teeth were perpetually nicotine-stained. Lydia radiated health and good humor; Danger was always nervous and irritable—she made a romance of self-destruction. Danger was wearing Foster Grants the same as everyone else in the Shrimp-Pot that morning. But she always wore them. She read too much, wrote poetry at night and suffered from insomnia. Her eyes were always afire and always hidden.

"Got anything for me?" asked Julius, insistently. His

voice boomed off the bas-reliefs and coffee urn. This was Julius's personal brand of character assassination; he implicated everyone he came in contact with.

I considered not replying, but my feelings had just taken a beating, my self-esteem had been bludgeoned. (Not to mention the fact that all that Darvon had dulled my natural survival instinct.) Julius had offered friendship when no one else would; he had spoken kind words when others scorned me. I was suddenly filled with warmth toward this unlikely G-man with his polished skull and horse teeth and a pot-belly straining at his elastic waistband.

He had been exiled to Gomez Gap two years before as punishment for arresting his boss for possession of controlled substances at the latter's college reunion. Persistent rumors had raised suspicions that the Gap, with its isolated airport and marginal fishing fleet, had become a major entrepôt for international drug traffickers. Before Julius's arrival two FBI operatives, known in the local bars as "The Lost Patrol," had disappeared in the mangrove swamps without a trace. Everyone knew that Julius was a narc, and it was commonly believed that he'd been ordered to Gomez Gap to perish. That he hadn't died, that he'd grown fat and tanned while failing to uncover a shred of evidence, was a tribute to Southern rebelliousness and wit.

"As a matter of fact," I said, "I've got a lead for you."

I don't know why I said it. It came out pretty loudly. It just entered my head and I blurted it out before I could get hold of myself. Even Julius was surprised. Suddenly the room went silent. I could hear waves lapping at the pilings beneath the restaurant, fat sizzling on the griddle, Wheezy breathing.

"I can get you protection," squeaked Julius, "new identity, plastic surgery, the works." He had tennis-match eyes, darting back and forth with anxiety. "You want to

talk outside?" He was whispering now, making a fast recovery from his earlier astonishment. He glanced at the
coffee urn. "This place might be bugged."

"I don't care who hears me," I said, loosing all sense of
proportion. "I'd do anything to put an end to this vile
trade in human misery. Killing is too good for that
human vermin. Bloodsuckers. Snakes in the grass. I'm
ready to make a full and complete statement. Just show
me where to sign. I'm your man, Julius. Together, you and
me, *kemo sabe*. I'm sick and tired of the way you've been
treated in this town. It's men like you who've made this
country what it is today.

"Sssshhhh!" hissed the intrepid Agent Wachtel. I had
him worried. He was wise enough to know that if he ever
did turn up a clue about drugs in Gomez Gap he had better be out of town yesterday.

"I don't care," I said, babbling. "It's a rotten shame. I'm
ready to name names. You'll get a medal for this, Julius.
You'll be able to write your memoirs in Switzerland. I
know Mr Big."

Julius blanched; sweat began to drip down his cheeks.
His madras was getting ready to run. I kept my eyes on
the row of faces up the counter. Nobody moved except
Danger, and she was finally looking straight at me. She
had her sun-glasses down on the tip of her nose, her eyes
rising behind them like twin moons. I could have
drowned in those eyes.

I was jabbering away to beat the band. Julius tugged my
arm, trying to make me shut up. But I had the bit in my
teeth and the wind up my nose.

"He's right here in Gomez Gap," I said. "I can lead you
straight to him, or give you directions. He thinks he's safe.
You can arrest him yourself, no problemo. I presume
you're armed, Julius. You'd better be armed. I know for a
fact Mr Big carries a gat. You wouldn't want any nasty sur-
prises for the folks back in Washington, no Julius-in-a-box,

would you? He's travelling with a female companion, an innocent dupe, a mere victim of his insidious lusts. I can vouch for her character. I'll take custody of her myself as soon as you get him out of the way."

Danger gave me the fish-eye, washed blue buttons behind the rims of her glasses. She'd never seen someone commit suicide before. Half the men in the restaurant had started for the door; the other half had their hands on the countertop, ready to jump. No one, not even Wheezy, had taken a breath in the last minute and a half. You could have cut the air with a butter-knife.

Julius himself was up and straining to get away, held only by the force of my oratory and the hand I had curled in his waistband. Terror ticked across his face like summer lightning—the price of knowledge, the sin of the Fall. I held him closer, whispering.

"He's at my place this very minute debauching the poor woman. You'll catch him with his pants down. Nothing better. He'll never know what hit him. Shoot first, small talk later. Believe me, this is your chance."

Wheezy, Edgar Demming and Roy Maberly now huddled in the doorway, tilting their heads to catch my words, puzzled. Their brows knit whole sweaters. Danger rolled her eyes; I was no longer impressing her. I was merely making an ass of myself. The usual thing.

"His name is Walter Hebel," I said. "There's another guy there. Otto. Watch out for him. He's difficult to see sometimes. I myself was in bed with him this morning without being aware of his presence. He could be the brains behind the whole racket. I wouldn't be surprised at anything."

Julius had broken free, ripping a belt loop. He stood on two legs in the middle of the restaurant, puffing like a blowfish. He thought I was crazy, I could tell. He looked as if he were going to puke. Crazy people have that effect on you. Whenever that girl from Elysium got talking it was like riding a roller-coaster in my head.

Bubba Driscoll hadn't moved. He remained hunched over his coffee next to Danger's right hip. But his shoulders suddenly relaxed when I uttered Walter's name; I could see his deltoids sag. Bubba had reason to be anxious—the sheriff's son was the biggest purchaser of stuffed game fish in town. A dozen a week sometimes. If he had all those stuffed fish in his house, I don't know where he had room to change his mind. It made a person meditate, it did, the popularity of stuffed game fish in Gomez Gap.

"I'll check on it," said Julius at last, summoning his reserves of courage. "I'll check it out, Tully, but it doesn't sound like much of a lead." He said this with conviction in a voice like a bishop's, and I saw the boys glance at each other with evident relief.

Danger had turned her back on me again. She and Bubba scrutinized the insides of their sun-glasses in silence. I suffered a pang of jealousy. Bubba sat as if he possessed some territorial right.

In fact, I realized I'd been getting upset. Forces had been acting on me which I did not admire. Briefly I considered taking the now vacant seat on Danger's right and striking up a conversation about life in stir, hard time, homo-eroticism in Crowbar Hotel. Bubba would hate it. It would put him off his coffee. In bawdy moments, when she was drunk, or before or after making love, Danger was apt to satirize his squeamishness when it came to sex and feminine hygiene, how he called her cunt her "thing" and classified it as a war zone, supplying her with unguents, ointments, douches and sprays and counselling constant vigilance.

But I had begun to sense a sea change; a cold wind, a regular ball-freezer, was blowing from the direction of you know who. And it hurt. In jail, I had mailed her five dirty letters signed "A Lonesome Con." I had dreamed of us together (she liked to sit on top, touching herself), of damp, musky sheets on hot summer nights with the windows open and the heavy scent of flower blossoms muffling her sighs (only sighs with her daughters sleeping down the hall). I had pined and grown exceedingly horny.

This new Danger-Bubba situation, following so quickly on the new Lydia-Walter situation, had me flummoxed. Besides I never like to make my moves in public. We Stampers prefer to cloak our hearts with night, we of the slow fuses and quiet passions.

8

It was mid-morning by the time I stepped out of the
Shrimp-Pot and clattered down the stairs to the break-
water. The sun was high and hot and felt like the proof of
God to man just out of prison.

While I had been inside the restaurant, a fleet of motor
homes, utility vans and huge semis full of costumes and
props had sprouted like mushrooms on the waste ground
by the old fiber factory. Hordes of new faces rummaged
around the decaying buildings, throwing up barricades,
roping off street corners, setting up little traffic signs.
Skinny women in tight shorts, with silk bandannas tied
over breasts that hung like grapes on the vine, sauntered
about or sprawled under awnings fixed to the campers,
sipping cloudy beverages from tall glasses. Nervous boys
with beards and creeping hairlines, consulting clipboards,
peering through monoculars, sighted vistas and camera
angles. Film crews swinging precariously from the beds of
Japanese pick-ups, zipped and buzzed up and down,
wheeling their cameras, looking up the legs of the sprawling beauties.

Walter Hebel and my wife had just stepped from a steel-
grey stretch limousine at the corner of Dixie and Water
Streets where my store stood. They were immediately
caught and nearly crushed in a knot of movie people,
tanned and glistening in the sunlight. Behind them a row
of earth-movers filled to the gunwales with fresh earth
began making passes along the street, distributing a
generous layer of sand on the municipal pavement. As I
watched, Walter swept irritably at the storefront with a

clipboard. Before I could utter a scream of protest, half a dozen men with stepladders and claw-hammers were after my sign like a school of piranha fish.

It was an old sign. An irreplaceable antique dating from the late seventies. It came off in pieces. I made for the spot as quickly as possible, already calculating restitution. I was so earnest and insensible that I nearly went down in front of the first earth-mover. Brushing the dirt from my knees, I strode up to Walter and opened my mouth.

Just then a gull went by, before I could speak. I mean it was flying, yet it was unlike any gull I had ever seen in my life. A neon gull. It looked like a laughing gull, smaller than a ring-bill, dark over the shoulders and on its wing-tips, black feet. But it was day-glo orange from beak to tail feathers.

We were all staring at it. In fact, Walter's mouth had dropped open with surprise and I could see him struggling to get control of himself as the gull touched down with a hop on the dirt half-way between my store and the Gap Hotel. It gave us one of those birdy expressions, as if to say I know this looks silly but mind your own god-damned business. Then it began pecking for breakfast along the trail of the earth-movers.

"Sabotage!" screamed Walter. "It's sabotage! Someone's fucking up my shot! Someone's—" He gave a start as his gaze fell on me. "You did this, you schmuck. I'm ten days over schedule; I'm paying through the nose in per diems; I deferred salary and gave up points against overruns; and you're fucking around with the pigeons. You envious wimp! You failure!"

"What about my sign?" I asked. "Who's going to pay for my sign?"

I caught sight of Kinch hovering in the doorway in Ina's peignoir, an expression of wonder and delight playing over his features. He was watching the gull. He pointed. There was a second circling above the crowd.

This time only the left wing and its head were painted orange. A piebald gull. It fluttered down to join its cousin.

"Shoot them! Poison them! I don't care what you do!" shouted Walter. "Get those fucking pigeons out of my shot!"

He was spluttering, losing composure. Oddly, though, the crew huddled close and seemed to be taking his tantrum seriously. Worry clouded their faces, turning their tans olive drab. Someone popped a pill and handed one to his neighbor. A girl in shorts and a halter top broke away from the group and approached the birds with her hand outstretched, making throaty clucking noises. Little silver crescent moons of white cheek winked back at us.

"Did you do this, Tully?"

It was Lydia, calm, icy. She fixed me with those cool green eyes. Evidently multicolored laughing gulls were more than just a curious natural phenomenon; they were a category of insult or catastrophe ranking near act of God. There were now half a dozen of these little affronts to nature pecking daintily away at the fresh topsoil, rubbing shoulders and wingtips with a flock of ordinary gulls, adults and youngsters, all come for the free meal.

"I swear to God," I said, eyeing the gulls. I was also watching the girl with the half-exposed buns. She had long black hair down to her waist and skin as tawny as a doe in the forest.

"Otto is obsessed with perfection," said Lydia. "Someone has done this deliberately to annoy him."

There was Otto again. I had the impression that Walter was some kind of advance man for the Great One, that at the last moment, with the sets set, the lights lit, the cameras loaded with film, the actors, actresses and assorted extras on their chalk marks, a bald man with a fat cigar and dark glasses, dressed in riding pants and boots, would appear from the biggest, sleekest motor home to whisper the magic word "ACTION."

But I wasn't really paying attention. The girl with the dark hair had flung herself at the nearest gull, missing by the breadth of a pinfeather and causing the whole flock to flutter upwards and circle noisily before landing again a few feet away and resuming its meal. Five Confederate soldiers tumbled out of the Gap Hotel and began advancing with fixed bayonets, forcing the birds to skitter down the street at intervals, but not otherwise discomfiting them to any degree.

"What are you doing with Walter Hebel?" I asked, somewhat dreamily.

Walter heard me. Suddenly, he stopped clutching his throat, throwing fits. He appeared diminished, more like the Walter of old than the ranting figure of a moment before, his dark eyes darting behind the thick lenses of his glasses like mice in a cage.

Lydia took me by the hand and led me quickly out of the ruck, down the alley beside the store. In passing I noticed a plank missing by the base of the building. Kinch was becoming devious.

"You fool," said Lydia, plainly irritated. "You ape, you'll ruin everything."

"I didn't paint the fucking birds," I said. "For all I know it's a late adaptation. You know—mutants from Miami. It's those Cuban breeding Technicolor laughing gulls."

"Not the birds, Tully. That's Otto Osterwalder back there. Walter Hebel no longer exists."

"Are you sure?" I asked.

"I ought to be. I married him."

"You're married to me," I said, suffering a temporary bout of amnesia. This happened from time to time. I was always expecting to find Lydia home cooking spicy duck over the range, a kerchief tied round her forehead to catch the sweat, her hands dripping with oil and spices. It is a fact that I never wanted a divorce, never wanted to be unmarried. I had only wanted a rest, a respite, a chance to forget my hideous failures.

(I had made her pregnant by mistake, making love while she was napping, without her diaphragm. When she begged me to go to Lamaze classes, I was too busy trying to avert the lamp-factory débâcle. Walter the Troll always ended up taking her. When her water broke, I panicked. I was reading baby books and popping Quaaludes in the back seat while Walter drove us to the hospital. In the delivery room, I looked on helplessly while she suffered and stony-eyed Doc Birdsong played mumbley-peg on her belly with his scalpel. In the delivery room, she said the words.)

In short, in my mind I had never abandoned Lydia; I had always intended to return when my heart had healed.

"All right, we're not married." I said this as a concession, as proof that I could touch base with reality as well as the next man. "But that is Walter Hebel out there."

"Sssshhhh," hissed Lydia. I admit I had raised my voice. I believed that my sanity was being called into question. She had done this often enough at Elysium. "It is, but it isn't. You see?"

I didn't see. There was a tone of intimacy and mild reproval in her voice, that masked a moral imperative I could not apprehend. But I wanted to make her happy. That was all I ever wanted, along with the frame house on Long Island, two dogs, a half-dozen little Stampers, a gallery in Soho that would sell my work with seemly regularity, a Swedish car in the garage. I swear to God I thought fucking made Lydia happy, even when she was asleep.

"All right," I said. "It's not Walter Hebel. What happened to Walter Hebel?"

"He changed his name."

"To what?"

"Tully, don't be stupid. We went to Germany. We changed our names. In Iowa, I'm Lydia Hebel, but everywhere else I'm—"

"I don't want to hear it," I said, clapping my hands to my ears. She reached up and gently pulled them away.

"Tully, Tully, Tully," she murmured soothingly. "Osterwalder's his nom du cinéma. Changing names made him what he is today. In Germany they loved him."

I shook my head in denial and disbelief, with tears in my eyes. Somehow I had managed to keep hope alive as long as I could believe there were Walter Hebels in the world. There was still someone worse off, less graceful, more bumbling, more luckless, more stricken by the Fates.

Now I had to face facts. From the mouth of my loved one. I didn't blame her. The truth is, irrevocably, the truth. Lydia and the doctors at Elysium had cooked up a theory based on Freud and my postcard parent: I had read his absence as a message; deep down I was guilty, unworthy of affection, doomed to fail. Those blank cards were a constant judgment on my futile efforts to succeed, to redeem myself in Daddy's eyes.

The truth was, the doctors said, I failed because I wanted to. And I'll tell you they were half right. I wanted to inoculate myself with failure. I wanted to protect myself from the inevitable. *Sweetheart, I just don't think this is going to work out.* And just as surely Walter Hebel had succeeded because he wanted to. It was Lydia's luck to see which way the wind was blowing. No, I didn't blame her. But it made me sad. There I was, the last failure on earth. I was done. I wasn't dead, but I might as well have been. I was done.

9

I shuffled along the alley, away from the crowded street, my hightops stirring up the dust, and tried the back door of my store. Unfortunately, we had nailed this shut some time before as a security measure and I couldn't get in. It wouldn't have done any good to knock since Kinch lacked the rudimentary mechanical sense to pull a nail with a claw-hammer.

A laughing gull shot by at shoulder level, shrieking alarm, navy blue this time, a welcome distraction from thoughts of Lydia and woe. It had exploded cloudwards from the waterfront, where a pile of boulders extended the breakwater and obscured my view, just a few steps over waste ground from the back of my store.

Tide was in, but as often happens in Gomez Gap the easterlies had pushed the Gulf out farther than usual, exposing a stretch of sand beyond the restaurants, right out to the ship channel. Sea gulls spiraled, plummeted and soared above the spot where the blue fellow had just come from, their wings flickering like leaves in a wind storm. They were mad after something down below which I couldn't see until I stepped onto the topmost boulder.

The lady from New Jersey, Ina's boarder, knelt on the wet sand, involved in some macabre ceremony using a bicycle pump, yards of clear plastic tubing, and bottles of paint. As I watched, she threw slices of Wonder Bread toward a target area that corresponded with the nozzle of one of her paint bottles. The gulls were dipping and diving at the bread, crying to one another about it, or about the paint. (Who can tell what gulls are thinking?) Whenever one landed within range, the lady would shove down on her bicycle-pump handle like some lunatic bomber, sending a squirt of paint into the unsuspecting bird.

It was too surreal for words. I had a dozen theories at once. Perhaps Walter was right. Someone was trying to sabotage his movie. But why pick on the laughing gulls? Why not deface buildings? More than likely, I reasoned, she was one of those bizarre conceptual artists from the North. I had once known a woman who made a career out of photographing the movement of shadows behind a patrol of cereal-box soldiers. If people can wrap sky-scrapers in plastic baggies or bury cars in Arizona and call it art, I didn't see why painting punk seagulls couldn't count.

Whatever she was doing, it didn't look good for the gulls. What if she was using lead-based paint? I asked my-self. I knew these head-in-the-cloud artists. They wouldn't think of a complication like that. I had visions of a whole gull colony suffering lead poisoning, blindness, drowning. (Could they float with all that stuff on their feathers?) Not to mention the ill effects of Wonder Bread on gull digestion. I hated people doing things like that. Tourists hauling shells away from the beach, feeding the wildlife junk food.

Without thinking what I was up to, I leaped from the rock and sprinted toward the paint bottle, whooping and waving my arms. A plump young bird, looking bigger than the rest, was lollygagging around the last crust of bread, not sure what he was supposed to do with it. The lady had cocked her elbow, getting ready to fire. I threw myself at the gull, which stood paralyzed with his beak open. The paint hit me in the ear. But I had the gull in my arms. With a deft swing of my foot, I knocked the paint gun over before she could shoot me again.

"Are you bats?" she yelled. She was shading her eyes against the sunlight. It was a strange expression to use. A little old-fashioned. And she didn't sound afraid or angry, just mildly surprised and exasperated.

For the first time I got a good look at her. An elf, under five feet in height, she was dressed like a mannequin in a secondhand-clothing-store window: army fatigue pants, K-Mart sneakers, a painter's cap and a faded T-shirt that bore the motto NO JOB /TOO ODD. She had those binoculars around her neck and wore a pair of glasses with flesh-colored rims.

"Are you bats or something?" she repeated. She peered at me through her binoculars. "Don't let that little fucker go."

I was stretched flat on the sand, breathing hard, the gull nestling contentedly between my extended forearms, plainly not interested in escape. I had cut my elbows and knees on pieces of shell. The army fatigues jogged toward me. I could see the lady's breasts flopping back and forth inside her shirt. She saw that I was watching her and stopped jogging. She started to blush. I'm not sure of this. It looked like a blush. She was tanned, so that I couldn't tell for certain.

Walking up to me, she squinted down at the gull. Gently, she extended a finger and stroked it under the chin, her beady little eyes darting nervously.

"Birds are dumb, you know," she said. "All those guys," she added, pointing above us where the rest of the gulls were whirling and calling in a frenzy of warning, "all those guys are telling him to get the fuck out of here, but he hasn't got a clue."

She dabbed a finger in the blue paint that was dripping from the side of my head. It wasn't a caress. It was just a dip, a disinterested dip, but something about it stirred me. It reminded me of Lydia reaching to pull my hands away from my ears. It reminded me of Ina testing my forehead for fever when I was very young. A woman's touch always brings out the child in me.

"I christen you Baldy, little guy," she said, wiping her finger on the gull's chest feathers. "Baldy after Baldossaro the Great, who would screw us both if he could. Now beat it."

She guided the young bird away from me with the back of her hand, then gave him a couple of pats on the rear. Nothing happened. The bird stood still, cooing in my direction.

Suddenly the lady from New Jersey jumped up. Knotting her fists in her armpits and flapping her elbows like wings, she stuck out her chest and cried, "Kekkekkek! Kekkekkek!" It was a weird high-pitched performance, very convincing, very gull-like. The young laughing gull blinked rapidly and stumbled back a few steps, keeping his eyes on the woman. Then he made a series of bowing motions, dropping the top of his head toward us.

"Submission behavior," said the woman. "He thinks that we're big gulls." She peered upwards again. The gulls scooped and hovered about her head, some coming close enough to fan the strands of her hair that hung loose from the bun she had tied at the back.

Her whole improvisation was so entrancing I didn't feel any hesitation in reaching up and touching her cheek. I don't remember if I thought she was pretty. But she was matter-of-fact and friendly and I realized she wasn't trying to hurt the gulls.

"Get your hands off me," she said, crossly, pulling away. It took me by surprise. "I saw you sneaking around the bulkhead this morning. I don't care what you guys do over there in your spare time. Just don't try to suck me in."

"Mating behavior," I said. "Human."

"Listen, Jack!"

"Tully," I said. "The name is Tully Stamper. I live there. At least I used to." I could see then that she wasn't pretty. She was interesting, but not pretty. My introduction somewhat mollified her. We watched the gull in silence as it stumped off along the tidal flats, pecking randomly in the sand.

"Dumb," she said. "He gets that from the adults. He still isn't sure what he's supposed to be pecking for."

I'd never looked at a gull this closely before. Birds are part of the landscape. They dash about in their own world, trying to keep out of the way of cars. Now that I noticed, the big youngster did seem confused. He was pecking, then looking about sharply to see if any other gulls were pecking and what they had discovered. Somehow I had always thought they were born knowing what to eat.

"Who is Baldossar?" I asked.

"Baldossaro Azzopardi," she said. "Niko Tinbergen's brightest student, the world's foremost expert on gull communication, my post-doc supervisor at the Institute."

"Is he here too?" I asked, glancing up at the rocks that hid us from the town. I was trying to wipe the blue paint from my face.

"No," she said. "That fucker hasn't been in the field for years. He just sits on his ass in New York. He's into marathons and sex now. Don't worry about that stuff. It'll wash off with soap."

"What's it for?"

"I mark individual gulls to make them easier to identify when they're exhibiting behavior. I want to see how they relate inside the group."

"A scientist," I said. "I get it. You're an ornithologist, a bird-woman."

She was standing with her hands in her pockets, not paying much attention to me, watching the birds. She was not pretty but when she was watching the birds she had a kind of charm and aloofness. Yet everything about her said, "Don't get too close." Somehow she was vulnerable and she seemed to know it. Her prickliness was her way of forestalling complications. I could see now that she dressed that way deliberately, marking herself as less attractive.

"You'd better stop painting the birds," I said. "It's interfering with the movie. The locals are pretty star-struck. I expect they'll start shooting your gulls if they get in the way. You haven't introduced yourself."

"Ruth," she said. "Ruth E. Appeldorn. I'm not a birdperson. I'm an animal behaviorist. I have a grant for laughing gulls. You want a curriculum vitae? I'm thirty-one, in case you're wondering. So don't get any ideas about me being some dumb young co-ed on the make."

She looked twenty, but maybe it was her size. Somehow you always expect small people to grow up one day. She wasn't any bigger than a kid and the T-shirt and cap made her look even younger.

"Why would I get any ideas?" I asked.

It was a little cruel. I saw her wince and recover. Her eyes were like bits of coal behind those absurd frames. We watched a plane zoom down behind the live-oaks heading for the airport. Dr Coyle's Cessna. A flock of skimmers and terns rose up above the trees, disturbed by the plane.

"Yes, I'd hide this equipment," I said. "Otto Osterwalder is a powerful man in Gomez Gap."

"Who the fuck is he?"

She was a woman unafraid of the stigma of ignorance.

"Never mind," I said, turning toward the store.

I knew it was rude to rush off, but there was something irritating as well as curious in the way Ruth E. Appeldorn combined frank friendliness with prickliness. It takes a good woman to bring you back from the abyss, the bright face of a young girl who's never been there and takes things as they come. This woman was an intellectual sort of woman, independent, very independent, a regular dark horse. But I was convinced she had none of the qualities I was looking for in a redeemer.

She was co-operative as long as you talked about birds, but whenever the conversation veered toward the personal she put up her guard. She was just the sort of person I didn't have time to fathom. I was waving goodbye over my shoulder when she suddenly said, "Look!" and pointed toward the stratosphere.

I glanced in the direction indicated by her index finger.

"Osprey!" she whispered. "The pair from the airport. They're up—they're hunting. See!"

She pointed low this time. A single skimmer was zigzagging across the mudflats, crying his fear. The air was tense and electric. The gulls had disappeared. The whole waterfront was waiting and listening as the osprey swung lazily on the thermals, uttering their short harsh calls. I had never seen it before. I turned to the lady from New Jersey, with her baggy pants and thick-lensed glasses and her chestnut-colored hair tumbling unkempt down her back from beneath that painter's cap. She was lost in watching them.

10

Five minutes later, just inside the door of my store, I collided with Bethamae Hamsett eyeing the walls with critical displeasure.

"Tully!" she said, in a voice that sounded like a carpenter hammering nails. "I've come to take my painting back. I wish to offer it to Otto Osterwalder as a token of the town's appreciation—"

Bethamae was about fifty, dressed in period costume, with so many stays and laces it looked as if she was wearing an iron grate beneath her bosom. She had hair like milkweed flax, eyes like new pennies, and oil paint under her fingernails, and chain-smoked a woman's cigarette called Eve.

Coming from the Midwest with an invalid mother who later died, she had fallen under the spell of the South with a capital S. She resembled Danger that way, though what Danger admired most was pure pigheaded cracker cussedness, while Bethamae's interest was mainly prurient. She was always talking about the "contradictions of a slave-owning aristocracy" and "William Faulkner's poetic values," but what really got her excited was speculating on whether the Driscolls had a lick of the tarbrush in their family tree or finding out that a black man named Vernon Mooers had had his balls cut off and fed to dogs on April Fool's Day, 1933.

Of course she took care to disguise all this, even to herself, as civic pride and antiquarian curiosity. Kinch called her an improver "in the worst sense of the word." Besides owning the Art Co-op, she sat on the executives of the

Friends of the Gomez Gap Library, the Arts Festival Committee and the local chapter of the Loyal Daughters of the Confederacy. She was also president of the Gomez Gap Historical Society (draping herself in a Rebel flag, she had recited the whole of Sydney Lanier's "The Marshes of Glynn" into the minutes of the inaugural meeting); at my tree-cutting trial she had testified for the State.

Around us, conversation crackled and spread like flames in dry tinder.

"Tully, you're out of jail!"

"Jail? I thought he was away in Ioway looking after that lamp business he's always jawing about."

"He cut down that tree and Audie Driscoll ran him in on a charge."

"Hey, Mister, can you stuff my kitty?"

"Jesus, how long has this been dead?"

"Tully, I've been trying to tell Oliver you oughta be stocking my purple-martin houses."

"—my waterfront water-colors."

"—my macramé plant hangers."

"What's going on, Kinch?" I yelled over Bethamae's sun-bonnet. The inside of my store looked like one of Brueghel's peasant comedies. "Is it a feeding frenzy? Did you fuck up the newspaper ad copy again? Are we giving something away I should know about?"

"It's Osterwalder," cried Kinch. He was battened behind the cash register, still wearing that peignoir. Next to him, two tiny heads, one blond, one dark, just reached above the counter—Danger's kids from her first marriage; my heart gave a little jump. "He hates members of the public walking through his set-ups, so they come in here and watch from the window."

The little girls waved, palms white as gull-wings. Cecily, ten, wore a checked workshirt, jeans and sneakers. Emily, eight, was haut punk in flame-red tights, ankle boots, a short denim skirt and a black pullover covered with sequins. Sometimes I thought I loved those fatherless orphans more than I loved Danger, though Danger always preferred to believe that I would be a baleful influence.

I waved back.

"Tully! Tully!"

Bethamae again, tugging the sleeve of my bowling shirt like a bell rope. I fought down a wave of murderous panic; I wanted to shove her false teeth down her throat. Instead I flashed her a smile that meant nothing and tried to think of something pleasant like taking Danger and her daughters crabbing in my boat, just the four of us with a bottle of wine, a ghetto blaster and a bucket of fish heads for bait.

"I came around yesterday," Bethamae said, "but Oliver told me he knew nothing about it. Of course we expect that sort of thing from Oliver. I must say, however, I am disappointed it was not more prominently displayed. You did practically beg me for it."

I glared at Kinch. Bethamae frowned—she was Christ's older sister. I had to concentrate hard to imagine the smell of oil and rubber boots, the putt-putt of the boat engine and the cries of the little girls as they spotted my buoy markers.

"If you're worried I'm going to bite your head off about that lynch tree and the Society's commemorative plaque," she said, showing an uncanny ability to read two percent of what was on my mind, "I must confess this movie business has driven such trivialities *completely* from my thoughts."

I broke out in a sweat. There was no telling what lengths she would go to to punish me for destroying her painting. Depression bled into daydream. Actually I hated crabbing with Danger. Alone I always let the crabs go. But with Danger there I had to keep up appearances: save blue crabs for the boiling pot, rip the claws off the stone crabs and throw the amputees back to regenerate, or die.

"It's Kinch's fault," I said in desperation. "He sold your picture by accident. He won't admit it. But when I came in this morning I noticed it was missing right away."

"I beg your pardon."

Bethamae had never sold a picture in her life except one to a blind aunt in Wichita. Her body stiffened; her thin wattles grew taut as drumheads. She looked like a waxwork prairie pioneer.

"Kinch sold it," I said, neither knowing how nor wishing to turn back. "I meant to tell you."

"Who did he sell it to?"

Who indeed? I scented fresh hazards. How did I see myself? Blue crab or stone crab? Would I ever find peace?

Cato French, my cellmate, came to mind. Briefly, I reflected nostalgically on our time together, his love of music, his uncritical acceptance of my right to exist. But, no, Bethamae would want an address, zip and phone number.

"Some Yankee," I said, "obviously a man of great wealth and superior discrimination."

She beamed at me like a mother.

"Who?" she asked. "What's his name?"

Raising my voice above the roar of the crowd, I announced that the store had to be cleared because of fire regulations. No one paid any attention to me.

"Who?"

I ran into the stuffing room, shutting the door with a slam.

There I found precious little consolation save for the Darvon capsules huddled together like a herd of tiny sheep on the plywood tabletop where Kinch had virtuously left them. I ate several without anything to wash them down, not bothering to count.

Bethamae's canvas stretched upright like a rebuke from God in the center of the room. Difficult to ignore because it took up so much space. The ghost of her painting. My dry throat suddenly seized on the last Darvon, throwing me into a coughing fit.

Voices emanated though the plasterboard walls like voices from another world.

"We saw Tully talking to Otto Ostermonger. Do you think he could get Peggy Rose his autograph? I brung her autograph book. She's made up a special page for the stars in Gomez Gap, right next to the mayor and the council and Sheriff Driscoll. She's just crazy about the movie."

"Did you hear? Tully Stamper is just like that with Otto Hosterbalder."

"Say, what are these little rocks with feathers pasted on 'em like hair? I never see'd anything so cute."

I could sense Bethamae's presence on the other side of the door. She was nonplussed, no doubt, by my sudden disappearance and obvious reluctance to return. She waited; I waited. I could wait her out; I had chemicals. I closed my eyes. Nodded off.

"Tell Tully he must give me a call," I heard her say to Kinch. "Tell him we have much to talk over." The sound of her footsteps diminished across the sales floor, like sonar blips in a submarine, then stopped altogether with the clang of the trip-bell over my front door.

"Hello, Tully."

"Hello, Tully. Did you have a nice time in jail?"

I opened my eyes. How long had I been like that? The little girls, elfin creatures, had appeared at my knee as if by magic.

"Emily! Cecily!" I exclaimed. "What are you doing out of school? Danger's going to have a fit."

"It's all right. We're in the movie," said Emily. "We're going to be stars."

"What do you mean you're in the movie?"

"Bubba Driscoll got us parts in the movie. We're going to play little girls in the town," said Cecily, enunciating politely but nervously. "Mama gave us a dollar for lunch.

We thought we would invite you out."

"Ma and Bubba been out every night this week," said Emily. "They go out after she comes home from work. Last night the crew held a barbecue for the extras. Ma says Bubba threw up and had to go home, but she stayed out till morning."

"Shut up, Em."

"Bubba's got a horse part," said Emily sniggering behind her hand.

"She means he's going to ride a horse," said Cecily.

Her words sliced through my brain like a meat-saw. I felt that familiar kernel of self-hatred driving me toward chaos. I thought I was going to be sick, even felt a little unsteady on my feet.

"I'm on a diet, Tully," said Emily, hands on hips, admiring her figure. "I'm afraid of getting stretch marks. Stretch marks could ruin me—"

"I'm in the movie too," I said, cutting her off. I was tired of letting an eight-year-old push me around the conversational ring. And I wanted to hear what the words sounded like—kind of a trial run before I tried them out on real people, people over three and a half feet high. "Probably not as big a part as Bubba has—a speaking part though. Has Bubba got lines?"

Cecily rolled her eyes, her mother's eyes.

"Cecily," I said, but suddenly things began to get vague. It must have been the Darvon; I felt like my brain was being sucked through a tube. Her eyes were huge and seductive as truth; I was falling into them.

"It's true," I managed to say, slurring the words. I was giddy. I felt like a man going off the high board for the first time. "I've been cast for a special role—a Rebel hero. You've heard of him—Colonel. . .Colonel what's-his-name. I'll probably get billing—it depends on the cuts—totally—but if I look good, Walter—I mean Otto says it could mean something big."

The eyes grew larger with every word I said. Suddenly, I realized I had started with the wrong audience. It was like speaking into a tape machine; these words were written on stone. I willed that my heart should stop right there, that I should stop talking forever. But my mouth went on; it had a mind of its own.

11

I woke up, stretched on my stuffing table like a corpse with a tin of car paint for a pillow. It was late afternoon. The chaotic sounds of the morning had abated in the salesroom. Kinch hummed something familiar yet unrecognizable on the other side of the workshop behind our communal canvas.

A faint buzzing noise attracted my attention. I peeked under the table and discovered my dog asleep, dreaming of rabbits, resting from his night's exertions in a pile of dirty laundry.

The canvas divided the room down the middle, one side for art, one side for the stuffing table, sink and freezer. Lately the freezer had been on the fritz and some of those trophies had gone bad. Kinch, who slept on the studio side, didn't seem to mind.

As I say, he was humming to himself, mixing paint, wiping his brushes on Ina's peignoir. I had never seen him in such a state. During the day he generally avoided the front of the canvas, the smudged, accusatory emptiness, a palimpsest of old paint. Or else he would stare at it for hours, silently weeping, sipping sherry loudly through a straw.

Occasionally I would arrive for work to find that overnight he'd painted something in one corner, a couple of lightning bolts not more than three inches long, a straight line with a bulge like a goitre, that sort of thing. He would whistle cheerfully about the place for an hour or two, then rush back to look at his masterpiece. By mid-afternoon, he'd have scraped it off or painted it white again.

To tell the truth, I was a little superstitious about Kinch. He was mascot, charm, fetish and minor household deity, all rolled into one. Sometimes he put me in mind of the father I had never seen—they'd have been about the same age; sometimes I trembled at the thought that I'd end up the same, a cinder dropped off the tail of life's gleaming comet. Most of all he reminded me of what I had lost, the desire to paint pictures, which once, for me, had been indistinguishable from the desire for food, sex and air.

Thinking about it made me tired: this vain craving after immortality. A man is nothing but weak flesh and brittle bone; he is born, is ashamed of his parents, finds a job, wishes he was in some other line of work, falls in love, wishes he had fallen in love with some other woman, has children who are ashamed of him, fails at his job, loses his wife, goes slightly mad learning the wisdom of acceptance, and dies.

In Tahiti the natives called the painter Gauguin "man who makes human beings." I must have been fourteen when I read that; I was at the age when you read anything that has naked women on the cover. *Man who makes human beings.* It made an impression; I felt like somebody had walked over my grave. I told my mother I was going to be a painter like this fellow Gauguin. Unaccountably, she began to weep, blowing her nose in an old bra she used as a duster, mumbling something about artists being "nothing but lousy heartbreakers." Later, I found out that my father had started in life as a commercial artist for a Boston ad agency. Ina thought Gauguin was someone he had gone drinking with.

Right away I discovered I had a talent for drawing from memory. Street scenes mostly. The more complex the better. I revelled in spider webs of overhead wires, jigsaw puzzles of overlapping store signs, tricky perspectives and architectural festoons. It was a gimmick, a shtick, a trick I learned to impress my classmates.

My teachers thought I was a species of idiot savant. They gave me da Vinci and Klee to copy with just a quick look at a print or a picture in a book. It worked; I was a born mimic. They sent me to a psychologist; one glance and I could reproduce his ink-blots. By the time I was ready to go to college, I could pay Ina's rent selling pictures "in the style of Wyeth" or "the school of Renoir" at knockdown prices to a Newark (we were back living in New Jersey then) wholesaler named Lipnick who supplied the parking-lot art trade.

But that wasn't what I wanted. *Man who makes human beings.* I started night classes at the Art Students League. I couldn't afford most colleges, but the University of Iowa offered a scholarship. I sent them my slides, paintings in the prairie school, Grant-Woody, and they telegraphed acceptance. Ina wept—in those days she hadn't met Tex Baxter yet, she was still mourning the loss of my father.

My junior year I met Lydia. She was working at the art gallery, minding the reception desk, part of her art-history degree. To tell the truth I'd been so busy learning to paint like a real artist I hadn't paid much attention to women. I didn't know what to say; I drew downtown Iowa City on the back of a flyer in ballpoint pen. I drew the river bank, a night scene with the gallery, the theatre, the footbridges and glowing lamps along the footpaths. All from memory. A tour de force.

Later, after we'd gone out, after we'd made love, I told her about Gauguin. She said, "Tully, you have a big bone and I love you. You're going to be a great painter, better than Picasso, better than Van Gogh. Someday I'll see your picture on the cover of *Time* Magazine." The words frightened me, even then.

I watched Kinch's feet behind the easel legs. He was practically dancing; spatters of paint like cow flops dripped to the floor. Some massive alteration had taken place; he was a man possessed. I hopped around to have a look, taking care that he wouldn't notice. There was a sketch, and he was brushing on an undercoat of gray and white, a dead painting like the Old Masters used to do. I could see that he had something that looked like a sun in the middle, or a volcano, a dense orangeish object built up with layers of thick paint like a bas-relief.

I didn't know what to make of it and this worried me, for I wanted something worthy to show Lydia. But I didn't want to hurt Kinch's feelings, he seemed so happy. So I tackled the topic obliquely.

"That's a lovely bit of background in the top corner," I said.

"Oh, Tully! You took me by surprise. D'you really like it? I'm out of practice."

Kinch frowned. He spoke in that stiff, clipped fashion he used when he was angry with me. I couldn't think what I had done to offend him.

He slapped some paint on the orangeish thing with a kitchen knife, putting arms on it, it seemed. For the first time, I noticed his hands weren't shaking. His palette strokes were firm and energetic. I still failed to see what he was driving at, but he appeared satisfied.

"I'll be bringing Lydia around tomorrow, Kinch. You think it'll be finished?"

"I can't say," he muttered, picking up a brush and beginning to push the paint across the canvas. "It's coming quickly. But I haven't done a major work in seven years."

He wouldn't look at me, a bad sign in Kinch, a sign of censure, of grave disapproval.

He was a gentle man without a harmful thought in his head. Life had simply been too much for him. Life (details were lacking, Kinch claiming, at various times, that he had Alzheimer's Disease, amnesia, a brain tumor and Farzey-Burkes Syndrome) had simply rolled him up like sheet metal on a roof in a hurricane and dumped him on a trash heap. He didn't know what had hit him, or even that he'd been hit.

"Happy?" I asked, trying to get him to talk, to get his mind off whatever was bothering him. For Kinch loved to jaw while he painted, to reveal his hopes, his inspirations, his little technical secrets. And, briefly, I thought it was going to work because he suddenly turned from the canvas and began an animated discourse, punctuated with paint-spattering stabs of the brush handle.

"It was that bird," he said. "It seemed magical, Tully. Suddenly I saw how I could paint it. You know—because before everything looked so dull, so gray, so bland. I just couldn't get excited about it. But as soon as you put an orange bird at the center the whole world changes. I'm going to make it the biggest, orangest laughing gull on earth!"

I could see now that there was something gull-like about that orange patch. Those appendages could have been wings. It did my heart good to see Kinch had a subject at last, although I was uneasy about Lydia's reaction to nature studies. I had never painted wildlife before.

"I see," I said, hesitantly, "but I don't think Lydia will buy it. We don't have to shoot for the moon, Kinch. What we really want is something competent, even a little conservative. Can I make one small suggestion?"

Kinch turned his back on me, brushing furiously. The hunch of his shoulders read like an indictment, and I feared that I would throw him off his stride, perhaps stop him completely.

"Nothing you can't paint out, Kinch. A detail or two for Lydia's sake. I thought you could put in an apple-green house with a copper-beech tree in the front. She'll know what it is."

He pointed, a brusque interrogative, drawing invisible lines with the wooden tip of his brush on the bare parts of the picture.

"Yes, that'll do nicely. And perhaps you could work in a couple of the lamps."

Kinch stared at the canvas, licking his cracked lips. I nodded encouragement, for he seemed to be getting the idea.

"There was a church next door with a piano in the window and black people in the pews."

"Apple-green house—black people?"

"If you could make them look like they are singing—"

Suddenly he rounded on me. His eyes gleamed venomously. He'd been holding them in so long his words came out like spit.

"You told those little girls you were a star in the movie."

"What if I did?"

"You lied!"

"I prefer to call it a semi-conscious pathetic plea for attention."

"Tully, when are you going to change?" said Kinch, getting fierce, looking as if he was going to give me a punch. "You think the world is just another one of your ideas. If you don't stop, your life will end up being nothing but a gigantic hallucination."

Wiping his nose on the paint-spattered hem of the peignoir, he added, "I'm sorry I said that."

"I'm sorry, too, Kinch," I said, feeling deflated, feeling his words in my flesh like barbed hooks. He had given me a tiny vision of the truth almost too terrible to endure.

"No, no, I shouldn't have brought it up."

"That's all right, Kinch," I said. "I won't mention it if you don't."

12

I walked shakily out into the street, which was busy and, I noted with irritation, manifesting signs of the movie everywhere you looked. The cameras, the cable snakes, the crowds of kibitzers only served to remind me of my foolish undertaking in front of Cecily and her sister to personify a Southern soldier in the battle scene, and for a full minute I raged inwardly against Lydia and Walter.

As I watched, a car careered round the corner, scattering movie sand. It was a vintage Dodge Dart, one of those old slant sixes, rusted up to the windows—Danger's car. It braked to a halt in front of me; the passenger door swung open.

"Get in," she hissed. I did. "Get down! There's Audie!" She pushed my head down with her free hand, at the same time jamming her foot on the accelerator. I cracked the dashboard with my brow. A sickening wave of pain passed into my stomach, and I slumped sideways onto her lap, out of sight.

Almost as soon as we'd started, we stopped. Danger cranked her window down. I heard the sheriff's dog Vince barking a few feet away.

"Afternoon, Audie," Danger called. She was leaning out the window with her elbow wedged against my neck to hold my head down.

"Hey, Danger, din't I just see you parked in front of Tully Stamper's store?" Audie's tone was impatient, shading into anger. Most of the locals didn't trust or understand Danger; to them, she was an eccentric outsider, fiery if crossed, not to be taken seriously because she was a woman. Since she had left Bubba, their interest had increased considerably. Much time in bars was allocated to discussing "what the fuck that dip-shit Babcox broad" was up to.

Danger replied, girlishly, "Hey, why'd I be doing that? I just come around the corner too fast and had to stop and collect myself. I'm on my way to take Momma Driscoll some key-lime pie—I don't want it to melt."

"You know you aren't supposed to drive down here when the movie's on." Audie seemed relieved. Nobody, not even the sheriff, liked to tangle with Danger. And now that Danger was moving back with Bubba, they were almost in-laws again.

"Sorry, Audie. I forgot. You ain't going to give little old me a ticket, are you?" Danger gunned the engine and patted my knee. "I've got to get this pie over to your momma's place."

"Shit, I ain't going to give you a ticket, Danger. Just get on out of here now and don't cause any more disruptions."

Danger accelerated slowly, waved back at Audie, turned a corner, then another.

"Shit!" she said. "Are you all right?" She sounded exasperated, not necessarily anxious about my health.

I said nothing; I had my nose against Danger Babcox's love box. When I turned my head I could see five joints taped underneath the control panel. I was getting to where I wanted to be. I sighed and snuggled against her belly, disposing my cramped limbs in as comfortable a position as I could manage.

"Asshole!"

Her favorite song was Shelly West's "Jose Cuervo"; her favorite poem was Allen Tate's "Ode to the Confederate War Dead"; she was forever looking down her nose at me (especially when she had had too much to drink, which was fairly often) and saying things like: "People from the

North have a limited sense of human liberty." Her father
was a lawyer, a "will and deeds man," up in Thomasville,
but Danger hadn't gone home since she left for university. She had turned into a lush after Willie Weber died.
For three years, she'd lived in the Keys with her daughters, migrating from one swimming pool to the next, doing crazy things.

One day she had drifted into Gomez Gap, dressed in
black, the little girls in torn frocks, quiet as mice. She was
tired of the cokeheads and gays, she had said. She wanted
a real man. She saw Bubba one night when the mullet
were running, poised like Poseidon on the prow of a
johnboat, stripped to his waist with a torch in his hand
and the silver fish seething in the nets. He was six years
younger than Danger, just out of the army, and she asked
him to marry her. On their wedding night, she got dead
drunk and set fire to the minister's car.

She liked to remind people that Florida was the only
Confederate state that didn't surrender at the end of the
Civil War. To Danger, drug-smuggling, like moonshining,
was an ember of revolt in the tradition of the Confederate
blockade-runners. Gomez Gap was a backwater on the
very edge of the American Dream and a refuge where
what she called "the keepers of the faith," the alligator-
poachers and whisky-haulers, the dregs, outlaws, holdouts
and rebels, could hide out from the BMW-drivers and
tennis-players of this modern not-so-palatable world.

She drove for five minutes or so with my nose crushed
against her jeans' zipper, taking several curves at speed,
making the old car rock on its broken-down shocks. I
didn't know where we were until she stopped, and I
risked raising my head for a peep. We were parked in a
grove of splash pine at the end of the airport runway. In
front of us a sandspit stretched half a mile from the tip of
Piney Point to a marker buoy by the boat channel.

My heart gave a little bump of pleasure. This was where

Danger came to collect sand dollars for the tourists, where she came when she wanted to be alone to mourn Willie Weber, and where we had first made love.

"Get down," she snapped as I made to sit up. "I don't want to be seen even talking to you, much less sitting in this car alone with you in the woods."

I snuggled against her again; I didn't mind. Beneath the black cloth of her skirt, I could feel the warmth of her skin. I could smell her deodorant, the sweat from working at the bar, the smoke from her cigarettes. I reached up and undid the top button; she pretended not to notice.

"My girls say you were passed out drunk in the back of your store this morning," she said in a tone of sharp reproof.

"I had a mild reaction to medication," I said. "I wasn't drunk."

"They say you got a part in the movie. Is that true, Tully? I told 'em you might be exaggerating. I don't want you fucking with my kids' minds."

Danger could be as self-righteous as the next person when it came to her children. I don't mean to disparage her intentions; she really believed she protected and cared for them. That it was her children who generally took care of her was but a grain of truth against the mountain of her conviction. Time and again, I had met Cecily picking up a few things at the Seven-Eleven Store, telling everyone "Momma's in bed with viral dipthemosa." Or "Momma's got spinal mennonites."

"I've got a part," I said. "I won't disappoint them. What the hell—I used to be married to the director's wife."

"That's another thing," she said. I nuzzled the pale undersides of her breasts with the tip of my nose. "What's going on between you and her? As soon as she showed up I thought there was something funny about it. And Audie said Osterwalder called in a sexual-assault report on you. Did you fuck her?"

She sounded jealous; she was five women all jumbled together; it made me crazy for her. I buried my tongue in her navel. I remembered that other time, how I had just strolled to the point for some spin-casting when I spotted her trapped on the sand spit, water up to her knees and the tide racing in.

By the time I reached her, the Gulf had risen to our waists. Danger was crying, confused; she hadn't moved. "Don't touch me!" she said, looking out to sea. I grabbed her arm but she struggled. "Leave me alone. Just let me be." She'd already left Bubba by then; I knew she was having a hard time. We fell in the water, and I slugged her and carried her to shore fireman style over my shoulders. Hidden in the trees, we stripped off our wet clothes and made love.

Afterwards she pretended she had only been hunting sand dollars, that I had made a fool of myself running out like that to rescue her.

"Stop that," she said.

"What?"

"What you're doing and thinking."

"I didn't have anything to do with Lydia coming here," I said. "It was a complete surprise to me. Honest, Danger. What do you care for anyway? You're back with Bubba and all."

"I can care about what I want to care about and I don't give a flying fuck what you think."

When she tried to do up her buttons, I put my face in the way. I kissed her nipples, her throat and then her lips. She gave me a little kiss back, a half-kiss, then thought better of it. She pushed me off.

"Why'd you cut down that tree?" she asked.

"I thought it'd impress you."

"People around town are up in arms. They're keeping quiet about it while the movie's going on but cutting that tree has been seen as major criticism of the way things are in Gomez Gap. Some would like to use you to inaugurate a new tree. You should leave."

"I'm not scared." I kissed her throat hard and felt her thighs go slack.

"Yes," she said, when she had caught her breath, "and you have solid bone between your ears, too. Listen, Tully, I'm going back with Bubba. It's final." She grabbed a hank of my hair and dragged me off her chest. "Now get out. And don't come walking out of these woods till I'm long gone. So help me."

Then she kissed me. I felt her tongue playing hide-and-seek in my dental work, her arms crushing the back of my neck, her breath going in and out against my cheek. I shut my eyes, then opened them—a tear dribbled down her nose.

"I love you," I whispered.

"Get out," she said.

I watched her go, the car zigzagging crazily down the runway, sending flocks of terns and willets into the air.

13

The sun was lowering over the horizon, shiny as a brass carpet tack. The line for extras snaked around the stone cairn and drinking fountain in front of the Bayard Onions High School. The head of the snake was inside the fieldhouse door, its snout against the basketball coach's desk where three assistant directors in tennis shorts and rayon-rhinestone cowboy shirts sat appraising prospects.

A brass plaque on the cairn bore the inscription:

> Site of the Onions Battery, Battle of Gomez Gap, 1864. Col. Bayard Onions accompanied by a force of local Confederate militia mounted six field guns on this spot prior to the landing of Union troops the afternoon of 22 March. The position afforded an unimpeded view of the enemy throughout the early hours of the Union attack. Col. Onions directed fire and defensive operations until repeated assaults forced his men to retire.

Another of Bethamae Hamsett's inspirations.

What the plaque neglected to explain was that Col. Onions lost a foot and an eye to enemy bullets that dreadful afternoon, that after three hours of intense fighting he mistakenly ordered his men to hurl chain-shot point-blank at a relief column approaching from the rear, that he fell into a disused outhouse hole during the retreat over Nigger Hill and died two weeks later of septicemia. His last words were, "I do not need the chamber-pot."

The line-up seemed impossibly long. Many of the faces of those seeking celluloid immortality were unknown to me. Word of the movie had no doubt spread and people were flocking from out of town to seek parts. I spotted Wade Fowler, Ted Maberly and his brother Orvis, standing to one side, sipping Budweiser from cans.

Ted and Orvis, with their elder brother Roy, had the garbage-collection contract for Gomez Gap. Orvis always wore a straw hat with a feather in it and carried a huge Buck knife with a wheel lock, which he used for cleaning his fingernails. Ted was the youngest of the brood, but looked the oldest, and lived in a shack on an out-island with a toothless welfare mother named Grace Flack. Wade Fowler looked like Hemingway with that white beard. He always wore the same clothes, Levi's workshirts, jeans with a Texas-longhorn beltbuckle Ina had given him, and cowboy boots.

"'Lo, Ted. 'Lo, Orvis. 'Lo, Wade," I said. They ignored me. "I hear Doc Coyle just flew in from Tampa to take a look at you, Wade."

"What the fuck do you mean by that?" said Fowler, moving his hips as though getting ready to leap at my throat. In a place like Gomez Gap, taking offense in ambiguous social situations is considered manly.

"Nothing. Nothing at all," I said. "Only Ma's Wasserman test came back from the lab positive."

"You son of a bitch, Tully," said Wade. "Your mother deserved better than you. I ought to—"

He was acting tough but I could see he was shaken.

"They say drinking's bad for it," I said, cutting him off and turning to Orvis who'd just thrown his empty beer can into a palmetto bush and slipped the knife out of his pocket. "You going to be in the movie, Orvis? They go for strong speechless types in Hollywood." Orvis was bashful and spoke with a stutter. He made a playful stab at me with the knife. Ted just stared with his mad little eyes.

Once he'd offered to show me the bodies of three hitch-hikers from the North who'd disappeared mysteriously into the swamps. I had never known whether to believe him or not.

I hate crowds, and, besides, one thing I could not afford was to have someone tell Danger I had been forced to endure a cattle call after I had already sworn to her daughters I was going to be a star. So I hurried away, affecting an expression of worldliness that bespoke superior connections, and went looking for Lydia.

I found Walter Hebel, a.k.a. Otto Osterwalder, brushing doughnut crumbs from his chest hair on the settee in the living-room. He had the TV on—he was watching a video tape of himself being interviewed by Johnny Carson. It was a bizarre juxtaposition, full of ironies. There was Otto in the box, sweating under the studio lights, staring goggle-eyed at the camera, replying in Hunnish monosyllables to Carson's glib questions. Otto was wearing dirty jeans and a denim jacket. His belly hung over his belt like a sack of fish. He was chain-smoking cigarettes and sipping nervously from a water jug. Meanwhile, Walter was stretched out on my settee in a T-shirt and jock strap, belching, scratching his armpits, obviously proud of his performance on TV.

"'Lo, Walter," I said, failing pointedly to knock on my own door.

"Good to see you, Tully," he replied, grinning sheepishly.

"Where's Lydia?"

"She's scouting for local color. Actually she went looking for you with that broad next door. Ruthie. Sit down and wait, why don't you?"

I noted with irritation the subtle alteration of my domestic arrangments. My stereo, my rubber and ficus plants, the hoyas that had once formed a zone of tropical vegetation around the window, had disappeared. An editing table stood against the wall, cluttered with film racks, rewinds, moviolas and a typewriter. Bits of paper, schedules, memoranda, legends, slogans, photographs and sketches of Civil War battles had been Scotch-taped to the wallpaper.

Walter farted. A wet one. The sound of hands clapping around his asshole. Right into my furniture. I felt sick. I knew it would never come out. Plainly, the man hated me.

"Sorry I smacked you this morning," he said. "I'm an animal when I'm shooting. Lydia'll tell you." His German accent had vanished. His voice sounded flat and twangy just like anybody else from De Puke, Iowa, where his family owned a house on a hill near the Mississippi River. "I was half-asleep. It's a real bitch. I didn't get a chance to prep this picture. I work on the script all night, catch the rushes at six A.M., start shooting at nine. Next week I gotta be in Cannes to get some award. You want a joint?"

His eyes lit up. This was a glimmer of the old Walter Hebel whose only social accomplishment was having learned the words "You want a joint?" He said this every chance he got; he considered it a universally appropriate conversational gambit. He said it even when he didn't have any dope. Now he had a new line to go with it.

"We got some coke in the bedroom."

He rolled off the settee and ambled, bear-like, hair sprouting like oiled springs from his jock, into the next room, returning a moment later with a silver gunpowder flask and a teaspoon. He was grinning.

"I'm a terrible infant," he said, nodding at the television. His alter ego had just mimed jerking off and poured ice water down the front of his pants. Carson continued to smile tolerantly.

He slipped the stopper out of the flask and tapped a cone of white powder into his teaspoon. Stopping up his left nostril with an index finger, he sniffed the cone up

into the hell of his right nostril, phlegm cracking like bedsheets in the wind. His eyes watered. His cheeks went
chalk-white. He sighed. He looked at me like a son. He
tried to say something, but it came out a grunt. He passed
me the flask. He made a series of snorting sounds, tossing
his nose higher and higher with each. Then he fell back
on the settee and sighed again.

I dabbed a little coke onto the back of my hand like salt
and sniffed. I am a man born suspicious of people who
offer salvation in a powder flask. I am a man born to disas-
ters which are always total. But this wasn't bad. I tried
some more. Before I could stop myself I was filling the
spoon to overflowing, spilling coke onto the rattan carpet
for the cockroaches, forking it up my nose as fast as I
could.

It burned. It fizzed. It caused me to snort and sneeze
like a hay-fever sufferer in a bed of pigweed. There was a
little cloud of white dust in front of me. I went sniffing
through it like a bloodhound after a lost child. I was
snorting the air like a vacuum cleaner. I wanted to pull my
nose off and get it down on the floor where the stuff had
fallen. It was all right. It felt good.

Walter was watching me.

I was all nose. There was nothing I could do about it.
My nose was a cock, an organ of pleasure and generation.
I wanted to shove my nose into some snatch. I could have
satisfied a cow elephant with my nose. Even Walter looked
good to me. I wanted to set fire to his hair. I felt sure he
wouldn't mind. I found some matches in my sailcloth
pockets and started tossing them at Walter's chest. Walter
was laughing.

"Take my wife," I said.

"Take my wife," he said.

He was a hell of a guy.

"What's burning?"

This was Lydia, some time later, back from hunting Tully.

"Walter," I said, though I couldn't be sure if it was true. He had disappeared into the bathroom. "I came to ask for a part in the movie and set fire to him."

Lydia's forehead wrinkled. She never knew with me. I was a psychological mystery. A surd, she called me once. I still don't know what she meant. But Walter was soon back to clear things up. He was laughing. There was a bare patch about the size of a drink coaster between his nipples. He pointed to it.

"Tully burned me," he said proudly.

Johnny Carson was signing off for the third or fourth time. On TV Otto's fly was undone and part of his shirt-tail was hanging out like rabbit ears. He had two cigarettes protruding from his nostrils and his eyeballs were rolled back so that only the whites showed.

"Pretty childish," I said.

"It's his image," Lydia snapped. "He has to look eccentric in public. It's very effective."

"You mean he's not like that all the time?"

The subject of our discussion had tapped a mound of coke onto the table top and was sniffing it up through a snorkel he had found in the bathroom. He was all hair and sweat, and his glasses kept falling off. He was making little woofing sounds, breathing through his mouth. Lydia looked pissed. I'd seen that look many times. The trouble with Lydia is a certain narrowness of outlook.

"Everybody wants to be in the movie," she said. "I thought you'd be above that. More original at least. When we were first married you wouldn't have wasted your time doing anything but paint and fuck."

Her cynical tone jarred within the context of the witty banter I had been enjoying at Walter's expense. Perhaps, I thought, it had not been a good idea to come after all.

Perhaps certain initial reservations, abandoned in the heat of the moment, had proved correct—that there was something seamy and undignified about asking my ex-wife and her husband for a favor in order to impress Danger and her daughters.

"Does that mean no?" I asked.

Lydia said nothing, but rolled her eyes and flexed one corner of her mouth, a piece of body language I had learned to construe as unwillingness to pursue a certain line of discussion.

She was wearing shorts and thongs and an embroidered smock that had tiny holes all over the front. I could see her nipples through the holes. I wondered what she and Walter did in bed and then banished the thought as not in keeping with the mood of optimism and bonhomie engendered by the cocaine. On impulse I touched the back of her knee with my forefinger. The skin shivered, little seismic disturbances of the heart. She loved being fondled behind the knee, just where the skin never quite tanned.

"I love you," I said. It was true. Seeing her only served to remind me of this elementary fact of existence. We had shared part of our lives together. And I figured it wouldn't hurt to mention it while Walter was making such a pig of himself.

For once in your life, Tully Stamper, be serious," she said, walking away from my finger and sitting next to Walter. "I've been looking all over for you. I thought by now you'd want to talk. We have to talk."

"About what?"

"About the baby—about Ariel."

I felt mildly euphoric. The coke had lent my thoughts a new clarity. And one thing I was particularly clear on was not wanting to talk about the baby. To me the baby meant nothing but sorrow, pain and tragedy.

"Where are you going?"

"Out," I said, a gloss on the obvious.

Lydia was plainly vexed, but I was in a sweat to get away from there. It had been the same thing at Elysium— therapists, hypnosis, truth drugs, shock. As though there was something morally bracing or curative about reliving horror. Remember, they had urged. And I did. Just as now I recalled the gory smile of Lydia's belly cut open in the delivery room. My God, at the time, I had thought she was dead.

I am not one of those cold Protestant souls who think the world is a better place for meeting it head-on. I was through the door before she could say another word.

Ariel. Ariel, I thought, running into the night.

At the gate I nearly tripped over Agent Julius Wachtel who had fallen asleep on a stake-out. He was snoring peacefully, his face hidden beneath a palmetto bush and a thermos of coffee, a notepad, a flashlight and a Smith & Wesson .38 within easy reach on the grass beside him.

I ran on. It was dark. Inside my head and out. Ariel Stamper. I had a rage to run, to burn off my misery like fat. But I ran out of breath and slowed to a walk in front of Ina's garage. The garage door was shut tight. There were voices inside.

14

I woke eight neighborhood dogs breaking into the boat-house, for which I had lost the key. Inside it was black as a licorice stick. I yanked the light cord, and the bulb blew out with a pop. I had placed boards over the boat slip to make a floor and piled lamp cartons around the walls up to the rafters. A little mountain of styrofoam packing chips had leaked out onto the boards. I unrolled an old sleeping-bag for a bed and composed myself for rest. I could hear the Gulf of Mexico lapping at the boathouse struts inches beneath my ears.

I closed my eyes and thought about the day: it had been averagely disastrous. I was empty and discredited, my fragile philosophy in tatters, my unreasoned code as full of holes as a sponge. Yet it could have been worse. When you touch bottom, you get a scrape, but it wakes you up. At least you know where you are. To tell the truth I was getting excited. We ought to pray to be resisted, I thought. Resisted to the bitter end.

My body and brains had taken so much abuse in the past twenty-four hours that it wasn't long before I fell asleep. I don't know how long I stayed like that. But when I awoke the darkness was exactly the same shade of black it had been when I shut my eyes. My mouth was full of styrofoam; I felt like a man in a box. There was someone beside me.

I threw up a hand instinctively to protect myself. It came into contact with something soft and spongy. It felt around—a little knob at the end. There was no doubt about it. I was touching a breast.

My heart leaped like a trout.

"Lydia," I said.

An alien hand came out of nowhere. Wham! It caught me right across the nose. I thought I was bleeding again. I was stunned.

My fingers scouted tentatively in ever-increasing circles around the breast. No one tried to stop me. I quickly located the other breast. The two of them were suspended above me like fruit. There was a bit of clavicle and neck about where you would expect them. And down below I was able to stick my pinky up to the second knuckle in someone's navel.

I was a little disoriented, waking up like that, the slap and all. But finding these anatomical landmarks in the right places somehow gave me confidence.

"Dange—?" I said, without being able to finish.

This time the hand had become a fist. It came in under my left ear. My ear was ringing. My head ached. Tiny red flashbulbs exploded inside my eyes. I had been dead wrong twice. It made a man lose heart. I decided to keep my mouth shut and await developments.

There were knees on either side of my hips. The hand, or maybe it was the hand's partner, reached down and began rooting around in my drawstrings.

I was prompted to speak again. But the hand came down over my mouth, gently but firmly. Then I felt someone's warm breath against my cheek. A kiss. The hand had finished fumbling with my pants. Her body pressed down, cool and anxious and dry. I didn't mind.

All around us were the cardboard cartons containing the Stamper lamps, fruit of my labor, hope of my future. On each of the boxes there was a logo I had designed myself: a generalized hand pulling a generalized lamp-chain and the words

AND STAMPER SAID UNTO THE WORLD,

LET THERE BE LIGHT!

But we couldn't see them. The styrofoam chips squeaked under my back.

I had met Colonel Parkhurst at Abe's Bar & Grill on Linn Street in Iowa City one hot Saturday afternoon while I waited for Lydia to get through visiting her obstetrician in the Medical Arts building next door. He had bought me a drink and showed me a smudged business card. No address. No phone number. Just PARKHURST/INVENTIONS. He looked exactly like Sidney Greenstreet in *The Maltese Falcon*, smelled of mothballs and infrequent bathing. He asked me how I'd like to get in on the ground floor of a million-dollar electronics deal.

I wasn't a lamp-stand mogul by nature, let me tell you. But my wife was big with child. Not big, titanic. She went in and out of rooms like a yacht under full sail. Across the parking-lot was my only source of steady income, a blood-transfusion clinic where I made $72.50 a month donating the maximum allowable number of quarts as often as medically possible.

Parkhurst had a patent on a process by which liquid plastic could be made to resemble marble. I suspected this was mostly bar talk, repeated a hundred times in a hundred deaf ears. But he used words like "minimal downside risk," "on-line capacity," "consumer research," and "aesthetic component." The words thrilled me. He was offering fifty percent in return for a small infusion of "venture capital."

To tell the truth, before I could see the drawbacks, I was hooked. It was a compromise, business with art. Aesthetics would play a key role, I told myself. I would shed light in dark corners while making money to finance Lydia's astonishing fecundity. I shook the colonel's hand on the spot.

You may well ask where a penniless art student with a pregnant wife, already maxed-out on student loans and with no prospects, could find the necessary investment

capital. I did it the American way—I sold drugs. Walter
Hebel was my best customer. With Parkhurst at my elbow
and a wad of cash in my back pocket, I bought a suit,
leased a BMW, looked at buildings, purchased machinery,
drills, vats, saws, lathes, polishers, found suppliers, retail
outlets. We threw away the first dozen batches of con-
gealed plastic marble because either it was too brittle and
crumbled, or it was too soft and melted when a light bulb
was inserted in the socket and turned on. Parkhurst called
this "tooling up." I was impressed with the words.

From the start I knew we had a hot item on our hands—
art lamps in abstract shapes, molded in plastic, veined to
look like marble. Green, blue, wine and cherry. Granted
the early orders were small—a craft store in Jersey City, a
gift shop in San Diego that catered to off-duty Naval per-
sonnel, Lipnick, the czar of parking-lot art—but I knew
the whole thing would gain momentum.

I rarely saw Lydia those days. She had failed to sympa-
thize with the lamp project from the start. "Anal reten-
tive" was her only comment as I gloated over balance
sheets and sales projections. "Feces fixation" was what she
said as I ran my fingers over the oily coldness of a brand-
new second-hand industrial jigsaw. She would lie in the
back yard in her underpants, letting the baby feel the sun,
looking like a lizard that had just eaten a small dog. She
would say, "Listen, capitalist pig, you can hear our baby."
But every time I put my ear down there it sounded like
triplets.

I had made my first delivery to Lipnick and shipped
lamps UPS to San Diego and New Jersey when Parkhurst
hit me with the small print. I was stunned. He had includ-
ed a buy-back clause in our partnership agreement—he
could purchase my fifty percent of the company any time
during the first year of operation with payment in kind
(with lamps!). He hired a Ryder truck and delivered
three thousand Stamper lamps to the Governor Street

duplex. They were in the yard. They were piled on the stairs. They filled the living-room. I had to get Rev. Penney to open up the church basement to take some of the overflow.

I tried to hide the whole thing from Lydia while I thought of a way out. But this was impossible. I mean there were a lot of Stamper-designed lamp crates. She opened one on the way upstairs—she was at the stage where she had to stop for a rest every few steps. It contained a wine-colored sailboat in plastic marble. I was pretty proud of it. When she opened the box, I had a feeling the day wasn't going to be a complete loss. Which just shows how wrong you can be.

I tried to stifle such negative memories while I dealt with the lady of the boathouse. But inevitably I would catch myself thinking of the lamps at the strangest times. The actual mechanics of sex are simple, as you probably know. By and large even the most inattentive lover can perform passably if his partner is eager enough. Peter-George, as always, was avid as a ferret after a rabbit to get into her hole. Meanwhile I tried to measure distances with my palms in an effort to arrive at an estimate of the overall length of the woman. But even at the height of passion she was conscious enough to slap my hands away. I closed my eyes and tried to imagine what color her hair was from the smell. Pointless.

It was a mystery all right. She was all darkness and heat, this woman. Her breath was like melted honey. And her pussy sucked up Peter-George so strongly that I feared for his return from that humid passage, that human labyrinth—my Perseus. But in all that drunkenness of arms and legs and heaving loins there remained also some essence of the act that was not just a proof for the inevitability of lust. I was there; she was there. Whoever she was. We cleaved to each other. Her hair was the color of night and I could see sparks fly off it. She was all female, all kindness and accommodation. Our lips flew like batwings, finding each other by sound and feel. And we said not a word after my first wayward greetings.

When we were done, she lay beside me, her chest rising and falling like breath. I pressed my hand against her ribs and felt them rise and fall. She left it there. I stayed awake, resolved to await the moon and by its rays solve the mystery of her identity. But I was too much satisfied and too fatigued by my exertions, and before long I slept.

An hour, two hours passed. Perhaps she was asleep as well.

She woke me with her hand.

"Who are you?" I asked.

"Sssshhhh," she said. It was the first sound she had made.

"I mean have we met somewhere before?" I asked. "Because if we haven't my name is Tully—"

"Sssshhhh," she repeated. This time I felt the hiss of her lips as they trailed down my chest, across my belly and tickled my pubic hair.

"Will I see you again?" I asked. "Can we make a date? How about a cup of coffee? I'll meet you. I'll be wearing. . .ouch!"

It was a playful nip. The lady was firm. She knew the rules. Hell, she made the rules. It was irritating. Men like to fantasize about meeting women of character, but the real thing is scary. I lay back, thought about lamps, resolved not to be an easy lay. But Peter-George was after it again. He was out of control. The dark lady took him by the neck and rammed him home like a professional bull-breeder, settled in the saddle with a sigh, eased herself, rolled her hips. We were away.

It was better than the first time. I don't know why. Maybe it was because we knew each other now. I really wanted to talk. I'm usually the one to be mum, but the situation intrigued me.

She was sitting on my belly, her hands on my shoulders—the watching position. What could she see in that darkness? What did I look like? It wasn't flattering. To be taken blind. I could have been a bald, one-eyed harelip and she would have loved me just as well. I opened my mouth to speak. She put her fingers there. I licked them; I worshipped them. She placed her hand over my eyes, closing them gently. The hand was cool. It seemed to vibrate. I wanted to close my eyes. I wanted to sleep again. I was dreaming the hand. I was dreaming the woman.

Later, I woke and she was gone.

15

I was awakened in the gray pre-dawn by the percussive application of clenched fists to the boathouse door. The neighborhood dogs were barking. Outside, my mother was crying, "Tully, Tully, wake up. There's been an accident. Wake up!"

It was difficult to make out what she wanted. I am always afraid of fires—the first thing that came to mind was that the boathouse was ablaze. I felt around for the mystery woman. Nothing. Ina was bashing the walls—I could see the planks heaving at each blow. I thought she was going to collapse the building the way she was handling it.

"I'm awake," I yelled. "Cut it out! I'm awake!"

"Tully, Tully," she went on, ignoring my pleas.

I was moving slowly, my mind taken up with the events of the previous night. Having convinced myself the threat of fire was remote, owing to the tell-tale absence of flames and smoke, I carefully unrolled the sleeping-bag and searched the folds for hairs. I found eight—three belonged to me, one was curly and blonde, which made me suspect Lydia again, one was red (incontrovertibly left over from an affair with a schoolteacher from Toronto three years before), the rest belonged to distinct breeds of dog. I threw them away in disgust.

Opening the boathouse door, tying my pants, I discovered my mother grossly underdressed in a scarlet teddy and hot-pink puffy bedroom slippers. It was a shock. I stared for a least a minute. It was the primal scene. The sort of perverse image that scars young male minds and hamstrings their relations with other women. I was about to explain this to Ina when she interrupted me.

"Oh, Tully," she wailed. Her mascara was running, creating black deltas beneath her eyes.

"Who did this to you?" I asked, suddenly full of righteous indignation.

"What?" she asked back, looking confused, hunted and scared. "What's wrong with me?"

"Don't you know?" I yelled, getting a little crazy. "Oh, my God!"

We were both hysterical. She dragged me across the bulkhead and up the path to the house in her teddy, both of us in tears. I loved my mother—every son does—and believed that something terrible had happened. By the time we reached the house, however, I was beginning to calm down. Ina looked so spry and energetic it stood to reason there wasn't much wrong with her. I had just had such a fright seeing her like that.

Turning into her driveway around the end of the overgrown palmetto hedge, we found Ina's 1959 Rambler American with its rear end smashed and gnarled into a knot of bent steel and its reclining front seats tipped back. The garage door had been bent outwards and was flying permanently at right angles like a bed-sheet in a strong wind. Evidently someone had driven the car backwards out of the garage without bothering to open the door first.

"Ina," I said, the soul of patience. "Dr Coyle warned you against driving while medicated."

"Accident," she whimpered shamelessly.

It was then that I noticed the body slumped in the front seat.

"Shit!" I said.

"He's dead. He's dead. I knew he was dead. I killed him. I'm a bad person, Tully. Tully, help me get away."

Ina was shrieking, doing a little dance in her bedroom slippers on the pine needles and pavement.

The body was Wade Fowler's. He was reclining in the

passenger seat, his head thrown back, mouth gaping gro-
tesquely, lips blue, very relaxed-looking. He had one hand
on the sill of the open window, the other rested on the
back of the driver's seat. His trousers and underpants were
tangled around his ankles. He had pale, hairless legs and
blue argyle socks. His Levi's workshirt was unbuttoned. His
cock lay like a turkey neck on his blue-veined thigh.

"Call Dr Coyle," I yelled.

"Couldn't we just dump him in the Gulf?" said Ina.

"Dr Coyle," I repeated.

Ina gave a squeal of protest and crumpled up on the
driveway. I walked into the house and dialed Dr Coyle's
number, which Ina had taped to her receiver. Coyle was a
Tampa osteopath who kept a second office in Gomez
Gap. He flew his own Cessna four-seater back and forth,
spending half the week with his family in Tampa and half
with his mistress and her family in the Gap. Sometimes he
flew to Las Vegas for a blow-out and the two families
would get together and have a picnic or go to Disney
World. Inevitably, they would end up trading Russell
Coyle stories; Coyle never caught on.

The mistress, Elaine Nightingale, came on the line at
the fifteenth ring. This was a relief, as I could count on her
to make sure the doctor got out of bed and drove over. I
ran back to the car. Ina was sitting up, dusting the pine
needles off her elbows.

"I expected better of you," she said sadly.

"What did you do to him?" I asked.

"Oh, Tully, it was an accident," she said with a resigned
shrug. "I wanted some help with the garage door. You
know it never worked. And Wade, I mean Mr Fowler,
seemed so handy with mechanical things, which is more
than I can say for some people."

"He didn't get like this fixing the damn door," I
muttered. I was dabbing at his wrist with my fingertips,
trying to detect his pulse.

"Of course not," she said. "That was last night. I asked him over to help with the door and—would you believe it?—he somehow locked the door while we were inside. It was awful."

The way Ina said the words made "It was awful" sound about as harrowing as "It was Tuesday." I dragged Fowler out of the car. I could see Ina's clothes in the back seat where she had thrown them.

"It was awful," she repeated. "What are you   doing?"

"Kiss of life," I said.

"It looks a little—you know."

"Shut up," I said.

It was all too clear what had happened. Ina had contrived to trap Fowler in the garage for the night and then seduced him. The poor fellow's ticker hadn't been up to the strain. He had congestive heart failure, no doubt, brought on by over-exertion.

I took a deep breath and blew into his mouth. His chest fell, then rose as I let up, just the opposite of what it was supposed to do. I blew in again, puffing till lights danced in front of my bulging eyes and my ears popped.

"I took his pants off to help him breathe," said Ina, adjusting her shoulder straps and patting her hair into place.

Recalling a dozen or so TV movies I had seen on the subject, I began thumping Fowler on the chest with my fists.

"Live! Live!" I cried, desperately.

At that moment, Dr Coyle drove up, parking his kid's dune buggy at the foot of the driveway.

"Nice morning, Tully," he called cheerily. Coyle was notoriously undependable at diagnosis. Usually he let his patients tell him what was wrong with them. He was happiest when they prescribed their own medication. A man lying stricken beside a smashed car with a second man pounding on his chest meant nothing to Dr Coyle.

"Ina," whispered the corpse. "Please, no more."

"I don't recall what happened, actually," said Ina coyly. "It's those drugs Dr Coyle gives me." She batted her eyes at the doctor as he ambled up, watching the palmettos. "When he went like that I guess I panicked and drove the car out. I'm sorry I killed him."

"What can I do for you folks today?" asked Dr Coyle. "'Lo, Ina."

"Dying," I gasped, out of breath from resuscitating Fowler.

"Nonsense," he said. "You're a little pale. I'll give you a course of Preludin if I've got any. Let me look in the car."

"Fowler's dying!" I yelled.

"Car accident?" asked Coyle. "Don't touch him, Tully. Wait for competent medical aid."

The doctor walked over to us and shook his head at the moribund painter.

"What's wrong with his legs?" he asked. "Why have you taken his pants off?"

"Tully thought it would help him breathe," said Ina.

"He was like this when I found him," I said, giving her a frank, mother-son look that implied great bitterness.

"Sugar," said Coyle inconsequently.

"What?"

"Sugar, I should think."

"What?"

"Diabetic seizure by the looks of it—though I'd prefer a second opinion. Just give him a little sugar water and he'll be right as rain."

Coyle was already heading back to the dune buggy, his hands in his pockets.

"What?"

"I'll see if I can't get you that Preludin, Tully. Fix you right up. Hear you're in the movie. Grand, grand. Catch you on *Celebrity Squares*. See you around. Bye, Ina."

Five minutes later, while pouring orange juice into

Fowler's parched and avid throat, I noticed the medic-alert bracelet on his wrist. It listed symptoms and disease in precise stainless-steel script and in three languages. I felt like a fool. I could have injured him slugging his heart like that.

Coming around, he sent me next door for his insulin kit. In half an hour, after dosing himself in the thigh, he was on his feet again. Ina and I watched him go from her Dutch door. He was not the man he'd been when he started his night's mischief. He listed heavily to the right. His gait was shambling. Holding his pants up with one hand, he walked with the other outstretched like a blind man in a furniture store.

"How was I to know?" said Ina mirthlessly, full of pique as she retreated to her bedroom, her teddy crimping and luffing like a sail in the wind. Pitiless, she seemed to me. But then she had always demanded a lot from her men. For a moment I almost felt sorry for the errant artist. With his superior attitude and sly desires and fading powers, he was a caution to us all.

16

Earlier I had spotted my mother's pocketbook on the kitchen counter. Taking advantage of her discomposure, I rifled the contents, palming the cash (all $1.87), dabbing a little My Sin under my armpits and giving myself a once-over in her compact mirror. Eyes like red caves, chin grizzled with premature white, nose as pitted as a photograph of the Mare Nubium on the moon—all I needed were a few paint spatters and a smelly sweatshirt to reproduce that artist-wrestling-with-his-demon look Lydia had fallen so hard for.

Skipping out the front door, I strode purposefully to the street with nothing more criminal on my mind than breakfast. But, passing my former home, I suddenly found myself turning up the path to the doorstep as calmly as if I still lived there and had just returned from a morning's crabbing. My intentions were innocent of malice; I swear I only wanted to make sure there were no misunderstandings about the role I was to play in Walter's movie and, perhaps, to trap Lydia into admitting she had visited me in the boathouse during the night.

The door was locked, but I always kept a spare key hidden in the crotch of a lime tree in the yard. In seconds I was inside, moving quickly toward the kitchen. The George Dickel was under the sink behind the cleaning bottles. Almost a gallon. Walter hadn't touched it. Above the sink I found the shoebox with my collection of potato chips in the shapes of state maps. I had fifty states, many duplicates and five islands of the Hawaiian archipelago.

With the shoebox under my arm and the George

Dickel hanging from my index finger, I tiptoed into the bedroom. It was still early. Outside, the morning sky which had promised so much had turned the color of café au lait. Once more Lydia was asleep, naked, on top of the sheets; Walter snored gracelessly with his head hanging over the side of the bed as though his neck were broken.

Silent as breath, I oozed over to the closet. At the back, hidden by Lydia's clothes (momentarily I was forced to lean against the doorjamb, insentient, dizzy with lust), there was a footlocker full of old tennis socks I'd forgotten to wash, a bird's nest, a shell collection and a Webley & Scott .38 I had bought on a trip to Canada in case of wolves. The locker made a hell of a racket coming out.

"You ape, you!"

It was Lydia, not asleep after all, sitting up with her breasts crushed against her knees like pillows and her fur purse pouting at me from underneath.

"What do you want?"

"Checking the meters," I said. "Ina wanted me to check the meters in the cottages since you are new renters."

Lydia's eyes rolled. She looked vexed. More déjà vu. I saw Lydia marching up the wooden stairs outside the Governor Street duplex with the sailboat lamp, blue, gold-veined, like neon Carrera marble. I held the locker in front of my face to shut out the vision. And remembered Lydia snapping her fingers, tapping her toes, impatient, while I cranked the arm of a fellow Elysium inmate who thought he was an antique Victrola. I am a man with many things to be guilty for.

Walter snored, drooling upside down into his nose.

The footlocker fell open; I grabbed the first thing that dropped out—the revolver. It was a relatively common World War I model, speckled with rust, lacking ammunition. Remembering Walter's actions the previous morning, I trained the sights on his head and breathed deeply.

"Get the fuck out of here!" said Lydia, a note of incredulity in her voice.

I could see her point of view. They were renting the house, not an ex-husband.

"Sssshhhh," I said, pressing the Webley's barrel to my lips. "Didn't want to disturb you if you were still asleep. I just wanted to pick up a few things Ina forgot to move to the boathouse."

I stepped over and sat on the end of the bed, staring at Lydia's feet. They were beautifully proportioned, tanned on top, oyster white underneath, five toes on each, all at the ends, little secret pockets between them. I knew these feet well. But it made Lydia uncomfortable, me staring at them like that.

"I love you," I said, meaning every word of it.

All of a sudden, I was overwrought, and Lydia could see it. To Lydia, I had always been an open book. The sight of me, all sincere and pitiable, at the end of the bed brought tears to the inside corners of her eyes. The sight of her tears brought tears to my eyes. I felt certain she was the boathouse succubus, the night maiden of my dreams.

"What's going to become of you, Tully?" she asked in a whisper, her eyes dripping onto her cheeks. "You're always doing crazy things, but you never get anywhere."

I'd have felt better if she had yelled at me. Feckless, confused, even dull-witted, I was willing to grant her. But not hopeless.

"You could have been a great artist," she said. I tried not to listen. "The week we were married Professor Lipshinsky nominated you for the Bellinger Prize. The Art Institute in Chicago tried to buy your mural "J.C.'s Last Stand, or Bad Night at Golgotha.""

"They were nuts," I said. "The art building would have fallen if they'd taken that wall."

"And then, when the baby came, you stopped, Tully. You just. . .stopped." Lydia was wailing quietly so as not to wake Walter. The effect was eerie. Her eyes were swollen and glossy with sadness. I wanted to kiss her knees, nuzzle her breasts, press my chin into the L of her jaw, which drove her wild, anything to make her stop this litany of my failure.

"You ran out on us. You used Ariel as an alibi, but really you just ran out. What's wrong with you?" she asked, giving me a look full of irritation and inquiry.

"I'm a deeply neurotic human being," I said.

"Is that an excuse or an explanation?"

I thought for a moment—"An excuse."

"Do you *like* living in a place like this?" she asked.

"Once you get past the violence, corruption, racism and paranoia, these people are really very nice," I said.

"What about the baby?" she asked. "What about Ariel?"

"What about her?"

"Do you remember her?"

"Yes."

I opened the potato-chip collection and nibbled Rhode Island. A tear slipped off my chin onto Manhattan, so I ate New York too. Walter snored on. Nothing could upset Walter's equilibrium. The man was a psychological bulldozer.

"You always remembered, didn't you? You always knew you had a baby. You weren't crazy. You just ran away, pure and simple. It makes me so mad to think about it. Such a waste. I used to think it was my fault. Maybe if I hadn't wanted you to be such a success—"

She began to sob quietly.

It had never occurred to me to blame her for my short-comings. Just as it had never crossed my mind that she ever felt anything but anger over what had happened between us. Certainly the day she had returned to our Iowa City duplex from her art-history class to find the lawn and stairway piled high with Stamper lamps in crates, she had cried. But she'd also been irate, with words like bullwhips.

"What is this?" she had demanded, holding up what was obviously a sailboat lamp minus bulb and wiring. "The marketing people say that will be our number-one seller," I said. "Crap," she said. "It's sort of art deco," I said. "What's happening to you, Tully?" she asked. "I'm in business," I said, pointing to a stack of *Fortune* magazines, heavily annotated and underlined. "What about your pictures? What about the baby?" she asked. "What about dinner?" I countered, attempting to deflect her with the thought of food. That was when she began to cry. She had only turned angry when she saw the crates in the shower.

"Gomez Gap has been good to me. I've done well here," I said, taking a sip of George Dickel to wash down the potato chips. "Nothing was your fault. I was mixed up. But I was on the right track. I'm painting, and I've sued Parkhurst's ass back in Iowa. Any day now that factory will be mine and I'll be able to give you everything I ever promised."

Lydia's expression suddenly hardened. She wiped her eyes on the sheets, wiped the little runnels on her breasts.

"I flew to Iowa to see the factory," she said, "when I heard Walter was bringing the crew down here."

I held my breath. Lydia had never expressed the slightest interest in the factory while we were together. In fact she had made me promise, several times, never to mention it again. This was proof positive her feelings for me still existed.

"There isn't one," she said flatly. "It's empty. There are bailiff's notices—I counted fifteen—tacked on the doors."

My mind went blank. I tried not to listen. I had to take a good grip on myself to keep my sanity. I had witnessed so much unreality in my life and Lydia was blasting away at the last pillar of everything I now held to be true.

"If you win your lawsuit," she went on, "if you win, you'll be taking over Parkhurst's debts. That's all."

"That's simply untrue," I said calmly. "The Stamper

lamp is known throughout America, and loved. They retail in every department-store chain in the country. I have testimonials from people who claim Stamper lamps have been beneficial to their health. What's more, I will never understand why you took this negative attitude to the lamps in the first place. It has completely colored your sense of the way things are."

"Bullshit, Tully," she said. "You have been wasting your life. I didn't come after you when you left Elysium because I thought you'd be better off without me and the baby. I thought you'd find yourself once you were shut of responsibility. I loved you, but I couldn't be with you."

"I never left you in my mind," I said. I was serious, too. "I used to go to the bus station and the buses north had just left—"

"I wanted you to be happy," she said. Her eyes held mine. I was vaguely aware of having eaten the Panhandle off a Texas chip. Walter had his eyes open now, but his head was still tilted back. He was staring upside-down at a bullfighting poster on the opposite wall. "I wanted to be with you, but deep down you were still a boy. You didn't want me; you didn't want Ariel."

"Not true," I said. I didn't understand how such an intelligent woman could be so wrong about so many things. "I was always on my way back. I loved you, both of you."

"Walter needs me," she said, offering her absurd companion as a contrast. "He likes having me around, even though he doesn't seem to notice sometimes. I'm not sure he's capable of romantic love, but I know he's uncomfortable and nervous when he can't see me. You were always trying to get away."

She had her hand on Walter's waist just below his appendectomy scar. Walter was flailing his arms and legs like an upturned sow beetle, his eyes fixed on the bullfighter, not sure he was awake or where he was if he wasn't asleep.

Suddenly, I was angry with myself, my paltry ambitions, my grand delusions. At the same time, I was jealous of her tenderness. I realized she had tried to be tender with me too, once. But I had resisted. I didn't understand that. Walter had let her care for him.

"I'm thinking about getting married again," I said, lifting the bottle to my lips again, depressed, unable to stop myself.

Walter grunted; Lydia gazed at me.

"That's wonderful," she said sadly. "It makes me feel I'm losing you all over again."

"I'm painting a lot, painting up a storm," I rattled on, feeling badly for hurting her even a little. "And I'm thinking of marrying Danger Babcox, the poet. Even if the factory's a bust, I'll be all right. In fact, I'd given up thinking about the factory until you and Walter showed up and reminded me. To tell the truth I'm so well adjusted it scares me."

At the mention of Danger's name, Lydia's mouth flexed and her eyes narrowed. She said, "I'm glad for you, Tully." But the words came out flat and constrained.

"Danger has kids from a previous marriage," I said. "I always wanted a family—I know you don't believe that. And now that I'm painting—well, you be sure and come down to my studio and see what I'm doing. You won't believe the new concepts I'm working with. Animals—nature. I put birds in now—"

I was babbling and I knew it. I had to get out of there. Lydia continued to gaze into my eyes, staring right through me, which was unnerving. I had too much to hide. Her expression was full of curiosity, not judgmental. She was rubbing Walter's belly, making him calm like an alligator. Wondering if it could be true, what she had said about the factory, I took my gun and my shoebox and the whisky and stood up.

"I'll come," she said, her voice husky with emotion. "I'll be there."

I nodded gloomily. I saw the cormorants and the pelicans out on the Gulf. I believed her. On the way out the door, I recalled my reasons for coming in the first place. I realized I still had no idea who had loved me in the dark boathouse. Someone out there was thinking of me, remembering what I remembered. But I didn't know who she was, and I was alone.

17

Stepping down the walk, I heard the screen door in the next cottage slam shut. The bird lady was on her porch. T-shirt, baggy pants, K-Mart sneakers, knapsack and her binoculars swinging at her chest, threatening to end her breast-feeding years before they started. She was watching me and scowling.

I waved. She gave an answering wave. Perfunctory. Reluctant. No doubt about it—the woman was hard to get along with. She started along her walk and I could see that we were going to meet on the street. She had her hands in her pockets, her eyes on the pavement. She was short and her elbows flapped like wings. I steeled myself, trying to forget my troubles: Lydia, Ariel, the lamp factory, painting, the movie, money, Danger Babcox.

"'Lo, Ruthie," I said as we nearly collided on the narrow path. Wind's up. We're in for a douser."

She peered up at the sky through her glasses as if for the first time that day, myopically. I guessed she probably couldn't see the clouds. Behind her, the birds on the Gulf were clucking to one another on their perches, nosing into the breeze for balance, their feathers ruffled like the water. Having looked at the sky, Ruthie went back to staring at the ground. She seemed irritated about something; I had the feeling it was her preferred state of mind. Until further notice, I wasn't going to take it personally.

"Well, have a nice day," I said, smiling like a check-out clerk at the Seven-Eleven Store, breezy as a Rotarian at a convention, already two steps on my way.

"Wait a second!" she snapped, exasperated. She was looking at me, at my face, now. She was angry. "You want a cup of coffee?" It was half-command, half-query. It was a strange thing to say in the situation, a beat off tempo, the way her slang had sounded the day before.

I was surprised, but not ungratified. Somehow this proved my theory about Ruth E. Appeldorn. She had one of those push-me, pull-you personalities. She expected everyone to be mean to her, so she beat them to it. All her invitations were destined to sound like negative RSVPs. I smiled, actually grinned, because, of course, it was a little funny, and she made a rotten face.

"Okay, forget it." She turned to walk away.

Two minutes later we were in the kitchen, a pair of half-clean mugs on the table, the kettle on the hob and a small-size jar of Nescafe sitting like a barrier between us. The table was ringed and speckled and strewn with crumbs. She'd spilled something viscous and yellow down the front of the stove. There were papers and books strewn around the living-room. And stretched on the welcome mat in the foyer, as though he hadn't summoned up the courage to walk right into the house, was my dog.

"I brought him from your store," she explained, straightening her shoulders self-importantly. "Oliver is a lovely man, but he was afraid to sleep with a dog in the room. He was afraid that if his hand accidentally fell over the side of his cot, the dog would eat it. I said I'd take care of him for you."

"Thanks," I said. "He's a good dog. I wouldn't sell him for anything. Been in the family for generations. He's old—that's why he doesn't move much."

"He's a pup," she said. "Oliver told me you had to sleep in the boathouse last night because I was here."

I looked up from the dog. Surprised. The woman sounded contrite. And it wasn't even her fault.

"Nice of you to mention it," I said shortly.

"I think there was some mix-up," said Ruthie. "I'll go around today and see if I can find somewhere else."

Her eyes were big, hoping for friendliness. She looked as if she were trusting me with her life.

"Not necessary," I said. "Boathouse is more than comfortable. I've fixed it up."

"No, no," she said. "This place was empty. You could have moved in here if I hadn't barged in first." Her eyes were clouding over. I was rejecting her. I knew her type; you had to work eight times as hard in any conversation with them as you did with normal people. Listening to her, watching the expressions of vulnerability chase each other like squalls across her face, made me think how short life is and how little time there is to waste.

On one side of the table she had set up a portable type-writer next to a pile of loose papers. I pushed at them with my fingertip and uncovered the photocopy of a journal article by Dr Ruth E. Appeldorn, Ph.D., fellow of the New York Institute of Animal Studies. "Tail Positions of *Cercopithecus Aethiops*" was the title, and it contained cute diagrams of slender long-tailed monkeys signaling to each other in semaphore.

"This is what you do for a living?" I asked.

"I'm not a bird-watcher," she said defensively. "Actually, I don't make a living. I don't get to do as much of it as I'd like at all. When I'm in New York I have to do Baldossaro's research for him. I burn out tiny sections of brain tissue in male ring doves to see how it alters mating behavior."

I felt simultaneous twinges between my legs and behind my ears. Some people say I have the gift of empathy to an excessive degree, but the cold-blooded way she said it made me shudder. I had a vision of the the dove, his head wrapped in bandages, his eyes fevered and wandering, trying to mount a feather duster, billing and cooing, lavishing all his male passion and gallantry in vain. As if life wasn't confused and meaningless enough. I glanced at the dog, tail and ears docked for the ring, and hated myself for being part of the murdering, torturing human race.

"Why don't you cut off their feet?" I said quietly. "That would have a considerable and interesting effect. Their wings? How does the male ring dove fuck with only one eye? No eyes? Love your work, do you, Doc?"

I was incensed, but she had her back to me as she fiddled with the kettle and seemed to think I was making a joke.

"Someday I'll chloroform Baldossaro and do it to him," she said as she poured. "But it's the only way I can make any money for my own work."

The two cups of coffee she made were black and clear respectively. Her milk was sour.

"You could get a job," I said.

"You don't understand."

I remembered the painted laughing gulls on the beach.

"Eichmann," I said under my breath. There were no spoons. I swirled the coffee in its mug.

"You don't understand," she repeated a little plaintively. "If I'm going to get anywhere in animal behavior, I have to stay at the Institute. Otherwise I won't get published and if I don't get published I won't get a teaching job and if I don't get a teaching job I'm a failure. My daddy's a thoracic surgeon. I have a brother who's an analyst in New Haven. My sister married a man who owns a toilet-float factory in Newark. I can't just be a bum. I took Baldossaro's fellowship so I could spend at least part of the time doing my own field work."

Two pelicans sailed by, setting almost still in the wind like prehistoric gliders, rocs or pterodactyls. The idea of sizzling the minds of innocent ring doves had thrown me into a depression.

"I have to go," I said. "I have to keep an eye on Kinch."

"Do you want some breakfast?" she challenged. Even seated, I found myself peering down at her. Her little birdy eyes flashed.

My mind had strayed suddenly to thoughts of Lydia and Danger. The more I thought about them, the more I balanced pros and cons and relative character traits, the more I became convinced my night visitor had been none other than the sultry and secretive Danger Babcox. But imagining myself in the boathouse with Danger had the strange effect of making me feel guilty towards Ruthie.

I nodded grimly.

Ruthie rummaged in the refrigerator, which was almost bare except for a milk carton, several unopened loaves of Wonder Bread, a bunch of blackened bananas, a can of tomato juice and a stack of baloney slices which she had left uncovered. She put the baloney and bread on a plate and glared at me.

"Mustard?" I asked.

"French or sandwich spread?"

"French."

She whirled around, yanked open a cupboard and banged a jar of mustard on the table with an air of domestic triumph as though I had asked for some rare herb which she happened to have cultivated in her windowbox.

"The monkeys talk to each other?" I asked, pointing to the papers with the end of my sandwich.

"Not exactly. But they're signaling continuously, you know," she explained with sudden warmth. "They're always saying 'I'm so-and-so and I am doing this sort of behavior' or 'I'm so-and-so and I want to fuck.'"

She was watching me with those alert little eyes. Her throat caught over the last word. And then she continued.

"It gives them a sense of who they are and where they stand in the world and their social system."

"Just like people," I said. The thought of all those animals sending messages to one another made me uneasy.

You never really wanted to think they knew what they were doing. It made you suddenly want to keep an eye out over your shoulder.

"Basically all they're interested in is food and sex," she said. "It's very limited."

For a moment I wasn't sure whether she meant animals or people. Of course it didn't matter, for I had suddenly perceived what she was driving at. Dr Appeldorn had opened her heart along with her larder, both queerly circumscribed. I had become the object of an awkward, not to say slightly inhuman, mating ritual. This aggressive sharing of food, the rebuffs, and the sudden starts of anger and submission reminded me of nothing so much as the gulls along the waterfront getting ready to nest. All of a sudden I felt sorry for her, for she was right—in a way we all wanted the same things.

I stopped myself before I felt too sorry. I was getting warm toward her. Her breasts made little tents inside her shirt. Her voice communicated a quality of earnestness. But most of all she had made me curious. I suddenly wanted to know what it was like to see the world the way she did. I had questions I wanted to ask.

Seeing that I was about to get myself into trouble if I didn't watch out, I pointed out the window.

"Great blue heron," I said.

The heron stood in the shallows near some mangroves, his head tilting one way and then the other as he eyed the water for his lunch. On the wreck of the *Sara P.* the lone cormorant looked down his neck with aristocratic disdain.

"That one's a cormorant," I added. "In Gomez Gap they call them nigger geese."

Ruthie was watching the heron through her binoculars. I tossed the sandwich over my shoulder at the dog. It struck him on the nose, waking him with a start. He leaped to his feet and circled the lumps of floury bread and leathery meat, sniffing suspiciously. I glared at him, mouthing the order to eat.

The dog extended his tongue and carefully palpated the baloney. Then he turned away and dropped heavily to the floor again with a sigh. Ruthie and I were leaning over the table toward the window. At that moment she turned to me, her eyes damp with passion. I noticed that our arms had touched at the elbow. I quickly pulled mine away. Her face was close enough that I could feel her breath.

We waited for several seconds, perhaps a year. I knew what was expected, but I had also reached an age when I knew the price of casual entanglements.

"I'm a married man," I said.

"No, you're not," said Ruthie dreamily.

"Did Kinch tell you that?"

"Never mind who told me."

"Well, I'll probably be getting married again soon," I said, feeling a chill in my spine. For I suddenly had no doubts, none to speak of, anyway, as to the identity of my boathouse inamorata. It had to be Danger. I recalled the vehemence, not to say violence, of her love assault and the fact that Lydia had given no indication whatever of having spent the night with me. Yes, yes, I thought, getting a little excited, seeing practically nothing standing between us.

"Besides," I added, "My ex-wife is in the next house. I can't take on any more right now. When there's a vacancy I'll let you know. Now look—that damn dog has taken my sandwich. Bad dog!"

I jumped up from my seat and rapped the dog across the nose with the flat of my hand.

"Teach you to take food from the table! Look, he's mangled it. Not fit for house-living, are you, you mutt?"

"That Danger Babcox has left you for good this time," said Ruthie.

By the expression on her face, I could tell she was only

lashing out in anger. Still, it was uncanny that she knew so much about me, that she could almost read my thoughts. I made a mental note to lecture Kinch on the virtues of keeping his mouth shut about my private life.

"I'll just take him outside," I said, ignoring her, feeling a little miffed. "Must go anyway. Drop in and see Kinch—he loves the company. And mind your own business."

I glanced over my shoulder at her as I shoved the dog through the door. She was slouched against the back of her chair, one arm propped on the table, the other hand in her lap, looking small and sad. I dragged the dog down the step on his rump and when I let him go he ran back up and whined thinly at the door.

"Watch it," I told him. "She'll be vivisecting you next. She'll fry what's left of your brains for science. You'd like that, wouldn't you?"

I opened the shoebox and fed the dog one of my Pennsylvanias, which he seemed to find palatable enough. It changed his whole attitude toward me and he followed me as far as the street, where it took Montana to get him to go any further. After two more states, I hit upon the ruse of moving ahead fifty feet and then holding out my hand as if it held a chip. The dog, saintly in his innocence, failed to catch on for several blocks.

Passing the alley between houses, I noticed a line of crab traps piled on the bulkhead to dry. A pair of sparrows had flown through the wire mesh to find food and a town tom-cat had trapped them there. He was crouched on top of the pile, dangling a paw through the mesh to excite the birds. His face was serenely intent. It gave me a chill to watch him.

18

At the corner of Rattlesnake Lane and Lime Circle I stopped and waved the pistol in greeting as Audie Driscoll hurtled by in the municipal Plymouth. A piece of pointless bravado, I knew. But I reasoned that the town was so involved in the movie that any sort of errant behavior would be condoned. The sheriff would probably think the gun was part of a costume. She didn't stop.

Cabbage palms tossed in a chilly offshore breeze. The Gulf looked black and spumey. The tide was up, splashing at the restaurant piles. At the foot of Water Street near the old fiber factory where the trailers and semis were parked, a film crew shot stock footage of Confederate soldiers in camp and cannons firing out to sea. Extras milled amid tepees of stooked muskets and ammunition wagons hitched to long-eared mules. The cameramen were doing their best with filters and giant arc lights to give the effect of a sunny day, while make-up artists flitted in and out between takes with spray-bottles to make the troopers sweat.

Sipping George Dickel to lighten my load, I pondered the soldiers in butternut and gray. The antique figures stirred fantasies of the past, fantasies I knew I had acquired from Danger. She had fallen in love with Bubba Driscoll, she told me, because every time she looked at him she thought of five thousand good old boys racing the battle flags to the massed Union center at Gettysburg, streaming to butchery. All because of slavery and some ideal of pastoral aristocracy foisted on those barefoot Southerners by their leaders and apologists. It fascinated her—she wrote about it in her poems, poems of beauty, cruelty and death.

Finding a piece of string along the way, I slipped a loop over the dog's neck and by dint of violent tugs taught him the command "Heel, asshole!" Together we walked through town and over Broward's Bridge toward Danger's house by Kiss-Me-Quick. At Broward's Bridge the dog paused to pee against a concrete pier. To the right glinted a shallow pool called One Indian Pond where a captured Seminole had drowned himself on the way to prison during the Indian wars. On the left lay a mangrove bog called Nigger Swamp where five black slaves had sunk in quicksand when they tried to escape internment during the Civil War.

Across the bridge I stopped at Acker Ottman's restaurant, the Rainbow, and bought a mullet out of his smokehouse. Acker's was the best mullet in Gomez Gap, fresh caught, sliced, salted and dried over smoldering bay logs, the orange flesh looking like melon halves on the wooden racks. Acker wrapped it himself and handed it to me still warm as my nose wandered happily in the wood smoke and fish odor.

Tying the dog to a peach tree that bloomed in the yard, I knocked on Danger's door with my pistol butt. Cecily opened, mute and haughty, her blond hair hanging over her face.

"'Lo, Cecie," I said. "Where's your mother?"

"Ain't here."

"Had breakfast?" I asked, holding up the fish package for her to sniff.

"Hours ago," she said, crossing her arms on her chest, eyeing the parcel like a fish hawk. "But I expect Em's hungry again. She might join you."

It made me sad hearing her say these things in low polite tones. It wasn't that Danger was a bad mother, she was forgetful. The little girls were in awe of her passion.

They didn't like to bother her with mundane things like food and cleaning. Inside the house was chaos: piles of paperback novels Danger bought for a dime at second-hand stores in Chiefland and Gainesville, stacks of lined notebooks where she kept her poems and diaries, dirty dishes in the sink and on the table, empty wine bottles, their shoulders dandruffed with dust, dust balls along the baseboards, bodies of crushed insects like skidmarks on the poorly painted walls, mounds of dirty clothes kicked off to the sides of a makeshift runway that led to a cracked three-quarter-length mirror nailed to the bedroom door.

In all that mess it took me a moment to find Emily, the eight-year-old, dressed in a pink leotard and curled up in her mother's raccoon coat, reading one of the paper-backs, one foot propped indolently on the other knee. It was Emily, the younger, who took after her mother. Cecie had had to look after both of them from an early age; it had made her tough and competent. She was dressed in jeans and a man's blue-checked workshirt worn through at the elbows. The tail of the shirt hung down to her knees. She was looking out the window as I cleared the table to make room for the fish.

"That your dog?" she asked.

"You bet, sweetie," I said.

"You fightin' him?"

"I'm thinking about it. He's a mean one. Have I told you about this dog? Been keeping him up in Stark County with a trainer. He'll tear your leg off as soon as he'll look at you. The man I bought him from said he looked like an alligator before they docked his tail."

"We had a dog like that," she said, her voice stagily tragic. "We called him Punchy. Mom fought him once over in Chiefland. The two dogs got a grip on each other and wouldn't let go. They was brave dogs. Specially Punchy. The crowd started shouting 'Ring 'em. Ring 'em.' Mom was stoned and she had a bundle on him. She let them go ahead. They chopped their legs off, one at a time. The other dog won. The man said we'd treated Punchy too good. He just lost heart and died when they cut his feet off like that."

"Jesus," I said. My palms were sweating. My hair stood up a little at the back of my neck. She had spoken in a monotone, never taking her eyes off the dog. "Jesus."

"Don't matter, Tully," she said. "Mom said he was happy going out like that. She cried more than Em and me. She had his blood all over her hands. And it wasn't because of the money."

"Come to think of it," I croaked finally, "I don't know as it would be fair to fight this dog. Leastways, not around here. He's already won a pile of money up in Stark County and he'd just rip through these puny Gap bulls like a chainsaw. I'm thinking of putting him out to stud. A good fighter like this, he's worth a lot of money as a stud."

"What's his name?"

"Nameless," I said.

"You mean he ain't got a name?"

"No, that's his name."

"He ain't got a scar on him, Tully."

"In Stark County this dog is famous."

She gave me a look that nearly tore my heart out. Just a peek from the corner of her eye, her pupils like tiny furry animals peeping shyly from the mouths of their dens. At the same instant the corner of her mouth tilted up—a smile and a grimace, a mixture of relief and sarcasm.

Emily had stood up and was simultaneously scratching her bottom through the leotard and examining the smoked fish on the table. Cecily glanced at the fish, then at Emily.

"You two eat. All right if I pet your dog?"

I watched as she ran out, her long legs already filling out a little at the top, her head held erect. The dog sat up as she approached. For a second I was full of fear, wondering if it could be true what I said about Stark County. After all, the animal had come without references. His tongue lolled. The stump of his tail wagged. And just as she got to him he gave a little jump, placing his forepaws on her chest. It was the most activity I'd seen in the animal since I'd found him in the swamp. My heart was in my mouth.

A little startled, Cecily stiffened. Her hands went up and grabbed his paws. For an instant she stood there, holding him in her hands. And I knew she was thinking about her own dog with his wounds.

And then they were dancing. The little girl and the dog. Under the blossoming peach. She was grinning and the dog was leaping, trying to lick her face.

19

"You and Mom having a fight?" asked Emily, sucking the meat off a piece of mullet skin. She ate like her mother— very little but with the maximum amount of epidermal diffusion. After two bites, she had fish up to her elbows and in her hair.

"Not a chance," I said, holding up two fingers pressed together. "We're like this. I don't want this getting around, but I think any day now she'll ask me to move in."

"I was just wondering," she said, wiping her hands on her leotard, "because she didn't come home last night and you're here'n all looking for her."

"She was with me," I said, hoping it was true. "All night."

"I'll tell Bubba. He was looking for her too. He said she left the hotel with somebody from the movie."

"That was me," I lied. "I'm in the movie. I told you I've signed up for a fat part in the battle scene."

I tapped my feet and drummed the table-top with my fingers. I had a headache. Emily was smart and coy. She already knew how to handle men. I glanced at the book she was reading: *My Sister's Keeper*, "a story of unnatural love." Cecily came through the door, her eyes laughing, the dog scratching the linoleum with his claws.

"They're talking about sending me to Hollywood or New York when it's finished," I said. "We'll have our pictures in *People* Magazine. You'll be able to go to good schools—"

"You mean you're leaving the lamp business?" she said with mild incredulity. "And I thought you were doing so well."

Emily reached delicately across my elbow for a piece of tail meat. She glanced at her sister.

"Roger Ramjet here wants to be our father again," she said. "If you ask me, he ain't no Willie Weber."

Flamboyant Willie had lived dangerously, flying low over the Gulf, chain-smoking cigarettes and reefers in that steamy cockpit, outwitting the Feds. Now Willie was dead and he had all the honor. Somehow Danger and Emily held the fact that I was not dead against me. On bad nights, Danger stood on the rocks at the foot of the airport runway. Waiting.

"I happen to know for a fact," I said, "that you weren't even born before that particular social misfit checked out. And if you ask me, for a long time before that he'd suffered from a condition we doctors call Flying Too Long With The Cockpit Open. He was nothing but trouble to your mother. Nothing but wormwood and aloes—"

"Stop, Tully."

It was Cecily. Her eyes glittered. Her cheeks were flushed. The dog was bounding at her outstretched palm, hitting it with his head, pretending she was petting him. Cecily herself was very still.

"Airhead," said Emily, tossing the dog a slab of mullet. "Here, Spot."

"I'm sorry, Cecie," I said. "I got carried away. You want some fish? It's from the Rainbow. Still hot from the smokehouse."

"I don't think you and Danger should get back together," she said finally.

Cecily looked me square in the eyes. For a moment there was complete silence. Emily stood between us, switching her gaze from one to the other. The dog watched Emily; either he liked fish or his name really was Spot.

"Why not, sweetheart?" I said. "You know I love you all."

"I hate mullet," said Emily. "mullet is a cheap bribe; red snapper is love."

I turned to her.

"Honey, when I said I'd send you to a good school I meant reform school."

"Willie went to reform school."

"I'll just bet he did."

Cecily walked around the table and stood close to me, her hands behind her back but her eyes on the mullet.

"You know we didn't really have any breakfast," she said.

"I know, Cecie."

"You knew she probably wouldn't be here too."

I kept my mouth shut.

"She's a rotten mother," said Cecily. "She'd make a rotten wife too. Bubba just wants her back because he doesn't like to get beaten. He still doesn't know what hit him the last time. He thinks that because he can't figure it out that makes her mysterious or deep. She ain't deep, Tully. She's ordinary."

Emily did a pirouette, rolled her eyes and fell in a mock swoon into a pile of Danger's underwear.

"Did I ever tell you the story of how I met your mother?"

Cecily shook her head.

"It was when I was new in town. I came here with a woman I'd met in Louisiana and we landed on Ina's doorstep without a cent."

"Was that the crazy one?" asked Cecily.

"She just took a shorter run at things than most people," I said. "Anyway I was drinking George Dickel in the Gap Hotel one night. Danger was working at the bar same as she does now. And these three computer salesmen from Rhode Island came in for a shrimp supper and beer. You know the type—cowboy hats, bolo ties, pot bellies underneath seersucker pants. They were rowdy and they started coming on to your mother, laughing at her cigars, joking about her black clothes. One man asked her when she got off work. Danger just laughed in his face. The next guy yelled, 'Hey sugar, how's about some hot pickled sausage? You got any hot pickled sausage?' And the third guy hollered, 'To hell with the pickled sausage. You got a daughter you'd like us to meet?'"

"Then what happened?" asked Cecily.

"I broke a chair over the third guy's shoulders," I said. "I wasn't anybody to her, you see. I was just a patron of the bar and these Northerners were insulting her. She just made you frantic to fight for her honor. She had something, maybe it was only expectation. Danger, your mother, wants everything to be better and more exciting than it is. She never really loved Willie Weber any more than she loved me or anybody else. She's in love with Rhett Butler, a character in a book. And that's the worst thing to fall in love with. It makes real people seem lifeless. You can't blame her for letting it happen because it's like any other great idea—it inspires us to betterment. But it's difficult to live around somebody with a great idea."

I was looking sternly into Cecily's face and talking in low tones. Her eyes were pooling a little and I could smell her warm breath like freshly cut hay. She was about to speak when Emily piped up from the floor.

"What happened after you hit the guy?"

"His buddies beat the crap out of me, that's what."

"I knew that," she said smiling. "Mommy told me that story a long time ago. She said you were real cute hitting that guy out of the blue when he wasn't expecting it but not so cute afterwards. You got shit from your girl-friend too."

Ignoring her, I turned to Cecily.

"Does that make you feel better?"

She shook her head.

"She'd still make a lousy wife."

"Cecie wants you to wait for her, stupid. She's had the hots for you since her last birthday," said Emily scornfully.

"I'm going to marry a South American diplomat."

"Shut up, Em. That's not true." Cecily put her arms around my neck and leaned her head on my shoulder. "I want you to stay, Tully. But I don't want you to count on Mom so much. She messes up so bad. You'd go away and hate us. And I just want you to be around for always."

Emily rolled her eyes, then covered them with her hands.

"And this girl is supposed to be more mature than me!"

"Shut up, Emily. Just shut up! You like Tully too. You know it. You just can't see that he might go away like everybody else."

"We had better chances in the Keys," said Emily. "What about that guy Leopoldo?"

20

I left Cecily and her sister debating the pros and cons of my potential marriage to their mother while making desultory and delicate attacks upon my fish. The dog accompanied me like silent misery. I wanted to leave him and, God knows, he wanted to stay. But Cecily was worried about Danger getting her hands on another pit bull, even one as obviously unpromising in the violence department as Nameless.

I had the gun, the bottle and the makeshift leash at the end of which the dog was suffering intermittent paraplegia and, as I headed toward town, I was pondering the abruptness with which major changes occur in life. For the past five years I had done little but fish, mind the store and get drunk, frequently. Lately taxidermy had begun to occupy more and more of my time, and I had started seeing Danger, but the general tenor of things had not changed. Now, all of a sudden, with Lydia in Gomez Gap, my life had been wrenched from its accustomed peacefulness. I no longer knew what to expect. Around the corner, there might wait a column of Confederate infantry, a Hollywood starlet, or even a daughter. It was too late to jump. All I could do was hold on for the ride.

As an example of this I can tell you what happened next. Coming out of Danger's yard, the dog in tow, I turned left on the gravel shoulder which ran past a palmetto border and a billboard erected by the Historical Society to advertise the town's notorious past. The billboard showed a bird's-eye view of the Gap, with gray and blue arrows and printed legends telling you how the battle had gone.

I paused for a moment, thinking how logical and well planned the map made everything look. Admiral Farragut's landing boats hitting the shore *en échelon*, the Florida militia's counter-attack, the Union breakthrough where the airport is today, the house-to-house fighting as Confederate troops and townspeople stubbornly retreated to the old bridge over Kiss-Me-Quick Creek, and the demolition of the bridge which, separating the two armies, ended the battle.

The truth was that hardly anything had happened the way it looked on the map. The Union boats had blown ashore in a gale, taking both sides completely by surprise. High seas had capsized two of the boats, dumping Federal soldiers into the Gulf of Mexico. The locals heard them screaming over the wind, though, with the tide out and the water only three feet deep at the time, they didn't really have much to scream about. Union shelling knocked over some trees and set fire to Grandpa Winslow Maberly's smokehouse. Confederate return fire knocked the end off the old railway pier, killed some fish and decapitated a palm grove. Fighting grew confused and hot. Troops in small batches blundered around town, discharging their firearms and then fighting pitched battles with their bare hands. When it came time for the Rebels to retreat, the bridge over Kiss-Me-Quick Creek was blown up before they could march across it, and many had to wade through the marsh between the railway pilings.

I was thinking about this, wondering how Walter was going to film the whole fiasco, when I noticed Audie Driscoll's Plymouth parked on the other side of the billboard. I peeped round the end of the board and there was the sheriff resting on the hood, her feet on the bumper, her riot stick handy. From where she was sitting I knew she could see over the hedge into Danger's yard, and I knew she knew I had just left the house even though she wasn't paying any particular attention to me at that moment. In fact, as far as I could tell Audie was showing a marked and unusual interest in the weather, watching the clouds, watching the wind whip the trees, her face a mask of calmness. Right away I knew I was in trouble.

With the billboard between us we were just five feet apart. My only chance was to hunch down and run back toward the bayou using the palmetto hedge as cover. Then I could cut along the shoreline keeping out of sight behind the neighbors' cottages. This seemed like such a good idea that for a second or two I even thought it might work. But then Audie cleared her throat.

"'Lo, Tully," she said. Her tone was funereal.

"'Lo, Audie," I said, still not coming around to her side of the billboard. From where she sat, I figured, she could only see my feet. I tucked the gun into my trousers and pulled my shirt-tail over it.

"Come round here, boy!"

It was one of the perks of being sheriff that she got to call everybody "boy."

"I can talk just as well from here," I said.

"Kinda hard to reach you."

"That's all right. I don't mind." I could hear Vince snarling and thumping the cruiser window with his head.

"You try to escape, Tully, and I'll run over you with the car."

"I'll just stand here."

"Might as well come round and take your medicine," she said, after a pause.

Audie's voice struggled to maintain a measured rhythm. She must have sensed the indignity of having to come to terms with a man standing behind a billboard. If she got off the Plymouth and chased me, she would have to run across Danger's yard, an absurd picture. If she didn't chase me, I could stay where I was and force her into embarrassing negotiations. Either way, it was bound to be bad for her morale.

I said nothing. I read some of the map legends, reac-
quainting myself with the various movements of the
battle, wondering what role I would play in the next day's
recreation. I imagined myself in officer's rig, plumed hat,
epaulets and trouser stripes, leading a serried line of gray-
clad troops against the Union beachhead. I saw myself
wherever the battle was hottest, Colt pistol in one hand, a
saber in the other, rescuing the wounded, saving the flag,
holding a bridge, mesmerizing the camera crews with my
acrobatic grace and nobility of mien.

Audie cleared her throat again.

"I was only going to bust you a couple of times with the
stick, Tully. But if you make me mad I'll likely as not
cripple you for life."

"You wouldn't want the little girls to see that," I said.
"They adore me. They think I'm the cat's ass. If you want
to keep Bubba in good with Danger's kids you'd better not
touch me where they can see it."

I said all this regretting that I had had to bring Cecily
and Emily into it and passing over, for the moment, any
mention of my wedding plans.

We were at an impasse. My dog sniffed grass at my feet
and scratched his fleas. Audie tapped the Plymouth's grill
with her riot stick. Just then a cream-colored Coupe de
Ville swooped by and drifted to a halt on the shoulder in
front of Danger's house. Gravel showered almost to the
raggedy flowerbeds Cecily kept against the clapboard
walls. The Coupe de Ville had California license tags.

Audie stopped tapping. I heard her feet hit the dirt. She
stepped suddenly around the end of the billboard, without
paying any attention to me, her good eye on the Cadillac.

The car had air-conditioning; all its windows were up.
They were tinted blue against the sun, so there was nothing to see except two shadowy figures in the front seat.
Then the passenger door swung open and Danger stepped out.

I felt Audie stiffen; we were an arm's length apart. Together we watched Danger. She was dressed in her bartending clothes, all black. Her face was white as a corpse, the little scar on her lips shone. Her eyes were hidden behind the sunglasses and her hair was wild. She suddenly broke into laughter, throwing her head back and showing her teeth, her lips like blood. Then she turned toward the house, angling unsteadily for the front door, her limbs somehow loose in their sockets. It was almost noon, with a storm in the offing, and Danger was so beautiful in that mysterious, infuriating, self-destructive way of hers it almost took my breath away.

She made it to the house, fumbled in her pockets for a key and nearly fell through the door when it opened for her. I turned to the Coupe de Ville, knowing that the girls would be taking care of their mother. Audie was already out of sight, moving swiftly behind the billboard again. The Coupe de Ville idled, emitting exhaust plumes like ostrich feathers, then eased into the road for a U-turn. Audie hit the siren before the big car could get all the way round. The emergency lights on top of the Plymouth began to whirl in silent triumph, as she shot its nose into the Cadillac's path.

The Coupe de Ville braked to a stop. Audie went on the loud hailer, ordering the driver to step out with his hands in the air and his back to the cruiser. The driver's door opened quickly and a tall tanned blond man of indeterminate age hopped out with his hands up. He wore a fancy warmup suit, a hooded sweatshirt, baseball cap and Ray-Ban aviator shades, the kind with red, white and blue laminated frames. His socks were pulled up over the legs of his warmups so that their brand name could be seen—Logos. His sneakers were by Nike.

Audie darted at him from behind with a shotgun in one hand and the riot stick in the other. I felt a sudden, shameful thrill of sadistic delight. The guy in the warmups had gotten me off the hook. But at the same time I held him responsible for the secret smile of delight on Danger's lips as she staggered toward her house.

"You're under arrest," said Audie.

"What's the charge, officer? I swear I wasn't doing anything."

"Speeding," said Audie.

"But I wasn't moving!" squealed Warmups, half turning his head.

Whap! Audie pipped him across the side of the neck over his jugular and the guy went down on his knees.

"Resisting arrest."

Warmups reached to rub his neck. He was whimpering.

"Oh, my God," he said. "I'm the screenwriter. You can't arrest me. The star simply will not work without me on the set. I wasn't doing a single thing wrong."

Audie whacked him across the knuckles.

"What's this?" She leaned her 12-gauge against a rocker panel and pulled a couple of joints from her hat band. Reaching over Warmup's shoulder, she stuffed the dope in his sweatshirt pocket. "A dope fiend. Looks like I caught me one of those traffickers I've been hearing about. You going to come peacefully, boy? Or am I going to have to lay you out?"

Warmups gave a shriek of dismay.

"You're framing me. You planted that stuff. Oh, my God. Please, officer, this must be a mistake."

Audie grinned.

"Kidnap. Possible sexual assault."

"Assault!" squealed Warmups. "I was only driving her home. I couldn't possibly assault anyone. Talk to my analyst. You have to let me go. You can't know what this could do to my career. Otto Osterwalder depends on me. I'll do anything to make it up to you."

"Attempting to bribe a peace officer," said Audie, little nervous tics playing across her features as she fought down her glee.

"Love your outfit," she added. "We got a new weight room over at the jail. It's a pleasure to know there'll be someone using it. And if you're bad, we'll strap you to the bench press and spank your little botty."

Warmups shrieked again. Audie whacked him across the shoulder and he went down on his face. After handcuffing him behind his back, she jerked him to his feet and led him to the Plymouth. His knees buckled when he caught sight of Vince slavering all over the back seat in expectation.

Audie nodded at me.

"Tully," she said, pointing her stick at the Coupe de Ville, "I have impounded this automobile. I want you to move it off the road and then get the fuck away from here. I'm just going to run my suspect over to Bronson which'll take me about an hour, and if I find out that you messed with Danger Babcox while I was gone, I will feed your balls to my dog, hear? I ain't finished with you yet."

21

The Cadillac had blood-red leather upholstery, a control panel like the space shuttle's, a digital tape deck, and a soft feminine voice that whispered instructions whenever you tried to do anything with the car that was against its nature. I believe it was that voice that put the dog off, for I had to lift him bodily into the front seat and he barked when the car spoke.

Before leaving, I rapped on Danger's door. I am not the jealous or vengeful type; I was just curious as to where she had been all night and who with. When no one answered my knock, I tried the doorknob. I was just getting a rock to break the glass when Cecily appeared at the front window, signaling for me to beat it, her face a mask of mortification.

We (the dog and I) drove off at walking speed with the windows open and the tape deck blaring Vegas Soul: "Lady," "Feelings," "MacArthur Park," "I Cried a Tear," "Little Green Apples," "Out of My Mind"—that sort of thing. But as we crossed the bridge over Kiss-Me-Quick Creek and drove past Acker Ottman's restaurant it started to rain and, by the time we reached my former home, hail was clapping against the windshield like No. 12 birdshot and the wheels were awash in movie mud.

I honked the horn twice.

Walter appeared at the door, dressed in L. L. Bean hip-waders and a grasshopper-green rain poncho with hood and visor, a clipboard and bullhorn clutched in his hands. The bullhorn had his initials on it. O.O.

"Where's Lydia?" I asked, when he reached the car.

Walter looked at me with an expression of startled recognition but said politely enough, "She's gone to the Gainesville airport to meet somebody. Where the fuck is Wally? He said he'd have the car back first thing this morning."

"Tall guy in a sweatsuit?"

"That's him."

"Tells everybody he's a screenwriter with the movie?"

"Tully, you're such a fucking wimp."

"He's gone to Bronson on police business—at least for the night, maybe more. Did Lydia talk to you about me being in the movie?"

"Get out of this fucking car," said Walter. Rain-water was dripping off his poncho visor through the open window onto my shoulder. "It's movie property. You're not supposed to be driving movie property."

"You're wrong there, Walter" I said. "Or should I call you Otto? This car has been impounded by the Gomez Gap Sheriff's Department as evidence in a felony case. If you want to go somewhere, you can get in the back and I'll take you. But otherwise I can't just turn it over to you."

"I wouldn't give you a part in a dog show," said Walter.

I pressed the UP button and shut the window.

Walter banged on the glass with his knuckles, then jerked open the back door and got in. His hipwaders squelched as he sat down and the car windows began to steam up. The dog raised its head and sniffed warily, then went back to sleep.

"Drop me at the Shrimp-Pot," he said. "I've got a production meeting in five minutes."

I glanced at his face in the rearview mirror. Walter grinned. Steam rose from his shoulders. The Cadillac carved a bow wave in the water-logged street as I made a U-turn and headed toward town.

"I was just joking about the part," he said. "You wanna be a hometown movie star, wear funny clothes and make

faces in front of a camera just to get laid, it's okay by me."
He leaned forward and put his hand on my shoulder. The
dog suddenly snapped awake and looked at Walter, who
took his hand back. "Seriously, Tully, we're all worried
about you."

I slammed on the brakes. Walter came half-way over the
seat with a grunt. The dog slid onto the floor.

"Just who the fuck do you mean by 'we' and 'all'?" I said.
"And who asked you to worry anyway?"

"Honest, Tully, I just meant Lydia and Ariel and me.
Well, actually, I don't worry much. But Lydia does. You
really put a kink in her life leaving like that. She'll probably never get over it. The baby's cute as a button. She
makes up little stories about you. Every time she sees a
painting, she says, 'My daddy did that.'"

A profound depression settled over me as though a
large black bird had landed on my head and folded its
wings across my face. I stared through the window,
blurred with rain, seeing nothing.

"I'm really scared about this one," said Walter, also looking at the rain (anxious as an expectant father). "I know I
say that about every movie, but this one is the worst."

I remembered the trip to the hospital (it was raining
that night as well, a regular Iowa douser with tornado
reports on the radio), Lydia sitting in the front seat beside
Walter, me in the back, wallowing in guilt and panic and
Quaaludes, skimming a book called *Natural Childbirth
Made Easy* by the roof light.

"I'll have five big mother Mitchells and a dozen hand-
held Panaflexes aimed at the beach. We'll do the whole
thing in one shot to keep the intensity going: slow-mo
violence, Russian cutting, collage. . ."

Walter, who had only taken time to throw a coat over his
bathrobe, was hunched at the wheel, squinting into the
liquid darkness, timing her contractions with his wrist-
watch, breathing in unison with Lydia to help her

concentrate. They were old pros, partners. Every time she shouted, I would shout. And Walter would say, "It's all right, Tully. She has to relax. She has to let go."

"There'll be two thousand extras, more ships than the Mexican navy—hell, some of them *are* the Mexican navy—eighteen assistant directors with walkie-talkies. . ."

He had stayed with us, still breathing, still timing, to the o.b. ward where the nurses turned him away. I will never forget the look on his face, forlorn, helpless, disappointed, as he watched them tie my gown and mask and lead me in.

"I play the explosions from a detonator keyboard on the top floor of the hotel; I keep the barrage ahead of the advancing troops. . ."

I was not myself. I was not as calm as I would have wished to be. The lamp-factory debacle had been preying on my mind; my art career was in the dumper. We waited in the o.b. ward sixteen hours, the delivery room for three, though somewhere along the way I lost track of time. I held Lydia's hand, watching her grow pale like a rag in the sun. Around the twentieth hour, fatigue and the rhythmic onslaught of her pains (not to mention the drugs I had taken) drove me right out of myself into another plane of consciousness, the zen of childbirth. I was one with the eternal suffering of women, or thought I was till a nurse shook me awake and I found myself under a gurney with a face mask over my eyes.

"The keys to a good battle scene are blood and body parts—"

"Body parts!" I said, startled, thinking of hospitals, sterile gowns and a doctor named Birdsong who mumbled ju-ju words and did a raindance between Lydia's legs to speed up a difficult delivery. She had turned to me and said, "Sweetheart, I just don't think this is going to work out." What? I thought. Doc Birdsong's antics? The baby? Our life together? What? What? What?

"Yeah, arms, legs and heads, exploding bodies, blood bullets, blood everywhere, blood splashing the camera lens. . ."

Suddenly, the room was abustle with gowned and masked figures moving about as though on wheels. Doc Birdsong pressed his stethoscope to her belly, his brow wrinkled with worry. Lydia was slurring her words; no tears now, she was all cried out. When the doctor muttered, "We can't wait any longer. We'll put her under for a c-section," Lydia heard him and her eyes blossomed with alarm.

They were too busy to push me out the door. Someone lunged for her throat, choking her. Later at Elysium, a doctor explained that the anaesthetist did this to keep her from vomiting into her own lungs. But all I could see was this Neanderthal's fingers jammed in her throat, and Doc Birdsong cutting a line across her belly and her blood everywhere.

I must have blacked out; I just blinked and it was over. Birdsong held a baby in the air by its feet while somebody snipped its cord. He shoved a finger into its tiny mouth and smacked its bottom. The baby shrieked. I stepped forward, slipped on a patch of blood, and went down on my knees. My wife was dead; I was certain of it; I was responsible.

I snatched the baby out of his hands and ran to a corner of the room where they couldn't come at me from behind. My mind was a tangle of horror, sadness, remorse and ignorance. Ariel's shrieks went through my eardrums like needles. To this day I don't know exactly what I was thinking except that somehow, no matter what, I had to save Lydia's baby.

She was already awake, mind you. It had been that quick. The anaesthetic had only vagued her out for a moment or two.

"Tully," she whispered, a sad ghost of a reassuring smile

on her lips, "Tully, give them the baby. It's all right, sweetheart."

It did not seem all right.

Sweetheart, I just don't think this is going to work out. I heard the echo of her words in the words.

I was not all right.

Sweetheart—

When Walter saw me in the corridor, he knew I wasn't all right. When he saw the blood on my gown, he nearly puked. He had gone home to get his clothes; his jacket pockets were full of pills. I took several. He didn't press them on me; I begged him; I threatened to brain him with a rubber tree. Pills became an issue of contention between us. It was easier to deal with the problem of pills than with the memory of Lydia.

I tried to leave the hospital with my gown, but Walter made me take it off.

I walked over to Abe's Bar & Grill, ordered a drink and left. Booze, I decided, just wasn't going to cut the mustard. I needed to be unconscious; I needed the U.O.D., the Universal Oblivion Drug.

Later, I fled.

"Tully, Tully, look at the fucking time, would ya?" Walter jabbed my shoulder with his bullhorn. "Earth to Tully. Earth to Tully. Let's get this shit-box on the road."

Then he began to talk about Howard Hawkes and Sergio Leone and was still talking about them when I delivered him to the Shrimp-Pot, where a bearded acolyte waited anxiously with an umbrella at the door.

I watched him go, sloshing in the gutters, hipwaders and all, happy Walter-Troll—the princess had kissed him and he had turned into a prince (though he still looked like a troll).

I sat for a while, staring at the gray spumy Gulf, sipping George Dickel from the bottle and scratching the dog behind the ear, which sent him into ecstasies of canine submissive behavior, and wondered what Sergio Leone would have thought about one-eyed Sheriff Audrey Driscoll.

Terns, skimmers and willets hunkered together in the lee of the pier and restaurants, disgruntled-looking. Deserted and rain-swept, the town reminded me of nothing so much as a reef, shells of old dead things occupied by lesser animals and squatters, nothing the outside world wanted any more. To simple people, content with themselves, the need to hide out in such a place must seem degraded. But I loved it, and anyway have never been content with myself.

I turned knobs and switched switches to get the car to say things to me. Whisper to me. "Please, fasten your seatbelt. Your parking brake is on. A door is ajar." I started the tape again and checked the glove compartment, hoping to find drugs. I also checked beneath the dash, behind the ashtray, underneath the seat and along the floor carpeting. The car was clean. Either Warmups had eaten the stuff or he'd thrown it away as he got out of the car.

Then I noticed the little garbage baggy and decided to go through it. Banana peels, used Kleenex, chewing-gum, one of Danger's cigar butts that had begun to burn a hole in a banana peel before going out, and a silver monogrammed cigarette case containing a half-dozen phials of what looked like amyl nitrite. Poppers.

I snapped one under my nose, sniffed, blinked and nearly went through the roof. My heart rate shot up. Something started in my gut, expanded into my chest, squeezed through my neck and mushroomed inside my skull. I sat there for five minutes staring at the dashboard clock. It was not the U.O.D. but it helped. It improved the mood. What I always say is, any psychic crutch in a storm. I suddenly felt very relaxed, content with the passage of time, unthreatened by entropy.

I slipped the remaining poppers into my pants pockets,

stuffed the .38 into my belt and hooked my finger around the neck of the bourbon bottle. I left the dog in the front seat with the tape deck on. He was sleeping when I shut the door. "MacArthur Park" seemed to be his favorite.

22

Kinch appeared surprised and elated to see me. He had shaved, combed, and washed, and was clad in one of those black Navy-surplus commando sweaters and new blue jeans. It was an experience to see his face fighting a half-dozen years of major depression, mouth twitching upwards at the corners, muscles making unaccustommed contractions. I didn't know what to make of it so I said:

"Had a bath, Kinch? Who do you know who has plumbing?"

"Bethamae let me," he said proudly.

"What's the idea?" I asked. "Got a date with one of those Hollywood starlets? Trying to pass yourself off as an artiste?"

Kinch frowned. It disappointed him whenever I let my breezy, cynical side show through.

"I just felt good, Tully. It was the painting, finishing it and all."

"The painting! You mean you finished it?" It was plain how pleased he was, but I couldn't restrain my sarcasm. This is what drugs and a terrible past will do to you. I didn't wait for him to answer. I walked straight back through the shelves of merchandise to the taxidermy shop to have a look.

Kinch had straightened the place up a bit. The smell from the deep freeze was gone, the fish scales had been rinsed off the table, my cans of automobile paint, brushes, thinners and glue had been set in order on the shelf. On Kinch's side of the room, the changes were even more significant. His bed was made, the tumbleweeds of dust that generally obscured the view of the base board had been swept away, there was a vase of flowers on his bureau and a genuine Stamper lamp on the card-table he used as a desk and dining-room table.

The painting itself was a shock. That orange gull was the centerpiece, very realistic, but larger than life, with a big pouty chest and fantastic wingspan. Back of it Kinch had painted the town in lush greens and yellows. The fish houses, Fedderberg's dry dock, the municipal pier, the breakwater and the Shrimp-Pot looked like aging sunbathers with their pants and skirts rolled up, wading up to their knees along the waterfront. Inland, I could see the Gomez Gap bank, gray and square, and the cluster of odd four-planed tin roofs gleaming white in the sun that made up the business district, and the nest of poles and power lines over the old tool-shed where Danger had her studio. In the middle background, rising like a Spanish ruin out of the live oaks and cabbage-plams, stood the creosote-stained Gap Hotel.

Kinch's version of the Iowa City duplex floated disconcertingly in the clouds in the top left-hand corner, looking like a huge lime-colored barn. Through the windows of the AME Church next door you could see a congregation of black faces with wide grins and orange teeth peering out happily at the gull. In the right-hand corner, for balance, Kinch had painted a picture of me holding two photographs. The photographs were real, glued onto my painted hands. I recognized one of them, a recent Polaroid of me taken standing beside a stuffed swordfish with a Greek fisherman's cap on my head. The other showed a chubby little blond girl in tiny jeans and a T-shirt, holding her palms up to the camera, fingerpaints up to her elbows. Across the sky, Kinch had painted the words MAN WHO MAKES HUMAN BEINGS.

It was strange to see, like meeting yourself coming around a corner. For a moment I felt stunned, empty, near tears. I couldn't take my eyes off Ariel. I'd only seen her once before, in that delivery room, small and bloody in Doc Birdsong's rubber hands. In the photograph, she looked like her mother, blond hair falling in loose strands over her ears, amused eyes, little white teeth with spaces between. But it gave me a chill, seeing that paint and her delight. It made me feel as if I knew her through and through, as if I'd known her all my life.

MAN WHO MAKES HUMAN BEINGS. Once I had been eaten up with the desire to paint, with wanting to get what was in my head onto somebody's wall. Put even a child's crayon in my hand and I would have been delighted. When I was being slick and glib, I would as likely as not say I quit painting because of the tenor of the times, that I ran away to Florida to escape the self-promoting, soul-destroying, production-line commercialism of contemporary art. But it really wasn't anything as conscious as that.

The truth was that after Lydia told me she was pregnant I had tried to paint, but the life had gone out of it for me. I didn't know why. Everything looked odd. Canvas. Brushes. Tubes of color. Colored marks on white ground. They didn't have eyes or mouths or bodies. They didn't speak. I suddenly didn't know why I put those splashes of carmine and yellow ochre and cobalt blue and burnt sienna on canvas. It seemed, all at once, like a dull thing to do.

I noticed Kinch hovering anxiously in the doorway, looking very dapper, his hands tucked into his pockets. His eyes were fixed on me, graceful interrogatives, waiting for my assessment.

He had once told me the effect of living in the South was to make everyone a little mad, and he was a prime example. But that didn't make him stupid. Once a year, like clockwork, Kinch would get the "flu" and lie in bed two weeks reading through the entire works of William Faulkner. Once he had looked up from a book Danger had loaned him and said, "You know, that man Freud must have been a Southerner."

He was blocked—when he tried to work he would rub out a hundred lines to get one down, then, on reflection, would rub that one out. But this is the riddle of genius; it goes its own way like one of those underground rivers that surface from time to time in the desert.

I stepped back and tried to look at his picture objectively. It was vigorous, puzzling, huge. With all that lush greenery it made me think of Douanier Rousseau. Taken together the corner pieces and the inscription seemed allegorical. The gull, soaring phoenix-like from the town, definitely pointed to eclecticism of a bizarre nature. The taped-on photos were montage-like, very contemporary. All in all, I had deep misgivings about Lydia's reaction, mostly on the grounds that I had never painted anything remotely like it in my life.

"Very nice, Kinch," I said. "You definitely finished it. There is paint all over the canvas. A big step. The therapy is working. Is this the kind of thing you used to paint?"

"In a way," he said, adding inconsequently after a guarded pause, "I sold two lamps."

"You don't say."

I found it difficult to believe, and in my present state of mind I wasn't all that interested. The lamps had suddenly slipped a couple of steps in the hierarchy of my immediate concerns. Kinch seem disappointed.

"I thought you'd be happy. It was one of those movie people from Hollywood. He was driving a big white car. He loved the lamps. He was a very nice man."

"When did this happen?"

"Last night. Just before I closed up."

"Come with me," I said, dragging Kinch by the shoulder to the front window from which we could see the Coupe de Ville lying like a beached porpoise against the sidewalk, the dog scratching frantically at the window.

"That's the car," he said, mystified. "What's your dog doing inside it?"

"Never mind. This has to be somebody's idea of a practical joke, a prank like on April Fool's Day. Is that where you got the money to buy jeans?"

"Commission," said Kinch brightly. The man had the mind of an M.B.A. when he needed it.

I went back outside in the rain and opened the trunk. Kinch was right. There were two Stamper lamps in cardboard cartons. A sailboat and a Michelangelo David in cherry marble. Somehow I had always suspected the David would go over with the decadent set.

The dog's claws clicked furiously against the glass. I let him out and he immediately fell through the hole left by the missing planks in front of the store. He sat there with his head up, looking at me, blinking in the rain.

I brought the lamps into the store.

"Put these back on the shelf," I said.

"But, Tully—"

"I've got my pride," I said. "Somebody's pulling your leg, Kinch. Now get a fire going. I want you to look competent but aloof for half an hour while Lydia is here. Competent and aloof—can you handle that? And call me Mr Stamper."

"All right, Tully."

"Mr Stamper. Start practicing. And for God's sake don't say anything that will make Lydia suspect that you did the picture. If you're a good boy we'll bring it into the front room and try to sell it. It ought to go about as well as the lamps."

That frown again.

23

It was half-past four when Lydia came in; I was dreaming.

In the dream I wore an $800 Brooks Brothers suit and Gucci shoes and people kept calling me Smith. I was on trial though the charge wasn't clear. "You're not Smith! We know you're not Smith!" shouted the judge, a black-robed porpoise of a man with thick glasses. "That's right," I said. "I'm not Smith. These aren't my clothes. I am somebody else." He whacked his gavel down on the bench. "Jail or exile?" Cato French, my former cellmate, greeted me with a huge grin as I shuffled through a door marked Losers and Obstructionists. "Back where you belong, Tully!" he crowed. "Back where you belong!"

Then I was awake, chuckling to myself, my forehead pillowed on the keyboard of my Underwood typewriter. A pile of letters, sealed and stamped for Kinch to take to the post office, was stacked neatly at the end of the stuffing table. The skin of a small sand shark, dried and fitted on a papier-mâché form, grinned hungrily in front of my face. It gave me a start. I had been touching it up before I nodded off.

For some reason I had decided to make the shark look like a speckled trout. Starting from the tail to about the shoulder under its pectorals it was a speckled trout. The rest was a faded-looking sand shark with angry teeth. I did this sometimes; my customers didn't seem to mind. The sportsmen of Gomez Gap didn't seem to care what the fish looked like as long as the mouth was open and they could stuff drugs into the form. My fish went all over the country, and as soon as they had served their purpose they were dumped. Mine was a throwaway art.

The letters were in response to certain urgent business matters.

> The Boathouse
> Piney Point
> Gomez Gap, FL

Ancel Ashbach
Waldron, Diltz & Ashbach
234A Clinton Street
Iowa City, IA

Re: the matter of Stamper vs Parkhurst re ownership of Stamper Lamps Inc. of Iowa

Dear Fishback,

This is to advise you that after five years of trying to light a fire under you gentlemen I have decided to allow my claim to said company to lapse as of this moment. Other methods will be employed to obtain restitution. Your services are no longer required.

Also re your latest billing, I consider $89.23 an exorbitant not to say outrageous fee for the amount of work you have completed in my case. Is this some kind of joke, gentlemen? Extortion through the mails is a federal offence (I have checked this with my good friend, Julius Wachtel, FBI). As to your threats involving turning my file over to a collection agency, I intend to respond with a defamation suit the instant I am contacted by anyone in this regard.

Enclosed please find a check for $5 on account

drawn on Stamper Lamps Inc.

Sincerely,

Tully Stamper, Pres.

TS/ok

• • •

Nowhere, FL

Julius Wachtel
Lot 33
Virgin Pines Trailer Park
Gomez Gap, FL

Dear Mr Wachtel,

The man living in Piney Point under the name
Wade Fowler is a phony. I have reason to believe he is
none other than D. B. Cooper, the man who hijacked a
Boeing 727 over Oregon in 1971 and parachuted into
the Columbia River. Cooper a.k.a Wade Fowler is also
known to inject himself daily with unknown but almost
undoubtedly criminal substances. Good hunting.

Sincerely,

Anonymous Well-Wisher

• • •

Island Art Co-op
Water Street
Gomez Gap, FL

Julius Wachtel
Lot 33
Virgin Pines Trailer Park
Gomez Gap, FL

Dear Mr Wachtel,

The man living in Ina Stamper's cottage at Piney
Point under the name Otto Osterwalder is a known
drug user and former campus radical at the University
of Iowa. He is wanted for mail fraud, traveling on a false
passport, alienation of affection and child abduction. I
will give you one hint—check out the name Walter
Hebel. Good hunting.

Sincerely,

Bethamae Hamsett

. . .

The Boathouse
Piney Point
Gomez Gap, FL

Roger Staubach
c/o Rolaids
Marketing Division
Avenue of the Americas
New York, NY

Dear Roger,

I caught your new commercial following the CBS
Evening News the other night. It was your best yet. May I
say that you have mastered the art of man-on-the-street

interviews—as I knew you would. A man of your talents cannot fail to succeed in any profession he chooses.

Of course we both know that the people you interview, the ones who spell out R-O-L-A-I-D-S on the spare envelope with the felt pen, we both know these are trained actors and that with modern photographic and dubbing techniques you can't miss. Still and all, it's a remarkable accomplishment. And to see that you have bettered yourself through the years, from Heisman Trophy, to Vietnam, to Rolaids, has done my heart the world of good.

Yet, all kidding aside, as one veteran to another, I am writing to ask whether or not, deep down, you think the best interests of the nation are served by your continued appearance as a commercial tout on network television. This is the eighth letter I have written to you without a reply. For some time now I have believed in my heart that the Rolaids people were just not giving you your mail, that the true feelings of your friends and fellow vets were being concealed from you. But recent events have served to shake to its very core my faith in the innate goodness of man, and the realization is beginning to dawn on me that, perhaps, you too have sold out to Big Money.

I have had to sell *my* Purple Heart to pay for taxi fare to the VA hospital. The doctors say the other leg will have to come off soon. My friend Oliver, the one who inhaled napalm, claims he sees large orange birds. But I don't want to complain. The point I am trying to make is that I was no hero and no great shakes as a quarterback either, and no one really wants a former Phantom pilot turned taxidermist to endorse his product. Rolaids has not sought me out, nor has American Express knocked on my door. ("You don't know me, but. . .")

In your shoes, I don't know what I would have done. But I *can* tell you what I think you should have done. The Roger Staubach I knew and loved as a kid, the gridiron ghost, the Navy man who gave up years of pro ball to fight for his country, that Roger Staubach would have told Rolaids to use their product as a suppository.

I know I should be a little overwrought about this. It's just that when the youth of America need heroes, all the heroes are selling. Heroism has become a commodity, and we are daily treated to unabashed confessions by this or that champion that the glory was sought for the sole purpose of cashing in. Is this what my buddies in Nam died for? What kind of moral example are we setting for our children? (Of course, you'll recall that because of my wound I have been unable to have children; I speak figuratively.)

I myself, a former user of Rolaids, have stopped buying them ever since your first commercial aired. Rolaids no longer spells R-E-L-I-E-F for this man, Roger. It spells dismay.

Now that I have got this off my chest, I will say no more about it. But I hope you will keep it in mind. This country needs a man of honor, and right now I am pretty busy with the store and the lamp factory. Ina is well and sends her regards. My ex-wife and her husband (they have a daughter—not mine because of you know what) are visiting and we are one big happy family.

I may be getting married to Danger Babcox whom I think I mentioned in a previous letter. Her children are very much in favor of it. I have got Oliver painting again (his rehabilitation program, remember?). Incidentally, I have a dog now. Well, he more or less adopted me. Some kind of hound, I think. If you are interested, I could let you have him for $50 plus shipping.

Drop me a note when you get a chance.

May the Good Lord Bless You and Keep You,

Tully 'Death on Gooks' Stamper

I must have been drunk—the meniscus of the contents of the bourbon bottle having reached the bottom of the top third of the paper label, just under the words George Dickel. The expression on Lydia's face turned Baptist as soon as she saw me. Ina was behind her coming through the door, with her shiny black hair and eyelashes an inch long, looking like a police undercover man in drag. There were raindrops in Lydia's hair, dazzling in the light. Her color was high as though she'd crushed strawberries on her cheeks.

Right away she was at me.

"You're drunk," she said. "How can you paint if you're drunk?"

"Not drunk," I said. "Exhausted. I just finished the picture. I had to rush it. But I wanted you to see a complete work."

Kinch had thrown a sheet over the canvas, concealing it for dramatic effect. I spun around in my chair, nearly catching my fingers on the shark's mouth, and yanked the sheet. Lydia stepped back and craned her neck. Her eyes widened. She was shocked. The moment was good for me. I felt all right.

She was wearing jeans and a Mexican blouse underneath a cheap transparent raincoat I recognized as belonging to Ina. But even inside a tent like that she still had a way of looking like a filet steak to a man in a vegetarian prison. And her expression of astonishment was not far from the expression she wore when she reached the peak of passion while making love.

But it didn't last long. I rolled my chair over to the painting so that I could look into Lydia's face and gauge her response better, but the colors were so jolting that I decided I would feel better behind the canvas with Kinch. I thought about doing another popper, but there were too many people around. And Ina was already losing interest in the picture.

"I've never seen any of Tully's work," she said, lying. Or maybe she had forgotten. "It looks like a chicken or something, doesn't it?"

"It's magic realism," I said. "That's a laughing gull."

"Did you do this, Tully?" This was Lydia, her voice like a glass cutter, the first indication I had had that the painting wasn't going over well.

"I know it's not what you're used to," I said. "I've been cut off from influences. I'm only getting back to it now. I've got to work out my ideas."

"I didn't even know he was painting," said Ina, as if I wasn't in the room. "He's so secretive."

Kinch was poised in the doorway to the salesroom, his eyes full of terror, hanging on every word. He flinched every time lips moved, waiting for the words of criticism to fall like whips.

"Did you do this?" An echo. A little voice against the course of history. What was she getting at? I asked myself. Something in the way she emphasized the "you" made me look at her carefully. But her face was a mask.

You may well ask why I didn't just tell her I had not been painting in the first place. And I would have to say that having been such a disappointment to her already I could no longer fail her in this, the slightest thing. Leaving had been such a test of will that I had no more strength to resist her kind intentions. She wanted me to be a painter; she wanted our parting to have been of some consequence. She wanted to see herself as a tragic muse—who was I to deny her?

"There's our house in Iowa," I said, "Reverend Penney and the AME Church. That's me in the corner. That's Ariel, right?"

"What's this?" asked Lydia.

"A laughing gull. I told you. It's orange, but it's a laughing gull. It's local fauna. We have them here all the time."

"No, I mean this."

She pointed to a leaf near the bottom right corner. I

edged closer and knew right away I was in trouble. Kinch
had painted in the letters H.T., nearly as invisible as spider
webs in the ribbing of the leaf, where a signature should
have gone. I didn't know what to make of H.T. (Harold
Tawdry? Hakim Tantalus? Hezekiah Trench?) and I was
fairly sure Kinch didn't either. I tried to think of
something, tried to buy time, but Lydia wasn't selling. She
stabbed me with her eyes, little ball bearings in her head
shooting steel slivers into my heart.

"Who else paints around here?" she asked, turning to
Ina, her tone unpleasantly reminding me of the county
prosecutor at my recent tree-cutting trial. "Who could
have done this?"

"You mean Tully. . .didn't?" Even my mother was sometimes amazed at the depths of prevarication I could
plumb.

I tried to swallow. My throat was dry. I thought I was
going to be sick, even felt a bit unsteady on my feet.

"Well, there's Wade Fowler and Bethamae Hamsett,"
said Ina. "There's several women." Her eyes wandered
around the room. They lighted on Kinch. "Oliver used to
paint, but he's like Tully. They just drink."

"Who's Oliver?" asked Lydia, her eyes following Ina's
gaze. Kinch was cowering now. I'd never seen a man look
more aghast. He had gone completely white, his eyes
rolling upwards into his head, and his hands scrabbling
like crabs at the doorframe.

"I painted this, Lydia. This is my work. Someone must
have put those initials there when I wasn't looking. It's a
clear case of forgery." I was trying to take charge of the situation, not only to save myself but Kinch as well.

"I've seen paintings like this before," said Lydia, curtly.
"Only one man I know of does anything remotely like it.
Have you ever had anything exhibited in New York, Mr
Kinch? Or Dallas?"

Turning to me, she said, "There are two just like this in

the Dallas Art Museum, one in the Hirschorn, one at the Museum of Modern Art. I've seen dozens of reproductions in art magazines. This is a genuine Horne Tooke. H.T. That's the way he signs them, the signature almost disappearing into the paint."

24

A harsh gurgle emanated from the doorway. Kinch's eyes were like little birds' eggs. He shook his head from side to side as the three of us stared at him.

"Horne Tooke disappeared from his New York townhouse seven years ago," said Lydia, her voice rising with excitement. "It was in the middle of a divorce trial and everyone thought he'd gone bughouse or committed suicide. He just went out one night to buy a roll of toilet paper and disappeared. He was already famous as a painter's painter when he vanished. Afterwards prices for Horne Tooke paintings went through the roof because, of course, people figured there weren't going to be any more. But this is one. This is a brand new Horne Tooke."

She had her eyes glued on Kinch the whole time she spoke. Her words had the same effect as pouring acid on an earthworm. He trembled with shock, tears hanging in his eyelashes.

"Shit, Kinch!" I exclaimed incredulously, "after all these years, you go and stiff me with a forged painting?"

"No, Tully," said Lydia, sounding implacable, "that's not what I'm saying—I'm saying that man is the missing Horne Tooke, whatever name he goes by now."

"Kinch!" I gasped, the voice of a doomed man who sees the avalanche coming.

I flapped my hands at my sides, exhaled through my nose loudly. I felt at once migraine-ish and yet lightheaded, a strange mixture of imminent pain, blank desolation and airy freedom. There I stood, unmasked, stripped bare, suddenly unencumbered by the normal

154

day-to-day worries of life. It was the same way I had felt in
Louisiana, in Elysium.

Suddenly I didn't care any more. I was a man caught in
the exhaust of the flame-thrower of Lydia's scorn. I was
naked to her. All my illusions, lies, constructions were as
ash. I had nothing left with which to hide my egregious
failure. And yet, looking at her, I felt only the excitement
of being close to a woman I loved.

Lydia glanced at me, crushing me into the floorboards
with the weight of her contempt, then stepped toward
Kinch, her hand outstretched.

"Horne Tooke, I presume."

Kinch shook her hand weakly, his eyes pregnant with
appeal.

"There's a reporter from the *L.A. Times* on the set today," she said matter-of-factly. "We've got time to make
tomorrow's edition. We can send photos on the wire from
Gainesville. I bet I can have every major art journal and
the *New York Times* down here by tomorrow night.

"Mr Tooke, I can sell this picture for a minimum of
$80,000. I have a standard gallery contract in the bunga-
low. Have you got any more?"

Kinch shook his head emphatically.

"Good, then we don't have to worry about flooding the
market. We'll hold the painting back and concentrate on
selling the story—where you've been for the past seven
years, why you were hiding, what made you give up the
life of a famous artist for poverty and obscurity.

"Damn, I wish I had a line on some of your other paintings. I'll have to get on the phone to New York tonight before the story breaks—"

I had never seen her like this, Lydia as a business-
woman. She was thinking out loud, strutting the halls and
boardrooms of power in her mind. It put me to shame;
she was living my fantasy. I recalled the stacks of *Fortune*,
my three-piece suits, my dreams of six-digit bottom lines,

and Lydia's sarcasm. Out on her own she had blossomed. She was no longer the sleeping Lydia, the sexy Lydia, the Lydia of the suntans and graceful movements, or even Lydia the mother. Her tone was cool and calculating, her eyes like nailheads.

Kinch had slumped to the floor, his back resting against the doorjamb, his head sunk to his chest, his mouth opening and shutting like a fish in a tank. His eyes flitted from Lydia to the painting and over to me. He felt in his pockets for cigarettes, then spilled a whole pack of Picayunes onto the floor when he tried to shake one into his mouth.

I knelt down and gathered them up, then lit one in my own mouth before passing it to him.

"Thanks, Tully," he said, his voice a well of courtesy.

He had a face like a Labrador retriever's with its leg in a steel trap.

"It's not true, is it?" I said, half-asking, half-reassuring him.

Once a polite young man had come to the store, asking if I'd ever heard of a bird named Oliver Kinch. He had worn a tweed jacket and wire-rim glasses, and his head had been bald except for a jet black fringe at his temples. He had shown me an envelope with a Gomez Gap postmark and a New York address in Kinch's hand. My clerk was in his cups at the time and had taken to sleeping most of the day in my boat in the bayous. And the man had looked suspicious. So I put him off. On his way out the door, he had said, "Tell him Paul was here."

"It was my son," Kinch told me later, just before lapsing into the peculiar staring catatonia characteristic of Farzey-Burkes Syndrome.

"His wife sold everything that was in his studio," said Lydia, "right down to the rags he wiped his brushes on. She went on the talk-show circuit telling everybody who'd listen how she'd been his muse and collaborator, how she'd sacrificed her own career for his. She had a couple of one-woman shows on account of the notoriety, but she flopped."

"Oliver—$80,000!" murmured Ina, measuring my clerk with new respect. Though Bert Baxter had left her well off, from force of habit she still found men with money sexy, men with gold American Express cards and stretch limousines. Since I had never qualified for as much as a gasoline credit card, it was something she often used against me.

"How much does Tully pay you?" asked Lydia.

"Pay?" said Kinch.

"I made this man what he is today," I said defensively. "That painting is to be sold out of this store. I have an exclusive contract. Correct, Kinch?"

Conversationally, Kinch was batting behind the pitcher. He now said, "Tully did the painting," trying to mend the damage already done.

"Tully, I'm disappointed." Lydia said that. "I thought. . . well, once I had faith in you. I thought you'd make something of yourself. You're worse than when you left Elysium; you're corrupt."

"Liddy," said Ina. Liddy was her pet name for my ex-wife. "Liddy, he's not a bad man. It's my fault. I was a poor mother. After his father left, I didn't know what to do."

"That's right," I said. "I never had a chance."

"Oh Tully," said Lydia, her voice caught between sternness and pity. "Stop making excuses. Stop feeling sorry for yourself. You don't have to be the greatest painter in the world or the richest businessman or, for that matter, the best father. I just wanted you to be something, to be true to the best in yourself. But this—" She indicated Kinch's painting without finishing the thought.

"You did this," I said to Kinch over my shoulder. Then to Lydia, smiling: "Okay, okay! I haven't been painting. How was I to know you were going to show up in my bed one day like a goddamn fairy godmother and start nagging me again to make something of myself? I was afraid that if you really found out what I was doing you'd be ashamed of me.

"I haven't exactly been idle. I'm into nature reproduction now. I know it's not art with your capital A, not the $80,000 a pop variety anyway. But I take pride in my craft and people pay for it."

I stepped back so Lydia could see the stuffing table. I was sure she wouldn't know the difference between a sand shark and a speckled trout, sure she'd be impressed.

The general public rarely suspects the artistry that goes into successful taxidermy. I could do a dozen freehand pencil sketches an hour of game fish brought in for stuffing. Then, when the skins were mounted and shaped, I'd mix up some oils and car paint to replace the natural colors. Still, it's not the sort of thing people take very seriously, and Kinch, for one, professed to despise my craft, often making up excuses to leave the store when I was working.

Lydia glided over for a close inspection on those stilt-like legs, her body moving in a fog beneath its plastic wrapper. She reached with a quivering hand to poke at the fish and test its teeth.

"Tully, it's the most disgusting thing I've ever seen. . .it smells." She put her hand over her face and stepped back.

"That's the paint," I said defensively. "It's not dry."

"What are all those spots?" she asked, muffling her mouth. "I've never seen a shark like that. It's a monstrosity." Her shoulders began to shake; I thought she was crying. Then she began to laugh aloud. "I'm sorry," she snorted. "Sssshhhh! Oh Tully, it's the funniest fish. You're not serious! Oh God!"

I glared at Ina who was watching Lydia with her radar bowl eyes trying to keep up with the shifts and swerves of the conversation.

"It's not one of your best," she said to me.

"Oh, what the hell do I care," I said, losing patience. "Am I still in the god-damned movie?" I asked curtly. "I just want to know if I'm still in the movie."

"Can I use your phone?" asked Lydia ignoring me, her suppressed guffaws threatening to explode her lungs.

"What for?"

"I want to call my gallery in L.A."

"Not on your life." I said. "That painting is staying in this store. Horne Tooke is a personal friend of mine. The work was done on the premises at considerable out-of-pocket expense. What's more, I think Mr Tooke would prefer to do business through someone he knows rather than wake up one morning to find that his work's been whisked out from under him by another art-gallery barracuda. Am I right, Kinch?"

He was standing a little to one side, a forlorn sailor on the sea of life. I put my arm around his shoulder.

"You wanna stay right here, don't you, Kinch? You need people around who love and respect you. You need the tranquil family atmosphere and the knowledge that there are those of us who value you for the wise, witty, creative human being you are rather than for the money they can squeeze out of you, right?"

Kinch shrugged inside his commando sweater.

"Kinch, you'd better back me up on this."

He nodded.

"Let me use the phone, Tully."

I picked up the .38 and held it to Kinch's head.

"Touch that phone and I'll kill him," I said. Kinch stared at me, a little surprised, but he didn't try to escape. I pulled back the hammer. Lydia tossed the hair back from her forehead with her fingers and sighed.

"Don't go crazy on me again, Tully," she said. "Is that loaded?"

"No," I said. "I don't know. It could be. Just don't use

my phone, okay?"

"Tully doesn't have a phone," said Ina. "He owes the phone company for the last one."

"Am I in the movie?"

I knew it looked bad, holding the gun to Kinch's head like that, making an argument about the phone. But I was desperate. I had to salvage something from the tawdry mess.

"Sure," said my ex-wife, plainly vexed. "I wouldn't miss that for the world. You're in. Otto's fixed it. Mr Tooke, we can talk later. I think when we've discussed your position more fully you'll see that I'm being fair. You have a lot to come back for."

Kinch nodded like a dummy. I put the pistol back on the stuffing table.

"Give me the keys to that car," said Lydia.

"What car?"

"Tully, you're a spineless imitation of a man. Give me the damn keys."

I handed her the keys.

Lydia headed for the door. By the stove she paused and examined the David-lamp we had retrieved from the trunk. With a finger she rubbed its curly head. As she did so I had a terrible thought.

"You sent that guy to buy the lamps, didn't you?" I croaked. "You put him up to it. It wasn't a joke, was it?"

Lydia turned her head and our eyes met. Her irises glittered with hurt and disappointment. She had tried to make it perfect for me. She had wanted me to feel good about the lamps when she came to look at my new painting. She had wanted me to feel like a winner on all fronts.

That was Lydia, always trying to protect me, make things work. I don't know where she found the energy. It all swept over me in that moment, the waste, the misery, the missed chances and the chances I would miss in the future. And, worst of all, I wasn't just making myself unhappy, I was doing it to her and Ariel as well.

I reached for the pistol, cocked it, and, as Lydia jumped back, shot the head off the lamp. The bullet went into the cash register with a clang. The head of the statue went up in a puff. Lydia grabbed Ina by the sleeve and dragged her backward out of the store.

Kinch blinked and said, "It was loaded, Tully. Jesus!"

25

An hour had passed in silent meditation.

Looking posthumous, Kinch crashed to the floor like a wing-shot duck, nose down. He had a cigarette in his mouth when he hit. The cigarette bent at a right angle but continued to burn. I could hear him puffing and wheezing; from behind it looked as though his face were on fire. Gripping his shoulder, I jerked him over on his back. The cigarette butt disappeared into his open mouth. Using my stuffing forceps, I picked it out for him. He stared, unblinking, at the ceiling.

We had consumed the remains of the George Dickel by this time, and the amyl nitrites, and Kinch had gone on to sniffing glue from my taxidermy supplies. He had dripped glue down his chin and chest. There were three cigarette butts stuck in the glue and burn holes up and down the front of his sweater. The store reeked of burned wool and sand shark—I had stuffed the damn fish into the stove some time after Lydia left. It had failed to burn satisfactorily.

"God's balls," muttered Kinch. Something like that. It was all I could get out of him.

I knew how he felt. Old yearning-for-love-and-courting-failure Tully had struck again. It was a rerun of the lamp-factory disaster, the delivery-room fiasco, and my earlier abrupt exit from the art world. History repeats itself like hiccups, although this time with certain shameful variations, lying and fraud to be precise, and surprising revelations regarding my clerk's identity.

"This is the crossing of the ways," I said to him. "Tully

162

rotting in Gomez Gap; Kinch, or rather Horne Tooke, guesting on *Lifestyles of The Rich and Famous*. You won't have time for your old friends after this."

"God's balls."

"Say what you will," I continued, "it's goodbye to everything we've built here. No more kibitzing by the fire. No more afternoon naps under the boat awning. No more California Tokay in the Gap Hotel. It's going to be canapés and whisky sours and Beaujolais Nouveau and every aspiring artist and every envious critic with an axe to grind buying you booze and stabbing you in the back before you can say Pensacola."

"God's BALLS."

Perhaps those weren't the words. "Dog's balls?" "Hog's bowels?" He seemed to have burned the inside of his mouth with that cigarette and couldn't speak properly.

"You'll forget us soon enough. I know. . .I know, I could have made things easier for you. But I always said to myself, 'What Kinch needs is backbone!' and so I never did anything to smooth your way. And it's paid off, hasn't it? I expect your wife will be glad to see you. She'll have sold the last of your old stuff long ago. She'll be all-forgiving as long as she can get some new work out of you."

Kinch whimpered.

"You can't fool me," I said. "You're pleased as hell over this. Puts me in my place, doesn't it? Of course, I can't blame you. It's what the whole town wants. Tully Stamper with his face in the mud."

"Uuuurrrfff!"

"Sell me the painting," I said.

I said it offhand, as though I hadn't really been thinking about it. In fact, I hadn't. But talking to Lydia had planted the seed in my head. It was selfish to want to rob her of her discovery. Vindictive, petty, short-sighted, self-defeating. Aside from that I couldn't think of a single thing against it.

Kinch turned to me with eyes wide as paper plates.

"I can't pay you anything on account, but we have to remember the intangibles: the fact that you live here rent-free, the fact that the piece of canvas in question belongs to me, the fact that I more or less commissioned and inspired the work. What do you say?"

"God's balls."

Just then the door out front chimed in a visitor. I raised my head from the floor where I had been resting it close to Kinch's ear. I resented the intrusion; I was half-afraid Lydia had returned to berate me and take the painting before I had reached an agreement with Kinch. But the man standing by the stove was not Lydia.

A halo of wispy blond hairs circled his bald spot. A ring glinted in his left ear. He was wearing mirror shades, a flak jacket, bath sandals, and khaki pants without a belt. A cigar smoldered in one hand; an open Army-surplus canteen sloshed in the other. Over his shoulder hung a tape recorder on a strap.

"We're closed," I said. "Get out."

"Which one of you guys is Tooke?"

"Who wants to know?"

"Harry Bard, *L.A. Times* correspondent. Bard's the name; war's my game."

He grinned and extended the hand with the canteen.

"I'm here to cover the movie. My editors thought I needed a little R and R. Too many boom-booms. My last gig was Iraq. Tanks, mustard gas, human-wave attacks. Unlimited Dexedrine. Captain Pomboul got it in the face and I was calling in air strikes on the walkie-talkie. Next thing I know I'm on a plane to Florida."

"Get out," I said.

Bard sighed. For a moment his eyes focused, not on me, but on something invisible to the normal human.

"Not so fast, buster. Lydia Osterwalder says we got a scoop here. She says Horne Tooke's been hiding out for years like that French painter Gauguin."

"All right. . .all right," I said bitterly. "That's him—for all the good it will do you."

He bent over Kinch's body. "He looks like an artist, sure enough. Went under an assumed name, I heard."

Clinical depression set in. Kinch was going to be famous, famous in that instantaneous Andy Warhol way I had always dreamed of.

"This the painting?" asked Bard, stepping over my clerk's legs into the stuffing room. "My, my, this takes me back. Had a girl in San Sal who got stoned and sprayed her budgy with aerosol paint. Came out something like this. Osterwalder says it's Great Art, and she's supposed to know."

"Kinch," I said, giving his shoulder a shake, "sell me the painting and you won't have to go back, not to New York, not anywhere."

"He got more of these?" Bard interrupted. He knelt beside us and jerked his thumb at the orange laughing gull.

"We're not giving out that information until arrangements have been made for the sale of the work through a reputable dealer," I said.

"Why'd Tooke hide out so long?"

"No comment."

"You mean to say nobody knew who he was all this time?"

"Call our publicist."

"What's your angle anyway?"

"I'll take the Fifth Amendment on that. We'll issue a press release in the morning. Now if you'll excuse us. . ."

"Not talking, eh? You must be Stamper," said Bard. He was grinning again. "She told me about you, said you'd interfere, lie, threaten, beg; you must have been married to her once."

"Fuck you."

Bard puffed his stogie; his eyes went suddenly sad.

"No more boom-boom," he muttered.

He flicked the play switch on his tape recorder. Gunfire, explosions, confused shouts and screams echoed in the store.

"Fao," he breathed, somewhat dreamily. "Iranian break-through; Iraqi counterattack; bombers unloading too high, killing everybody: old Harry B. under a pile of bodies with the tape running . . . "

"God's balls," said Kinch, wincing at every fresh blast. His hands fluttered like injured birds.

"What's wrong with him?"

"I don't know. Could be a stroke. He may never regain consciousness, let alone talk, walk or paint again."

Bard rubbed the bridge of his nose and chuckled to himself as his tape-recorded battle raged on.

"Your ex gave me all the dope," he said. "Anything else I need I'll invent. Tooke here is in no condition to claim I misquoted him.

"I got a disguised-voice call this morning from an FBI narc who wants his name in the papers. A looney-tunes in the bar offered to show me the remains of three missing tourists out in the swamp. It's not as if I weren't up to my neck in story possibilities."

He switched the recorder off.

"No more boom-boom," he murmured, dropping his cigar butt into the stove and disappearing out the front door as suddenly as he had come. There was a soft thump as he went through the hole in the planking, followed by a string of curses.

I turned to Kinch, slapping his face with my open palm.

"Time's running out," I said. "We'll be partners; partners in the factory, partners in the gallery."

His mouth worked as he tried to speak.

"Sell me the painting or I'll turn the dog on you."

He gripped my sleeve and dragged me close to his face.

I bent my ear to his lips, feeling the harsh, corrosive warmth of his breath.

He sighed.

All at once his eyeballs rolled back, his hand went limp, and he began to snore.

26

Some time later, taking a small detour on my way to the boathouse, I found myself stepping through the bar entrance at the Gap Hotel. On the eve of battle the lonesome recruit is naturally apt to seek out the companionship of his fellow troopers. The wind in the palms sounded like distant hoofbeats, and, inside, fifty lusty throats vibrated to the tune of "Dixie."

Unpainted barnboard and cypress shingles on the walls. Fly-specked bar lights on the ceiling. An oil portrait of Neptune and his daughters, all naked with tails like sharks' fins, hung behind the bar. It was rippled and rent, courtesy of the 1905 hurricane. There was only one window and that had a piece of Turkish carpet nailed over it for lack of glass. The atmosphere was warm and wet and smelled of boiled shrimp and hush puppies.

Lydia and Walter sat in a booth against the wall with Ina, Wade Fowler and several men and women out of the *Enquirer* or *Star*. Danger and Ruthie, the birdwoman of Gomez Gap, whispered together over the draft-beer spigots.

Everywhere else it was standing room only. The usual row of moony faces, sweaty and blurred—Bubba, Wheezy, the Maberly boys, Pig Morton—posed along the bar, casting covert glances over their shoulders at the celebrities. The singers were mostly strangers, beer-ad jocks in checked shirts, jeans and tooled cowboy boots. A bald man with a handlebar moustache and a shiny pate had mounted the pool table in his stocking feet to act as conductor.

The instant I stepped through the door, the tumult subsided, a general diminuendo ending in silence. The
crowed parted like the Red Sea for Moses, giving me a
clear run at the bar. Everyone stared, waited.

Not five feet in front of me a man lay unconscious on
the floor in a pool of blood. Part of his face had been
smashed away, an eyeball hung on his cheek. From the
look of things his legs had been broken as well—his feet
pointed sickeningly in opposite directions.

It was a shock. If I had been less preoccupied, if I
hadn't had other matters preying on my mind, I might
have come unhinged at the sight. Instead, I nipped by
him, being careful not to get blood on my hightops, and
went straight up to Danger.

"Where were you last night?" I asked.

"Out."

Her eyes were chill; her speech monosyllabic. It's something I've noticed often enough—ask a woman a direct
question and she turns into the oracle of Delphi.

The man next to me nudged my elbow and nodded at
the corpse on the floor.

"I told him nobody wanted to sing 'Marching through
Georgia,'" he said matter-of-factly. He had forearms the
size of hams, a tilted-up nose beginning to blush with
drink and a thatch of brown hair clipped short over the
ears in a semi-military style.

"There's no accounting for taste," I replied, turning
back to Danger. "Who were you out with? That guy Audie
took in—what was he to you?"

"We didn't want to sing any of that Northern shit," said
my neighbor with the forearms of steel. "Tonight, we're
all Johnny Rebs."

I could see he was drunk. He spoke with a sort of wood-
en insistence shaded with belligerence. For some reason
he had picked on me. I noticed too that the rest of the
crowd had not gone on with its singing.

"Listen," I said, "I'm not interested in your personal problems, or his for that matter. I'm trying to talk to this young woman, trying to conduct a normal conversation."

"Where were you born?"

His tone became suddenly threatening.

"Is this a test?"

"No, no. You gotta say Virginia or Georgia or Florida. Something like that."

"I don't see what that has to do with anything. I was born in New York."

"*He* was from New York."

The crowd pressed in. Someone knelt by the corpse. I felt a hand on the small of my back, a female hand I hoped, rubbing ever so slightly. There was strange look in Danger's eye. The belligerent man prodded my breast-bone with a finger like a jackhammer.

"Where'd you say you were from?"

I turned to Ruthie. "Juvenile aggressive behavior—human."

"You calling me a juvenile?" asked the guy, his chin about an inch from my nose. He had been eating the house shrimp basket.

"Just what this town needs," I said, "an influx of new jerks to add to the old jerks."

I don't know why I said it. Perhaps the idea of being a Confederate gallant had gone to my head. The man was an inch taller than me; from the looks of those forearms he pumped iron for a living. He gripped my parrot-green bowling shirt in his fist and yanked me up on my toes.

I had had about enough aggravation for one day. I put my hands on his shoulder and shoved myself free. Then, taking up a stance, I threw a haymaker punch that struck him square on the jaw.

He barely blinked.

I slugged him again in the gut. Suddenly the place erupted in applause. The big guy grinned and made a playful feint at my nose. I ducked. Twenty palms like sides of beef bruised my shoulders. The corpse on the floor stood up and peeled gore and eyeball from his face. He came over and shook my hand.

"Welcome to the Suicide Club," he said. "These are the best damn stuntmen in America. We were having a little fun at your expense, friend. No offense. Let me buy you a drink."

He was acting the hail-fellow-well-met with me, his hand on my elbow, extra eyeball stuffed in his breast pocket. My knuckles stung. The belligerent man was already down the bar chatting to Roy Maberly's wife Molly, a buxom red-haired woman with come-hitherish eyes.

"I'll have a bourbon," I said quickly before his offer evaporated in the general air of admiration and good humor my heroics had engendered. "Make it a double, Dange. Straight up. No ice. And one for my horse."

She heard me but walked away, a vexed expression on her face, no doubt irritated that despite all my faults and weaknesses I had shown myself a man of mettle. Little things like that made dumping me for Bubba much more difficult.

Ruthie was laughing. It was the first time I'd ever seen her let go and somehow it pleased me.

"They blew into town this morning for the battle scene," she said, "a whole planeload of them from New York and points between. I gather they've been in here all afternoon finding the mood. You're the first one who walked through that door without falling for the corpse gag. I nearly barfed."

"What are you doing talking to Danger?" I asked.

"We're friends. I met her in here three weeks ago. I come in here for a drink at night. It's allowed."

"You're studying me, right? Everywhere I go you turn up. You take over Ina's spare house. You get Kinch to spill his guts. You befriend my dog, which, incidentally, has not been the same since the night he spent with you. Now you are conspiring with my future wife."

"She doesn't know about that. Keep your voice down."

"Doesn't know about what?"

"That you're engaged, or whatever you are."

Danger was down the bar out of earshot, satisfying the demands of commerce. She doled out boilermakers in a row, keeping a running tab in her head, concentrating too hard to pay attention to me. I took this as a slight.

Over at the booth, Walter leaned his head against the wall, staring at Lydia through the bottoms of his sunglasses, coked to the gills. Lydia was watching me. Her face wore a mysterious half-smile, a knowing smile, which seemed odd considering the disappointment she had suffered that afternoon.

"What's your angle anyway? What're you really doing here?" I asked, tapping the bartop in front of Ruthie with my index finger, giving her the third degree.

"Field work," she said.

"*Really.* I mean what are you *really* doing here?"

At this juncture the bar door creaked and swung open, admitting Agent Wachtel and Dr Coyle. The stuntman with the eyeball hit the deck again. His face looked as if he had been blasted with a .410 shotgun at close range. I got a couple of winks from the boys. I had done well. Stout CSA recruit that I was.

The crowd parted, offering up its dead. Coyle at first failed to notice; Julius looked sick to his stomach and went all rubbery in the knees, which you could see because of his shorts.

"Doc, look!" he squealed.

Coyle bent over the body.

"He's dead."

"Shit," said Julius. The drinkers and singer held their peace, letting the two men have the floor. "Somebody call the police. Are you sure, Russell?"

"Sure I'm sure. I'm a doctor."

Coyle knelt down and took the corpse's pulse for a few seconds.

"Dead. Dead as in not walking around, talking—several hours I'd say."

He lifted the gory head and let it drop to the floor with a dull thud, then repeated the maneuver.

"Yup," he said, confirming his diagnosis.

"You Southern boys sure know how to hit a curve," said the corpse, reaching for its eyeball. "This ain't fun no more."

Julius sagged into someone's arms; Dr Coyle helped the stuntman solicitously to his feet and brushed off the seat of his trousers.

"Remarkable recovery," he muttered. "Remarkable."

"Do you now where Danger was last night?" I asked, turning to Ruthie. "I mean, observing things, you might have noticed. We're talking about mating behavior—human—again here."

She blushed. I admit I was letting my sarcasm slip the leash a little.

"What do you want, Tully?" she asked, softly. "What is it you really want out of life?"

She was suddenly earnest and concerned, her face close to mine. It was a strange question and it triggered an absurd response. I believed she was trying to get at me.

"You know," I snapped, "you'd be a helluva a lot more attractive to men if you'd dress properly, take the rubber bands out of your hair and use a little make-up. This kind of get-up went out a decade ago. Somebody just might take you seriously if you'd stop buying your good shoes at the K-Mart Kiddy Counter."

"You should talk!" This was Danger behind the beer spigots, looking fierce.

I stepped back, for I thought she was going to give me a knock. My arm brushed something soft, spongy and familiar: Lydia's right breast. At the same moment, I felt her hand on my ribs, gently shoving me aside.

"Excuse me," she said, her eyes a lyric poem. "We have to go home. Otto will be up all night working on script changes."

Walter was hanging onto her other hand like a primate. He avoided looking at me.

It was a strange position to be in, caught as I was between Lydia's gland, Ruthie's sharp knees projecting from her barstool and Danger's fists. Ruthie was turning shades of red like a trilight, reacting to my insults. Her eyes flitted from Danger to Lydia. Danger was watching me; Lydia grinned, taking it all in.

"Have you two met?" I asked, indicating Danger and Lydia. "Danger Babcox, this is my ex-wife, Lydia Stamper Osterwalder. Lydia, this is Danger, the love of my life."

Lydia said, "Of course we've met. We're old friends, Tully." She winked at Danger. Danger smiled. There seemed to be an understanding between them.

Danger said, "The love of your life—shit!" She said "shit" in that way Southern women have, giving the word at least twenty-four syllables.

I recoiled a little, pressing myself against the warmth of Lydia's hand. All at once, I wanted to curl up in her palm and ride home like that; I wanted her to keep me in a box on her night table. I didn't care about Walter; I just wanted her to let me stay near her.

"Move, you ape!" she said, starting to giggle. She knew what I was doing, trying to make myself the victim of some low-level sexual abuse. "You're drunk. Don't you ever get sober, Tully?"

Everyone was watching, including Julius and Dr Coyle. Suddenly, I began to be suspicious. Lydia and doctors had colluded in my past. She had been very chummy with the medicos at Elysium, babysitting their kids, playing bridge with their wives. I suddenly realized I had to keep my head or circumstances might get beyond my control once more. I couldn't be sure—perhaps it was only the effect of guilt stemming from my attempted art fraud—but I thought I caught her winking at Doc Coyle.

"Ssssssst!"

It sounded like a slow leak in a tire. It was Julius on the verge of an epileptic seizure by the looks of things, blinking nervously, flicking his head to attract my attention and rolling his eyes in the direction of Walter Hebel.

I tried to ignore him; I was somewhat confused. All that femaleness was going to my head. Lydia's question about my relative sobriety had reminded me of so many diagnostic interviews in the past. It occurred to me that she had planned it for the doctor's benefit. I wanted to ask Walter about the precise nature of my part in the movie, but I had already drawn too much attention to myself. I detected a rift with Danger. I had a feeling the women had formed an insidious cabal against me.

Russell Coyle, looking pompous and medical, whispered in Lydia's ear, no doubt suggesting a diagnosis (manic depression? alcohol or drug abuse? unintegrated Oedipal conflict? hypoglycemia? I had heard them all before). I began to panic. I had a sudden attack of that phobia—whatever they call it—fear of people. I started to look for a diversion or a mode of escape.

"This is all your fault," I said, turning to Ruthie. "You've screwed things up. Why don't you—"

"Tully," hissed Julius, "We have to talk." He stealthily jerked his thumb at Walter. "I got a make on him from D.C. His name's not Osterwalder. That's just an alias. He could be you-know-who, Mr B-I-G—"

I turned my back on him, cutting him off, hoping he would shut up. No one else had heard him speak because the stuntmen had gone back to singing "Dixie," of which they plainly knew only the first verse and chorus.

I took Lydia's arm and dragged her and Walter toward the door.

"I have to tell you something," I said. "That man by the bar—he's a narc. Somebody tipped him off about Walter. This town's full of stoolies. Just remember who warned you."

Lydia seem incredulous. She said something I couldn't make out, then nodded to Dr Coyle. I took it for a signal to move in. I swung at Coyle. I had sworn never to go back to Elysium. If Lydia had come all the way from Los Angeles to put me away again, I was surely going to disappoint her. Coyle flinched, and my blow fell short. Even so he dropped to his knees, gasping, as I fled through the door.

27

Inside, the boathouse was pitch-black. Trying to be stealthy, I tripped over the threshold. But the place was empty and I was alone, my dreams of nooky dashed. I lay where I fell, staring into the Gothic vaults of night frescoed with the after-images of my desire, taking uneasy, faltering stock of my day. Had I done anything I could be remotely proud of? Had I done any good? Had I done anything thoughtful, unselfish or unmotivated? No.

I spent a good half-hour trying to convince myself to be sensible and stop wanting so many women. Wanting even one woman was dangerous enough but wanting several at once was like playing with plutonium beyond the critical mass. For a long while after, images of destruction seethed in my brain like a knot of snakes. And I did not sleep except fitfully and in terror.

Along about 3 A.M., though I could not be certain of the precise hour, I heard soft footsteps outside and the boathouse door complaining of its hinges. Beneath the floorboards the Gulf slopped nervously against the rotting piles and the shore rocks like a blind man touching the walls of his room. I took a deep breath as she stood over me. I imagined her head craned to see if I was awake, the look of love-hunger on her face.

I heard the hiss of her clothes coming off, sniffed the odor of her as the things fell in a heap beside my face. And then I felt her nestling against my body, shivering a little before she pulled the edge of the sleeping-bag across herself, not wanting to press too hard for fear of waking me. She was a sermon on gentleness.

I had a lump in my throat for her anonymous love. We lay for an hour like brother and sister, feeling the hot blood travel beneath each other's skin. I slept, I don't know how long, dreaming pleasantly of things I would not remember when I woke.

And when we made love it was like melting together like candlewax, with a quick hardening at the end.

I did not try to speak. We lay breathing each other's breath, ringed in each other's arms. Suddenly, I didn't want to know who she was. Never. I wanted it always to be like this, all secrecy and ignorance. Without names, without words to give us definitions and rights. I wanted my love always to be separate from the world of daylight, this drunkenness of limbs, this ghostly presence, absence of guilt and ties.

With Lydia, I had let other things come between us, painter's block and my desire to become a lamp-stand mogul, which were both symptoms of my anxious and excessive desire to please her, to be a good father to my child, to be worthy of their affection. To tell the truth, I had lost my nerve. I had cleaved to distraction and strayed from the mysterious center of our relationship.

It was clear there in the night that my folly had been to fear too greatly the loss of love. All along I had been obsessed with failure. Nothing short of brilliance, the aura of genius, would conceal from my wife and child the revelation of my ordinariness. I had invented lies, fantasies, selves to impress Lydia (and later Danger); but somehow I had forgotten what it all meant.

It wasn't anything I could stop either; in matters of the heart, I was always in a state.

The woman beside me sensed my sadness, the tiny muscular contractions of fear. She tucked me between her breasts and let my fingers explore the foothills of her spine. She allowed me everything. When she came, I heard the lust words catch in her throat. I wanted to stay like that, tangled among her limbs. Just the smell of her made me want to cry.

She gave me love without reserve.

But in the morning when the distant movie bullhorns woke me with indistinct instructions, she was gone and I lay for a while with my cheek against the place where her clothes had been.

28

Chilly morning. Like waking up in a cabin in Michigan in October. No wind, sky clear, tide out. Sun blazing through the oaks and palms, glistening off the mud-flats like polished chrome.

Ina was already up when I slipped through the Dutch door into her kitchen.

"Okay," I said, "who is it?"

"Who is who?"

"Don't play the eternal innocent with me, Ina. It's Lydia, right? Danger?"

"What are you talking about?"

She seemed genuinely confused; it gave me pause.

"Never mind."

Ina huddled in the breakfast nook with the floral tiles her last husband had hand-carried all the way from Tijuana. She was wearing a silver-fox coat, the one he'd given her just before passing on four years before.

With a pang, I realized she'd been crying, her face bedaubed with mascara deltas and powder arroyos.

"What's wrong?" I asked.

The sight of her crumpled up like that made the backs of my eyelids prickle, her sorrow clashing unpleasantly with my morning mood of post-coital optimism.

"I'm dying," she said, phlegm snapping like bedsheets in her nasal passages, her face a mask of reproach.

"Nothing new then."

I banged open the cupboards one by one looking for her kitchen bottle, suddenly wanting a drink to steady myself. I was beginning to feel unearthly with excitement, as though I might drift up to the ceiling at any moment, as though nothing held me down but the heft of my hightops and the change in my pockets.

"I came for a shave," I said. "I have to look my best for the movie."

Ina frowned, etching sour little darts at the corners of her mouth, and ducked her head like one of Ruthie Appeldorn's seagulls. Fishing in her coat pocket, she withdrew a bundle of soiled and shredded envelopes.

"These came while you were away. They came all torn up like that," she added, lying. "I think they open the mail of known felons they want to keep under surveillance."

Her eyes strayed to the window, which happened to give on the house next door, with the monkey tree in its back yard and the toolshed that Wade Fowler had converted into his studio. The shed was covered with stucco siding, what the locals called nigger brick.

There was a card from my father, the first in a year, postmarked in Terre Haute. No message. The usual. Also a letter from my attorney in Iowa City and a computer-personalized invitation to join the National Rifle Association.

Dear Long Time Patriot:

Patriotism, Old Glory, and good old fashioned national pride are back in the hearts of most Americans.

But for people like you and me and the NRA family, there is nothing new about our devotion and dedication to fight for Freedom, our families, our country.

NRA and our United States was founded by men and women who never ducked a fight. Military, business-men, clergy, farmers, doctors, and Americans literally from all walks of life—and every single one of them dedicated to the FREEDOMS that are the foundation of this country . . .

If I joined up right away, for only $15—a saving of $5 on the regular price, I would get my choice of the NRA's commemorative 'Made for the USA' shooter's caps and become eligible to win a Colt AR-15 semi-automatic, the civilian version of an M16.

My attorney's letter had been mailed the day of my trial. It looked as if Ina had used it to make soup stock. But the nature of its message was clear enough.

> Waldron, Diltz & Ashbach
> 234A Clinton Street
> Iowa City, IA

Tully Stamper
c/o Ina Stamper
Piney Point
Gomez Gap, FL

Dear Mr Stamper,

This is to inform you that the Supreme Court of Iowa has ruled in your favor in the matter of Stamper vs. Parkhurst (referred for upper court decision by Iowa Court of Appeals, December 24, 1983).

We are pleased to inform you that the title to Stamper Lamps Inc. of Solon, Iowa, has been transferred to you *in toto* along with all rights and perquisites pertaining thereto.

Enclosed please find a brief financial statement outlining the current status of Stamper Lamps. We would draw your attention in particular to the matter of TAXES (outstanding) and certain debts and liens that remain to be discharged.

Also enclosed please find a bill for our services to the amount of $3,892.83. As per our original agreement, we would have charged Stamper Lamps, but as the company is in no position to bear the additional debt load, we trust you will see fit to make restitution at the earliest.

Again we are pleased that we are able to bring you these good tidings and that the courts have finally seen the rights of your claim after your long and valiant battle.

Sincerely,

Ancel Ashbach

"This is what comes of going to the law," I said, "instead of, say, directly to the Mafia."

"I'm not lending you any more money," said Ina, as though she could read my mind.

"I could have had Parkhurst fitted with a cement suit and dropped off a bridge into the Mississippi for a tenth the price and saved myself all the heartache and worry."

I totted up the figures.

"I owe the IRS $8,295.38," I said, with a voice like a funeral director, "$913.27 for limousines in Des Moines, $387 to the Iowa City Grapefruit and Racket Club. Old man Sage wants $1,200 in back rent. I owe $17,000 to a dozen, count them, assorted machine-tool manufacturers, dealers, courier companies and maintenance outfits, $5,500 on a courtesy apartment in Chicago, and $37.12 to an art rental agency."

"I was thinking of Bert," said Ina, inconsequentially, oblivious of my personal misfortune.

Bert "Tex" Baxter had been the last great love of her life and a constant source of invidious comparisons with my errant manhood.

He was a muscly ex-cowboy with spindly shanks and a steel-ball gut that hung a good six inches over his longhorn belt-buckle. He had made a million dollars after turning sixty, financing mobile homes in Waco. He had collected bullwhips, dressed Ina in miniskirts, white leather stretch boots and rhinestone cowgirl shirts, and called her "Honey" and "Sweetie-pie."

His affection for her was not of the subtle variety. "Your Ma sure do love the rack, boy. I can't get enough of her hot hairy jumping doughnut!" He was always goosing her in the kitchen and when she'd complain he'd tell her to "Belt up!" and smack her across the jaw.

Ina sighed heavily and said, "You mustn't think too harshly of him, Tully, for he left me all this and he croaked quickly, which was a blessing considering he was so bad-tempered and impatient. Besides, you are an art fraud and a liar and can't make any money. When I die, everything I have is going to your baby, to Ariel. You will have to leave the cottage unless she lets you stay."

"I will beg in the street outside her house. I will embarrass her just like you have embarrassed me."

"You wouldn't say that if you knew her, Tully."

Before she could continue, I fled, loping toward her motel baroque bedroom in search of a razor and gin.

Turning through the door, I found myself face to face with the corpses of thirteen shore rats, lying on their backs on the parquet near the patio sliding door, with their little paws up like Christians praying.

"Jesus," I said.

"Aren't they awful?" Ina mumbled, dogging my footsteps like a bad conscience.

"They were making such a racket last night I had to do something. I ran across the way to get that nice Wade Fowler. But when we turned on the patio light to see them, he went all funny. He nearly barfed."

She uttered the last sentence in a tone of flat distaste.

"I made him lie down on the bed. I shot them myself with the gun Bert gave me for burglars and rapists."

She nodded to where her .22 long-barreled pistol with the ivory grip nestled against a pillow at the head of her bed.

In my mind's eye, I saw Ina trotting next door in her teddy, quivering and squeaking with feminine helplessness, and Wade, inspired to protect her, striding across the intervening alley with the distressed damsel caught in the crook of his large arm, only to fall, suddenly, inexplicably, faint at the sight of the gambolling, chittering rodents, and Ina firing two-handed over his recumbent paleness.

I began to understand her morning tears. The affair with Wade Fowler was turning into a bust. First the diabetic attack in the garage, then failure to evince masculine bloodlust. If she kept up, she'd probably badger the poor frail man to death.

It was no wonder her mind kept turning to Bert, who had consorted with her steadily for eight years and nine months and had suffered cardiac arrest, as it were, in the saddle.

She was all woman, was my mother, she needed that masculine attention. To her, allure was everything. And what with a good poke in the morning and a regular ration of gin, she'd always been able to float through the day in the afterglow.

Watching her, I realized how much alike we were. It was all up and down, peaks and valleys, and no predicting what would happen next. It wasn't a life for the squeamish or the nouveaux pauvres of the spirit with their stereo entertainment centers and their Japanese cars and their major medical plans and their IRAs.

"I guess you want to keep your mind on all the things a person can do and not go dreaming about what might have been," she said, turning off the bedside lamp with a shrug of resignation, leaving the pitiful row of nature's martyrs to rot in peace.

Now I didn't know what or whom she was talking

about—Bert, Wade Fowler or yours truly.

She shadowed me into the bathroom and sat on the toilet while I lathered my face with a bar of soap and began to shave with one of her Bic throwaways. Right away I nicked myself in the corner of the mouth.

"Shit!"

"Your father used to do that," observed Ina blandly. "He had laugh lines like yours. There's an amazing resemblance."

She sniffed noisily and tore off a length of toilet paper to wipe her nose.

"I think Lydia's still in love with you," said Ina. "But you know, it's hard to stay with a man who acts crazy every time you get near him. I don't understand it myself. Either nothing's important to you, or everything's just as important as everything else—which amounts to the same thing. With Bert I knew where I stood."

I nicked myself again. Looking into the mirror, I found that I was sweating under the lather. I needed a drink of water. But Ina's tooth-glass was full of gin and it went up my nose.

"Thank you very much, Mother," I said, hastily wiping my face with a towel. "This is another perfect day left in ruin by your realities."

"You're never going to change, are you?"

I said nothing. There was nothing to say.

I wanted the fantasy more than the truth. I had dreamed of being a great artist, then a captain of industry. Now I had it in my mind to become a Hollywood movie star. I was born six men and had six fates. Though there was some truth in what Ina said—I never knew what I really wanted. Image was everything. Tully Stamper, CSA scout, probably detached from Jeb Stuart's cavalry. Tully Stamper, failed canvas dauber, lamp-stand mogul, lover, husband, father, was about to pass out of existence, was about to be reborn.

29

Out on the street again, I heaved a sigh of relief and whistled a few bars of "Dixie." It was a fine day for filming a battle, not a cloud to blemish the cheek of the sky, and the Gulf running a low swell with white-caps flashing from time to time. The whole town shimmered like a postcard prop.

A stretch limousine idled patiently in front of my former home emitting translucent blue exhaust plumes, waiting for Otto to appear. Ruthie Appeldorn stood on the bulkhead, tossing Wonder Bread to the gulls, which swooped and cried above her head as though they'd discovered a brand-new garbage dump to pillage. I felt a pang of yearning seeing her like that: smiling, at ease, alone with her birds.

While I was watching Ruthie, Lydia emerged from the cottage with a hamper of food clutched to her breasts. Concentrating on her footing, she didn't notice me at first. I set off immediately at a brisk walk, pretending I hadn't seen her, hoping to avoid a confrontation over Kinch's masterpiece before I went in front of the cameras. But before I'd gone five paces, she spotted me.

"Tully," she called. "You'll be late."

"What do you mean?" I asked.

She wore bikini bottoms, thongs and a University of Southern California sweatshirt, with her hair tucked back in a bun. She looked cheerful and self-possessed, which irritated me. A show of anger would have been welcome. Something to indicate she still cared. Suddenly I felt foolish standing there in my parrot-green bowling shirt and hightops, with blood oozing out of my jaw.

"You'll be late. That's all. Don't be so paranoid."

"Oh," I said.

"Tully," she repeated, as I turned away. Her voice betrayed a note of hesitancy and misgiving. "Ariel's here. She's inside. Do you want to say hello?"

She paused to gauge the effect of her announcement, then added, apologetically, "She flew in yesterday afternoon. I wanted to surprise you. But after that painting, well, I didn't know how to handle it."

I was stunned. A flurry of thoughts raced through my head like urchins on a tear, nearly knocking me over. I tried to smile; I must have looked sick. I needed preparation, at least two or three years, before facing my daughter. What if, after all this time, she hated me? God knows, she had reason. Worse, what if she just didn't find me very impressive?

Smiling to herself, Lydia placed her basket on the sidewalk and took my arm.

"Come on," she said. "She could hardly sleep last night thinking she'd meet you today. Otto and she played Fish in the kitchen till 4 A.M."

I allowed myself to be led along the walk, past the lime tree, up the steps and into the living-room Walter had transformed into his movie HQ. A small child sat on the floor in the lotus position, with her elbow on her knee and her chin on her fist, staring at the television. She wore an undershirt and pants with bunny rabbits gamboling in circles round her torso. Her tiny foot tapped nervously against the carpet. She was watching coyote and roadrunner cartoons with the sound off. Wiley Coyote had just dropped off the edge of a cliff, and he had that look on his face, the dawning of disaster. Which was the way I felt.

Walter stood next to the moviola where my ficus had formerly flourished. He was wearing a stop-watch, which hung round his neck on a shoe lace. Nothing else. When I came through the door, he was shouting into the telephone.

"Phoebe, I want to talk to Bernie. It is imperative that I talk to Bernie this instant—"

"—"

"What do you mean he's dead? Did he tell you to say that?

"—"

"Phoebe? Phoebe, listen to me. Don't talk when I'm talking. Listen, Phoebe, it's a very sad day when a producer will not speak with his own director on the telephone. . ."

Lydia gave me a little push from behind just as Ariel turned and saw me in the doorway.

Her eyes widened, bright blue tiles in that munchkin face. Then she smiled. I stumbled forward, feeling utterly witless and ill at ease, entranced by her smile. When she stood up, her tiny belly button flashed beneath her shirt. I could have held both her feet in the palm of one hand. Her hair was still mussed from sleeping. Suddenly she put her fingers to her lips, shyly hiding her delight.

"Is it him?" she asked, looking up at Lydia.

My ex-wife nodded. Her arms were crossed over her chest as though holding herself in. A strange, complex expression played over her face, a mixture of sadness, pride and relief. Walter had stopped talking. I heard the telephone click as he hung it up. It sounded like kettledrums.

Ariel giggled. She shut her eyes and held out her arms for a hug. I knelt at her feet. When I touched her, she lunged. We bumped heads. I could feel her laughter bubbling in her chest like fresh water in a spring. Her lips moved against my collar bone; I could hear her whispering, over and over, "Daddy. . .Daddy. . .Daddy."

Out of the corner of my eye, I noticed Walter tactfully slipping from the room. It broke the spell. Ariel wrenched herself free and ran into the bedroom behind him.

"Don't you feel bad, you," she called out. "I can have two Daddies if I want. I can have a zillion. You come right back."

I glanced at Lydia; she rolled her eyes.

Ariel dashed out of the bedroom again, her white legs flashing like knives, with a sheaf of paper clutched in her fists. Pieces she dropped swirled in her slipstream and fell like leaves to the floor. She plopped down beside me and started scattering pages fanwise for me to see.

"This is Grammy and Grampy's house. This is Grammy in her rocking chair with Spike the cat. This is Momma's gallery with a picture you drawed on the wall."

"Did you draw all these?" I asked.

"Who do you think drawed them?"

Lydia placed a hand on my shoulder, bent forward and kissed Ariel's cheek, then followed Walter into the bedroom without a word. I wanted to put my arm around my daughter's tiny waist; I wanted to bury my nose in her hair again. But she was intent. She didn't want to be distracted. Seeing her like that made my heart ache.

"No, I mean they're so good," I said. "Who'd think a little girl could make such wonderful pictures?"

Ariel rubbed her nose with her palm, once again concealing her pleasure.

"This is Momma having a nap on the beach with a man trying to talk to her. This is one I haven't finished yet. It's your house right here. I started it yesterday, but the rain got on it. I wanted it to be a surprise."

"What's this?" I asked, hardly looking. I'd suddenly become enthralled with the way her hair was parted, fascinated by the wispy blonde fibers springing from her pink scalp, the perfection of this pint-sized shadow-self I'd helped create.

"That's Otto with a camera," she said, affronted by my ignorance.

"Otto," I said. "Is that what you call him?"

"Sometimes."

"No. I mean, does he like you to call him Daddy?"

"Not really."

"What then?"

"Well, he changes it all the time. Sometimes, he's Otto. Sometimes, he's Uncle Eddie Edelstein. Uncle Eddie makes me laugh till my stomach hurts. When we visit Grammy and Grampy Hebel, he's just plain Walter. And sometimes, he's Gimp the Dwarf. Mostly, around the house, he's Gimp the Dwarf.

"Don't you like my pictures?" she asked, looking a little sadly at the ones that remained in her hands.

I knew what she was thinking; I'd been a sensitive young artist myself one. I'd only spent five minutes with my baby girl and, in a fit of anguished jealousy, I'd already hurt her feelings. This was the kind of misunderstanding I had always had with her mother. My agonized mental contortions were as foreign to her as foot-binding in China.

"I know what we'll do!" she exclaimed, suddenly gleeful. She pressed a box of crayons into my hand and turned one of her own pictures over so that the blank side faced up. "You're a drawer, aren't you? Draw me something."

I tried to concentrate. But my fingers trembled as I fumbled a crayon out of the box. My daughter stared at the paper, her chin in her hands, waiting for something miraculous to appear. My mind was empty; I tried a line. It was only a line, but it looked awful.

"Tully can't stay, sweetheart," said Lydia, floating out of the bedroom to rescue me. She had red, rueful lips and her tongue in her cheek. "He's shooting an important scene with Gimp the Dwarf today. He's got to put on his costume and makeup."

"Oh," said Ariel with a vexed grimace. Clearly she considered my drawing more important than Walter's movie, which was gratifying. But in the interest of humoring the large people who shared her life she was willing to let it go. "I'll finish it myself," she added, turning to me.

"You will?" I said. "What do you think it is?"

"It's me, silly."

I examined it closely. You never knew with a line. They were slippery creatures. They could metamorphose into almost anything once your back was turned. This one had careered down the page like a drunk crossing a street, with a sharp little kink near the top. A face with an eyebrow? An elephant with its nose in a box?

"It's me with Grammy Stamper," said Ariel, "trying on hats in her closet. I knew you were going to draw me."

She seemed pleased; I held the page up to the light, getting a little excited myself. For, the moment she spoke, I could see them: Ina on the right with Bert "Tex" Baxter's Stetson perched on her perma-curls and Ariel caught against the curve of her hip, the two of them peering into a three-quarter-length mirror on the bedroom door. I was just reaching with my crayon to start filling in some detail when Lydia interrupted again.

"Tully, you really will be late."

Squatting on her haunches, she plucked the crayon from my fingers. She looked puzzled and sympathetic.

"I know what you're thinking, but you can't go back any more," she said. "It's too late for that. You've got to try to start over, to move ahead, Tully."

She pulled me to my feet, with her hand in my hand, and then propelled me toward the door.

"Now I want you to report on schedule, in costume, properly made up, and with a positive attitude. Don't screw up, okay? You can come over and see Ariel tonight."

"Bye, you," called Ariel from behind her mother's back as I slipped into the sunlight. "Bye, you."

"Goodbye," I answered.

"Bye, you."

The door closed. I heard Lydia laughing behind it. Two hands, one large, one small, waved in the picture window like ragged white flags.

30

I had some trouble with my eyes. Blurred vision, blinking, that sort of thing. At first I thought it had started to rain. I walked over to the bulkhead to be alone with myself till the feelings passed, but Ruthie was there and I found that I was having a conversation with her.

"I've got something for you," she said. "It's a house-warming gift—since you had to move into the boathouse and all."

She handed me a bottle of George Dickel corn whisky with the seal unbroken and a red bow round its neck.

"Danger Babcox told me what you like to drink. Is something wrong?"

"My past just hit me like a runaway train," I said. "I am in confusion. I have no more lies to tell."

"That's good, then."

"How would you know? Only one thing keeps me alive."

"What's that?"

"A secret. Nothing you would understand. Have you dissected any living organisms this morning?"

She seemed about to cry. What had she done to deserve this unprovoked daylight assault? This was life in a nut-shell: receiving pain and dishing it out, both karmas leaving you dry as a husk. I felt like taking a pill but was fresh out.

I tried to think of words to redeem myself.

"What is this?" I asked. "Some special scientific equipment?"

"A cassette recorder," she said. "These are binoculars. This is my field pencil. 2H. Medium soft. Am I that hard to take in other than minute doses?"

Avoiding her eyes, I said, "So, what are the birds up to today?"

"Mating."

"No kidding."

"Laughing gulls court from mid-February to the beginning of April, unlike primates which are never totally free from the tonic stimulus of sexual hormones."

A silence stretched between us like a piece of thin string. The gulls went about their marital chores, cooing, screaming, shoving, soaring. A veritable ferment of feathered domesticity. Oblivious of our presence.

"Speaking of courting," said Ruthie, "how are you and Danger getting along? Have you set a date yet? Will I be invited?"

"Well, we are trying to work things out," I said. "It looks like we'll either never talk again or get married."

She hid a furtive smile behind her binoculars.

"And they aren't necessarily the same thing," I added.

She seemed suddenly very bird-like, with her long neck and large, active eyes. I began to wonder if birds hadn't taken over her personality completely.

"It looks confusing," she said, peering through the lenses, "and sometimes the gulls themselves are confused. They get all balled up in ritual behavior. They're figuring out who is male and female and picking their mates. They do the long call which normally means aggressive behavior—'This is my name and I can fight!'—and they complement it with certain wing movements which make it into a proposition.

After a brief but significant pause, she added, "I like Danger."

"I wish you'd mind your own business," I put in. "I wish you'd stay right out of my life."

"I'm not in your life," she said, showing her feisty streak. "And don't worry—I don't want in. But you're fun to watch. You seem to have a weird capacity just to whack out in an unpleasant way over apparently imagined situations."

"Just once," I said, "—and I don't mean to be critical—just once I'd like to see you in a different pair of pants."

Ruthie sniffed. Her chin went down on her chest, as she struggled to control herself. I didn't mean to be always hurting her, but she was so bad tempered. Men and women are such pains in the ass to one another. It was amazing to me that we had survived so long without killing each other off.

"Why do you say things like that?" she said. "Why are you always trashing everything that's gentle and good in you."

I opened my mouth, but Ruthie said the words. She did not look at my face.

"I'm not supposed to tell you this, but Lydia was showing us slides of your paintings."

"Us?"

"Me and Danger Babcox and your mother and Oliver, although Oliver fell asleep. They were amazing."

It was demoralizing to think that even total strangers had this much command of my private affairs. It cast a shadow on my versions of the truth. It made me suspect conspiracies, or that I was not the man I thought I was.

"When was this?"

"A week ago. Before you got out of jail."

"What did Danger say?"

"She said it made her nervous thinking you were a real artist, not just one who talked in bars."

All at once I found that my hands were shaking. Boohoo, I thought, I had mislaid the better part of myself for five years and now it was probably too late to get it back. T. Stamper, Who was that masked marauder? Why is all love pathological? Why is philosophy never the consolation it's cracked up to be? I wanted to change. But it would be a bitch. I would need strength for the coming struggle.

"I must be off," I said. "I'm in a rush."

She managed a weak smile, a ghost of a smile, hardly a flash of enamel.

"I understand," she said. "There must be some good ironic quote about the understanding woman always finishing last, but I can't think of it."

"Thanks for the bottle," I said, heading for the alley between the cottages. "It's my brand. Danger wouldn't forget."

I scooted away along the street, then stopped as soon as I was out of sight of the cottages and broke the seal on the George Dickel.

I was standing alone on the pavement, a scruffy tall man in sailcloth pants and a bowling shirt, with my head back and the bottle pointing out of my mouth like a telescope, when the limousine drove by. Walter was in the front passenger seat. Lydia, Ina and Ariel sat in the back.

They pretended not to see me.

31

My spirits rose as I crested the hill on Rattlesnake Lane and turned toward the Bayard Onions Memorial High School.

On the dusty football field, husky stunt men, uniformed as officers of the Confederate States of America, drilled columns of extras in countermarches and precision firing. Knots of attentive Rebels were learning the ins and outs of musket-loading and bayonet-fixing. A hot-air observation balloon floated on the tether above the Onions cairn, with Confederate stars and bars flapping from its cable. Hoarse shouts and the clatter of arms rent the morning stillness.

I recognized several regiments by their guidons: the Quincy Guards, the 2nd Florida Infantry, the Crystal River Coast Guards, the Marion Dragoons, the Gomez Gap Avengers—all dashing in their gray and butternut homespun. Closing my eyes, mentally subtracting the milling civilians, newspaper writers and still photographers, the crews, the cameras, generators, lamps, cables, smoke machines, catering trucks, I could almost imagine that it was all true, that we had shifted a time zone or two.

The fact is that, at heart, everyone is a little Southern. We're all suckers for lost causes and underdogs. We all harbor a nostalgia for old things, for things in their place, and share the dream of the barefoot boys charging the guns at Gettysburg.

To tell the truth, and against all odds, I felt elated. I was a desperate character, a bankrupt, deadbeat liar, a man who had abandoned his wife and infant daughter on fraudulent psychiatric grounds. I wasn't even a very good taxidermist. But the night woman of my dreams didn't care. She took me as I was—unless of course she had mistaken me for someone else in the dark (the possibility was momentarily daunting)—and forgave me everything.

Perhaps it was only a hangover; I felt as if my brains would burst, as if they were boiling off through the top of my head. Seeing Ariel had been a shock, there was no doubt about it. But the reunion had gone well; my daughter had not berated me. I congratulated myself for handling the situation with such aplomb. Holding her crayon in my hand, admiring her pictures, seeing my line come alive through her eyes, though, had had a strange effect—my palms were itching, the tips of my digits were palpitating with minute contractions.

Art isn't thinking; it's all in the muscles and nerves. It's all eyes and hands, and who knows what goes on between them? I was torn, I'll tell you. Part of me wanted to get back to the cottage and look at that line. I hadn't seen a line with that much zing in five years. I was pleased and terrified by turns.

But I was in the movie. And at that moment being in the movie seemed like my best chance to get my life back to normal. Maybe I was deluded. Maybe I was in the grip of a collective fantasy, the infectious group hysteria of all Hollywood extras waiting to be discovered. But at that moment it did not seem impossible that I would ride Walter's coat-tails to the top. All I needed was thirty seconds of celluloid, a glorious dash beneath the colors and a good Roman death. The rest would be history.

Otto Osterwalder's limousine was parked next to the cairn. But there was no sign of Walter, Lydia or the baby. I fell into line with a crowd of strangers and pushed my way through the double gym doors under a sign that read:

EXTRAS
Costumes
Makeup
Ordinance
Lunch Vouchers
(The management will not be
responsible for the loss of
personal articles left on
the premises.)

Two harassed women with clipboards in their hands, Walkman earphones on their necks and sunscreen on their nose jobs, drove extras like cattle through roll-calls and supply points. I gave my name and a bright young man with shifty eyes, brown as a buckeye, clad in baggy rugby pants and an Izod shirt with a name tag that said FAUVE WELLBORN III/ASSISTANT TO THE DIRECTOR, took me by the elbow.

"You're late," he said. A stinging rebuke. He spoke with the air of a man who had much to do with the training of dogs.

"What's that?" he asked, pointing to the whisky bottle.

"Prop," I said.

"No, it's not."

"Yes, it is."

"Wait here," he snapped.

The gym smelled of sweat and wintergreen. Everywhere I looked men were changing into Confederate uniforms handed them by costume girls pushing metal clothes racks. The good old boys were in a rare mood, impatient of discipline and spoiling for a fight. There was much grabbing of genitals and nipple-pinching behind the backs of the ladies. Orvis Maberly stalked up and down, snapping suspenders and taking playful slashes with that knife of his. I spotted Wheezy and Edgar Demming in their jockey shorts, trying to conceal themselves from a tanned, wizened crone in a sweatsuit and eight diamond rings, who cackled with delight as they hiked on their battle-stained uniforms and tried to figure out how to fasten a blanket roll over one shoulder.

I was about to offer technical assistance when young Fauve returned.

"Try this," he said, handing me a suitbag on a plastic hanger. "Quickly, please."

He looked down his nose at me, sighed impatiently and checked his wrist-watch, doing his best to make up for that unfortunate name.

I unzipped the bag expecting to find the battlefield gray of a Confederate uniform inside. Instead, there was something that resembled a clown costume. Instead of trousers, I held in my hands a pair of baggy scarlet pantaloons. Instead of a belt, a pale green cummerbund. The jacket was a bolero bull-fighting item, short over the kidneys and trimmed with piping in elaborate Oriental arabesques.

"What's this?" I said. "What kind of trick is this, you little weasel?"

"Oh, I forgot. These too."

He tossed a tote-bag which fell open at my feet revealing a pair of spats, a turban, and a saber with sword-belt and scabbard.

"What the fuck?" I cried. "What war do you think I'm in, the fucking Crusades?"

I was so upset I was nearly rude to him. But then I thought, he's young, ambitious and unscrupulous. He doesn't know any better, being from California and having his brains baked in the sun all his life.

"Zouaves," he said.

"In English!"

"You're a Zouave, Mr Stamper. According to the research department, there were elements of a Zouave regiment attached to the invasion force. It's an authentic outfit, copied from an original in the Smithsonian."

"The invasion force! What are you talking about? This is the defence. This is the Army of the Confederate States of America. We're for the South, for Christ's sake!"

The gym fell suddenly silent. Half the Rebel army in Florida had paused with one foot down a trouser leg to see what the fuss was about. I caught sight of Wheezy's face, an expression of sharp inquiry etched on his features. He nodded to Edgar Demming, who tapped Orvis Maberly's shoulder.

Yanking a uniform rack between us and the rest of the gym floor, I shook the pantaloons under Fauve's superior nose.

"I'm going to look like something that walked out of a harem," I hissed, whispering so as not to tip off my neighbors.

"It was a highly respected regiment."

"On the wrong side, asshole!"

I tossed the pantaloons into a corner and grabbed my boy by his Izod lapels. I wanted to rip out his lungs and break his knees. He thought I was only an extra, a mongrel subspecies of the genus Actoris Hollywoodicus. It made me furious to be underestimated.

But then, I thought, why pollute the stream of my life with his bloated corpse? Especially since I was already under suspicion by those in authority, Sheriff Driscoll to be precise. Audie would have loved to ship me back to Bronson on a charge of common assault just as I was about to redeem myself in the movie.

"It's the wrong uniform," I said, letting him go, smiling amicably to let him know there were no hard feelings, that I was a man of reason and compromise. We could work this thing out between us. There would be no need for the police. "Now get me one of those gray ones just like everyone else has."

"They're all assigned," he said. "This is the proper uniform. Your name is Stamper, T., right? That's the name you gave. You're on my list."

I broke into a sweat; I suspected everyone of plotting to sabotage my role. Walter-Troll, mainly. I scented his crabbed and malevolent intelligence at work. All around me property men and wardrobe assistants were walking up and down, almost on tiptoes, and everyone was changing round about, quiet and constrained.

"You don't understand," I said, speaking with exaggerated calm and precision. "I am supposed to be in the Rebel army. All the extras from Gomez Gap are in the Rebel army."

"Well, you're not." My protests were beginning to irritate him. "I'm to deliver you at the municipal pier. The Transportation Captain has lined up a boat to take you out to the ship, ETD 1100 hours. The crew leader will fill you in when you join your troops."

"My troops!"

"You're an officer. You have lines, right? Put this on."

He handed me a tiny remote microphone with a clip.

"What do I say?" I muttered, dazed by the rapid reversal of my fortunes. A Union officer! A Northerner. . .with lines! It occurred to me I had just discovered a new natural law. Things always get worse. This was no mere run of ill luck; cosmic forces were at work.

"I don't have a spare script," he said. "You can peek at mine. It's fairly easy. One word. 'Charge!' If you need to rehearse, we can go outside."

The boy was getting his confidence back. He was being dry, very dry, at my expense.

I gazed about: Gomez Gappers everywhere. You had the whole town there with all its feuding, love-making and scandalmongering, a world in miniature; you could cover it with your hat. For five years I had called it home. It was my bolt-hole and refuge. I didn't want to turn that world against me.

Something, I thought, had to be done to alter the day's trend toward disaster. But what?

I reached for the sword and placed the tip at his throat.

"Listen, Fauve Wellborn Number Three," I said, "get me something to wear on top. I will not be seen walking around town in this belly-dancer outfit."

The color drained from his face. As soon as I let up on the saber point, he scurried off. Gone for good, I thought.

But I barely had time for a snort of George Dickel before he was back with one of those yellow mackinaw rain slickers over his arm and a sword of his own in his hand. His haste bespoke a new respect; the sword told me he was a man used to dealing with difficult actors.

"Get dressed," he said, throwing me the mackinaw.

I shrugged.

I tried to remember everything Walter had said about the battle scene: the hundreds of extras, the maneuvering ships, the batteries of cameras, the assistant directors with walkie-talkies, the special effects, the utter chaos and confusion of it all. It didn't make sense to think of Walter hovering nearby, shouting "Cut!" every time any little thing went wrong. Once those cameras started rolling he would be powerless. The truth was Walter probably wouldn't even notice me.

My brow furrowed in concentration, as I began to conceive my role anew. A Yankee, yes. A Zouave cutting an outlandish figure in that costume. A garish berserker storming ashore with his blue-clad troops. But also a man of hidden depths, of conflicting loyalties, in short, a Southern sympathizer who, perhaps for the love of his Rebel sweetheart, experiences a change of heart in the heat of battle and recklessly risks his life leading his men into a cunning Confederate trap.

The more I thought about it, the more I warmed to the idea. The scent of danger, even the imaginary kind, was heady. I would be playing a hazardous double game; I could be shot by either side. I could be hung for treason. I could be bayoneted from behind by my own men. I could end up on the cutting-room floor.

But none of that mattered as long as Danger, her girls and the rest of Gomez Gap saw me fighting for the glory of the South.

32

The mood of the crew was upbeat. The morning air was as rife as a barnyard with cluckings, guffaws and whinnies. Snippets of shoptalk assailed my ears like whispered warnings.

"No, shithead. Not even Abraham Lincoln had a quartz crystal LCD wristwatch."

"In New Guinea we were down to eight men and two units. Three caught bilharzia, six went down with heat exhaustion, and the others were stung by killer bees. We also had snakes and tick-bite fever."

"This time, if we lose anybody, we'll get Wardrobe to burn their clothes and say we never heard of 'em."

"So he said to me, 'I don't care what you call it. It's a camera to me and I want you to point it at that and shoot this. Now you're the fucking cameraman—you figure it out!'"

"Listen, dearie, as far as I know you're the only person in the world who thinks the Civil War is a metaphor for AIDS."

I emerged from the make-up tent, spitting Pan-Stick, sweating under the mackinaw. The make-up stung where it got into the shaving cuts. I carried the spats, turban and George Dickel safely concealed in the tote-bag. Fauve Wellborn had confiscated my saber; I was not to be resupplied with weaponry until we were well at sea. But I had strapped the empty scabbard on over the raincoat where everyone could see it.

He ushered me to the football-field end zone and parked me by one of the uprights next to an antique-gun dealer's display booth, with strict instructions to wait until he came to guide me to the pier. (It was no good telling him I knew the way.) Then he took a deep breath from an asthma inhaler, consulted his clipboard and dived precipitately into the crowd.

As soon as he was out of sight, I wandered toward my drilling compatriots. Picknickers, Civil War buffs, the women and children of Gomez Gap thronged the edges of the field. Kibitzers shouted advice to friends and kin in uniform, expressing a certain ribald delight in the spectacle.

Ruthie had left her birds to their own devices for the moment. She stood aloof, with her knapsack slung on her back and her hands in her pockets, looking out of sorts.

Danger was there as well, her hands clenched on a crowd-control rope, her eyes hidden behind sun-glasses. Dressed in black. Her daughters sat cross-legged at her feet, in period costume, waving little Confederate flags in their fists.

Wade Fowler had his easel up and was slapping paint on canvas like a house-painter; somewhere, in some bank lobby or dentist's waiting-room, not far in the future, there would be a brand-new set of Wade Fowler depictions: *Scenes from the Civil War.*

Ina, dressed gaily in a pink pantsuit, chatted amiably with Bethamae Hamsett. I had never known two women who hated each other so much. Yet in any public gathering they would inevitably gravitate toward one another and spend the whole time gabbing like schoolgirls at a reunion.

The troops were practicing fire control: loading, kneeling, pulling the trigger, that sort of thing, on command. An officer yelled, "Aim!" A dozen muskets barked in ragged staccato. Someone had neglected to remove the ramrod after loading. Visible in flight, the rod shot down Rattlesnake Lane and embedded itself in the hardpan at

Oliver Kinch's feet where he was climbing toward the school.

A fat-faced boy, with a beard that looked as if it had been dipped in red ink, gave a little shriek and dropped his weapon.

Kinch hunkered down, confused, peeping warily from side to side, unable to make out where the threat lay. The dog was with him. It sniffed inquisitively at the vibrating ramrod, then marked it for future reference with a squirt of pee. Kinch retreated, finally, into the palmettos that choked the roadway, flicking his fingers for the dog to follow.

"Tully! Tully!"

This was Cecily, standing now, waving her little flag, very animated. Danger had her eye on me, too, though she was making a show of being intensely interested in something in the opposite direction.

"Cecie," I said, as I ambled over, trying to hit a gait half-way between John Wayne and Jimmy Stewart. "If this keeps up there's going to be a heap of casualties by this afternoon."

Cecily was suddenly demure, almost subdued, embarrassed about the spectacle she had made calling me over.

"I wanted to see your uniform," she said, clearly disappointed. "Aren't you wearing one?"

I am a man used to the sight of disappointment in the eyes of others. But Cecily's tone was especially heart-breaking; she being so brave and trying to hide her feelings for fear of hurting mine.

But not her sister.

"He couldn't even get a job as a private," she said. "Are you expecting it to rain, Tully?"

"I've got everything right here," I replied stiffly, indicating my raincoat and the tote-bag. I had hiked my Zouave pantaloons up to my knees, revealing a hairy calf on each leg beneath the hem of the coat; I looked like a man about to commit an illegal sex act. "Only my part's kind of special, and I don't have to suit up so far ahead of time as the rest of these guys."

"Is that true, Tully?" asked Cecily, trying hard to believe in me.

"Of course not," said her mother. Danger glared at me, though all I could see of her eyes was the distorted reflection of my own face in her glasses. "He's lyin' again."

"Bubba told the movie he could ride, but he can't," said Emily. "We saw his horse take him down the Piney Point road heading for the airport."

"Shush!" said Danger. She was irritable with the girls on account of my being there.

"Well, I've got make-up on," I said. "And I've got a weapon here." I slapped my empty scabbard. "I'm in the movie all right. A plum role. But it's a secret."

Emily made a face and Cecily shoved her in the shoulder. Danger ignored me.

"I guess you're mad because I've been telling people we're getting married," I said. Out of the corner of my eye I could see Cecily's face cloud over. "I guess I don't blame you, Danger. I am a trial and a burden. But I have loved you since the moment I set eyes on you in the Gap Hotel five years ago and I know you love me because on occasion we have shared a bed and no woman would do the things you do unless she loved the man she was with."

"Don't shout, you asshole!" said Danger. "You want the whole world to know?"

"Then walk down the hill with me."

"Tully, I'm not in love with you. I ain't going to marry you either."

"You could learn to love me," I said. "I'll make an effort, wear decent clothes, lift weights, cut down on my drinking."

"He sure ain't Willie Weber," said Emily.

Kinch came up, finally, breathing hard and looking

outraged after dodging a dozen infantry columns and firing details. The dog went straight for Cecily and tried to lick her face off.

"Tully," he gasped, "I have to talk to you."

"You finish any more paintings?" I asked.

"It's only eight o'clock in the morning!"

"I knew you couldn't keep up the pace."

"Tully, this is important. It's urgent."

"All right. All right," I said. "I'll be back, Dange. Don't run away now."

Kinch and I stepped over the crowd-control rope and cut in line for a beer.

"That guy," he said, "the one with the big car, he came back this morning. He wanted his lamps back."

His clothes were in a sorry state; his thin white hair stood up in cow-licks.

"Forget the lamps," I said. "Listen, Kinch, I'm getting ready to start painting again. I'm going back to the beginning, back to the mother lode. I'm going to find a cave and hole up for a year, maybe two, make my paints out of dirt and animal fat and blow them on the wall through a bone the way they did it at Lascaux. It isn't going to be for anyone else to see. And I'm not going to make your mistake and sign it."

"He wanted more, Tully. He ordered a gross, a gross to begin with! Do you know what we clear on a gross?"

His eyes glittered. I wasn't sure Kinch even knew what a gross was. But as far as he was concerned, we were talking megabucks.

"I'm a father, Kinch. I have a daughter. She's here. I saw her this morning at the cottage."

"I know all about Ariel."

"I know you know," I said. "I just wanted you to know I knew. This is some kind of plot to make me sane, isn't it?"

"A gross *to begin with*, Tully!" said Kinch, his tone suddenly sharpish, as though he were losing patience with me. "I told him we had a whole boathouseful. He wants them all! He has to leave town on account of some trouble with the police, but he wrote a check to hold them."

Kinch fished a neatly folded slip of paper from his trouser pocket.

"I can't figure Danger out," I said. Just out of earshot she had struck up a conversation with a Confederate captain, a stranger in a long gray coat and plumed hat. "It's like she's afraid of something."

"Yes, you. She's afraid of what you'll do next, of maybe you disappearing."

"Once when a date stood her up, she shaved her head. And you're telling me she's afraid of a little emotional instability?"

"Look, Tully," cried Kinch, holding the check up to my face. "$3,500."

"Listen," I said, ripping up the check and tossing the pieces over my shoulder, "I'm not a charity case. The lamps are a bust, finito, caput! In five years, we've sold two dozen—tops—all to my mother. And that was only because she bought a new one every time a bulb burned out. I have put the lamps behind me."

Kinch gaped as a dust devil picked up the bits of paper and swirled them across the gridiron, scattering them among the drilling soldiers.

"Forget it," I said. "You're beating hell out of the Old Masters with that painting of yours, and I have joined the Union Army. What do you think of that?"

At first, he wouldn't believe me. I had to undo the snaps on my mackinaw and show him the turban.

"Are you crazy?" he said. "You should quit the movie."

"I can't quit. I won't quit. The word 'quit' is not part of the Stamper vocabulary."

Kinch regarded me thoughtfully.

"Walter Hebel, a.k.a. W. Troll, a.k.a. Otto Osterwalder,

has done this to me out of jealousy and spite," I said. "But I am going to desert to the South. It will all turn out. You'll see."

33

We were interrupted by the crash of trumpets and a sudden, throaty roar from the crowd.

All at once the gray-clad warrior horde broke ranks and funneled toward the far end of the football field. Shading my eyes, I spotted Otto Osterwalder emerging from a bunting-draped motor home, acknowledging the troops with a crisp salute.

He looked like a short Prussian general on inspection, or a meat block in jodpurs, not anyone I would take seriously for a minute. But as he climbed awkwardly into the box of a grounded cherry-picker, I became aware of a subtle atmosphere of militaristic expectancy.

And as the crane hoisted Otto aloft, the rent-a-cops in charge of crowd control let their ropes drop, allowing the spectators to surge forward, with a sigh of pent-up relief, till they came in contact with the back row of Confederate soldiers. The football field, which grew about as much grass as a billiard ball in good years, suddenly became a vortex of gaily dressed civilians, dust clouds and tossing flags.

The Gomez Gap Drum and Bugle Corps struck up "Dixie," and pubescent majorettes in spangles and platinum curls flashed their thighs in the sunlight. A line of concessions had sprung up overnight, manned by husky, tank-topped, florid, youngish gentlemen who had an air of attending their ten-thousandth Civil War re-creation. The smell of warm beer in collapsible plastic cups wafted to me along with the stench of hot dogs, mustard, fried frozen fish and hush puppies.

I caught sight of Danger again, where she was being drawn away from me in the suck of the eddying crowd, head erect, either out of sudden pride or to see better. Her sun-glasses gave off a mysterious glint. Her scar shone like a blade.

Otto perched high above the throng with a bullhorn poking out from his mouth, his sweat spattering the faces below. The band kept playing, Otto waited, and slowly the tension built, and all eyes turned to him.

I hadn't the vaguest idea what Walter was up to. It seemed like a lot of hype, a lot of snake oil, just to shoot a scene or two.

He fumbled with the switch on his bullhorn, at the same time motioning irritably for quiet. A half-dozen retainers exploded from the edge of the crowd like a covey of quail and rushed toward the band, waving their arms. The musicians straggled to silence, their conductor striving in vain to lift them to new heights all the while because he couldn't see the urgent signals coming from the movie crew to shut up.

A ripple of laughter filtered through the soldiers, towns-people and tourists.

On the cherry-picker, Otto, God-like, surveyed the mass-es beneath him.

Suddenly, he gestured toward the Gulf, sweeping the horizon with that bullhorn, and intoned, very low, but audible to everyone: "The enemy, ladies and gentlemen! The enemy is at the gates!"

As if it possessed but a single head, his audience swivel-ed to gaze in wonderment over the palm crowns and live-oaks and remnants of primordial hammock into the spar-kling sea.

The sun was like a torch; a heat haze made the horizon all rubbery-looking. Just on our side of the line that divid-ed the water and the sky, a dozen or so black dots bobbed gracefully in the gentle wash that was all that remained of the previous day's storm. Admiral Farragut's U.S. Gulf Squadron, up from its base at Key West, trailing here and there tell-tale wisps of black smoke from its antiquated steam-engine stacks.

It was a tremendous sight. The crowd gave a collective gasp, a thousand tongues began to yammer excitedly.

Otto's fist clenched skyward, bringing them to silence again. It was a masterful moment. I was full of admiration for Walter and his amazing concoction. He had transformed himself all right—these people believed in him.

"The enemy is at the gates," he repeated. He glanced at his stop-watch. "Already we are shooting footage from the shoreline. In three hours, they will be on the beaches and the battle for the town will commence. You are present at an historic moment. The Battle of Gomez Gap has been recreated to the utmost scintilla of accuracy. You who watch from the sidelines will witness the Civil War as it actually took place."

He had dropped much of the phony accent; he merely sounded foreign, which gave him authority. He spoke in a measured cadence, giving equal weight to every word. The crowd was mesmerized, the man had materialized an enemy fleet at their doorstep and metamorphosed them into soldiers of romance and myth. He spoke to them as a commanding general to his troops.

Almost at once I stopped listening for I could tell just from the tone of his voice that Otto Osterwalder was one of those who saw the rational and heroic side of war. He saw Gomez Gap the way it looked on the billboard next to Danger's house and on the plaques and cairns that dotted the town.

While he droned on through that bullhorn about the glory of battle and the town's proud history, I glanced around, surprised to see the faces, pale as upturned palm leaves, straining to catch his every syllable.

They were hungry faces—the same faces that fell for

the evangelists and the Amway distributors. He was telling them why they felt so empty—because they'd been beaten in a great and glorious contest and their way of life destroyed by the carpetbaggers and bleeding-heart liberals and New York plutocrats. They adored being told that their great-great-grandfathers had known what they were doing, herding slaves around, killing Indians and slaughtering each other over states' rights.

Like most of us, the people of Gomez Gap had a deep hurt and a yearning. They wanted purity of spirit and lives full of meaning, adventure and beauty. And what they got was a lifetime of servitude to the fish companies, a respite with the Army, a baton-twirling child-bride with bad teeth and sagging body. They were poor whites; they wanted to be told it wasn't their fault. And here was Otto Osterwalder, calling them to account, like a cross between Huey Long and Garner Ted Armstrong.

He gave them a dream all right, and a promise, and, as he spoke, I could see their expressions change, the men in gray, their wives, lovers, friends and children, as they rediscovered their ancestral instincts.

Slyness gave way to pride; their pale thin faces took on a nobility of mien. Their costumes gave them a mind and a soul. You could see them being swept away by a surge of enthusiasm much stronger than any power of rationality, an enthusiasm that annihilated inertia, caution and fear.

I spotted Danger, Emily on her shoulders, clutching her tiny Rebel flag. Danger was as rapt as anyone in that lake of faces; instead of Willie Weber, she had a regiment of Johnny Rebs.

At the edge of the crowd, Bubba Driscoll sat sternly upon a bay horse, like Robert Lee himself on the fabled Traveler.

There was scarcely a dry eye in the house. That entire gesticulating throbbing hubbub belonged to Otto. And the ersatz wunderkind, manipulator of men, mystic cinematic demagogue, sage of the mighty fallen heroes and demigods, was directing their emotions as a conductor conducts his orchestra.

"Don't think that because you are only an extra you will not be seen," he said. "You *will* be seen because my cameras will search you out. Every one of you.

"Don't exaggerate. Don't look at the cameras and crew. Forget about them if you can. Think only of what you are supposed to be, of your great-grandfathers and mothers, of the great and noble Confederacy. You are no longer in the 1980s. You are in the closing month of the War Between the States, with General Sherman's army pulling the noose tight around Lee in Virginia. It is the eleventh hour. The South is on her knees.

"They are coming," Otto hollered suddenly, his voice rising in stentorian cadenzas, reaching for a finale. "They are coming!"

A Rebel major ran the Florida flag up the high school pole; a snare drum commenced a low vibration, setting the blood aboil.

"The columns of bluecoats, the steamrollers of history, are on the march. They know the truth of the history books is on their side. But what they don't know is that the blood of the Army of the Confederacy still runs in the veins of the people who stand before me.

"I want to see surprise and dismay on their faces when those Union troopers hit that beach. I want to see those blue bellies sick with astonishment when they try to penetrate your thin gray line. I want them to come smack up against the spirit of the Old South as it lives and breathes in this town.

"I want you to go out there today and beat the living shit out of those damn Yankees!

"I know you can be winners, brothers. I know you can soar. This may be just another movie to the big-money boys sitting around their conference tables in Los Angeles and New York. But we know differently. When I look up at the flag fluttering above this town, I tell you I know it is our time to win.

"My friends, my people, I feel you called to destiny! The South will rise at noon!"

Otto finished with his fist punching the air, and the crowd growling, rumbling, and exploding into a roar of cheers and clapping. Not just a roar, but a sound like thunder. A thousand tongues baying, two thousand meaty palms pounding each other raw. Otto had them aroused and full of blood-lust. The band struck up "Dixie," and you could see the folks swaggering, almost dancing to the music. An ancient bag lady who lived on one of the out islands ran up to Bubba Driscoll and tried to kiss his hand.

In front of me, a knot of troopers talked excitedly.

"It's true, I tell you," said a man I recognized as a warden over at the Bronson jail. "They is offering us a $200 bonus if we win. He ain't kidding. They really wants us to go after them Yanks!"

I had a sudden foreboding, a prickle of fear up my spine. Either Walter was a fool or he had failed to understand the average redneck Southerner. It struck me that he had carried his vaunted desire for realism, for dramatic enhancement, too far. Most of the time the good old boys didn't even need an excuse, or a camera turned on them, to practice violence. Most of the time, they were just mean without any reason.

I thought, suddenly, of ditching the whole thing, going over the wall with my clerk and setting up again farther south. There were several careers I had not tried yet. I had a yen to do porno movies, sell condominiums, corner the market on some health-food item no one had heard of. But would the night lady of the boathouse know where to find me?

The crowd was thinning, extras heading for the beach,

spectators scurrying toward specially roped-off viewing areas. All at once, I found myself alone with Kinch on the moribund turf, snatches of song drifting back to us as the cheerleaders marched down the hill with the band.

I wish I was in the land of cotton,
Where old times are not forgotten. . .

34

A dolphin surfed our bow wave as Earl Albert's second best mullet-boat-turned-water-taxi sped toward the Union fleet. Earl Albert's second best son, Daken, the one with the fishhook ear-ring, stood at the helm, smoking a joint. Fauve Wellborn hovered anxiously at his side, his nose beginning to burn up with the Gulf sun, his body fastened inside a huge kapok life-jacket.

I sat astern in a K-Mart folding lawn chair Daken had nailed to the deck for sport fishermen. My saber, now back in its scabbard, rested across my knees.

I counted two dozen Yankee ships, from lighters and single-rigged sailboats to sleek paddle-wheelers and three-masted frigates with smoke and flame erupting from gun ports etched in their hulls. Waterjets from exploding special-effects charges pocked the oily water here and there, simulating return fire from the shore batteries.

Behind us, the town looked like an architect's model with its wharves and warehouses and railway spurs, the small mountains of cotton bales and lead pigs for bullets, meadows white with tents, and the bristling defensive line snaking along the waterfront. Hundreds of gulls were up and flying, made nervous and irritable by the booming artillery salvos.

"You want a hit?" Daken asked. He had to shout over the roar of the inboard Evinrude.

He was about thirty and, it was commonly acknowledged, had wasted his life on drugs and fancy women. As he seemed to be enjoying himself, I did not think it was such a waste myself.

"No, he doesn't," snapped Fauve, who was just the slightest bit impatient with me for insisting we stop at the hotel bar for a bon-voyage cocktail.

He had driven Kinch and me down from the high school in one of those Japanese ATVs with a roll-bar, tires like doughnuts, and a buggy-whip aerial. Twice he had gotten lost (driving over Nigger Hill we passed a new Historical Society cairn next to the lynch-tree stump; Kinch said they'd cut up the trunk for commemorative coffee tables).

In the bar, Fauve had told us his life story, how he'd been born in a tract house in Lubbock, how he had changed his life by moving to L.A., how he wanted to die there and have his ashes interred at Spago's or maybe Nicky Blair's.

Kinch had refused to come along on the boat for the ride on the grounds that just living in Florida, surrounded on three sides by water, made him seasick.

Ignoring Fauve, I accepted Daken's joint. The first puff knocked the top of my head off. My eyes rolled back. Everything went dark. I coughed until I retched.

Daken grinned. "Haitian weed," he said, "a little Laotian smack, PCP—"

Fauve made a panicky grab for the wheel as the boat bucked and side-slipped in the swell.

Daken walked away from the helm and started rummaging in an old tackle box. He held up a sweet-pickle jar for me to see. Something gray and shriveled floated in a urine-colored brine.

"Human dick," he shouted. "I bought it in Key West last summer."

I nearly lost my balance as Fauve suddenly let go of the steering wheel and bent over the side.

Daken staggered forward, the wind blowing his hair straight back, just in time to swerve clear of a square-rigged lugger wallowing in our path.

"Woo-woo, Tully," he yelled, grinning, "*Raiders of the Lost Ark.*"

We were slaloming among the lead ships now, heading for a decrepit-looking side-wheeler with chipped paint on its hull and a ten-pound Parrott gun poking over it bow.

I peeped into Daken's tackle box. The little compartments were spilling over with pills and capsules. Black Beauties, Reds, White Cross, Dexedrine, Librax. The bottom open compartment contained a dozen joints, a block of hash, a pack of papers, six Bic lighters and a pipe.

"Don't take those little gray things," he shouted, "they is lead weights for my fishing line."

A little chemical support to see me through the coming battle seemed like just the thing. I popped a Red and a thirty-milligram Dexedrine with time-release spansules into my mouth and sat back in my chair.

Two blue bellies on the deck of the side-wheeler waved; I flipped them a bird. It seemed to me it was bad enough that I had to be part of the invasion force; I didn't have to make friends with it. Anyway I would soon be showing my true colors, turning for the stars and bars when I hit that beach.

The troops on the ship had their flags out, Old Glory and regimental guidons, and bayonets fixed on their muskets. Their faces were camouflaged like commandos' with burnt cork or shoe polish. All at once, something about those faces began to bother me, a tiny nubbin of doubt tugging at the coat-tails of consciousness.

"How come I didn't get any of that camouflage?" I shouted.

Fauve frowned incomprehension and yanked back on the throttle nearly pitching Daken and me into the water. The prow of the mullet boat hit the side-wheeler with a thump and a crack. The huge paddle-wheel idled, still and dripping, just aft of us.

An agile little private with cheeks the color of soot threw us a line. Then he mounted the gunwales and beckoned me to throw my bag aboard.

"Jump!" shouted Fauve.

Daken grabbed the painter rope and wound it in a cleat, then cupped his hands to give me a leg up.

"Hey, is that guy black?" I yelled. I wasn't sure; it could have been the sun in my eyes and that make-up, not to mention the mind-altering effects of the George Dickel and those drugs.

A half-dozen black men leaned over the gunwale. Ebony hands reached over the gunwales to catch me. I beat them off with my tote-bag. Daken peered upward, an expression of sharpened interest etched on his features.

"Jump!" yelled Fauve, as the launch bounced under us in the choppy sea.

Sailors, I thought to myself. They're only sailors. It was a relief. I thought of that lynch tree; even Walter wouldn't be stupid enough to land black soldiers against the good old boys of Gomez Gap. But sailors on the boat, that was okay.

Daken grinned; I stepped on his hands. As the mullet boat rose on a wave, Daken heaved; I dived over the gunwale like a man shot out of a cannon, sprawling on all fours on the deck planks, barking my shins and running slivers into my palms.

I lay where I fell, somewhat dazed, vaguely regretting all the trouble I was going through, planning how one day I would get Walter Hebel's dick in a jar like that.

It was only when the tiny flash-bulb lights cleared out of my eyes that I finally peered about and saw that the entire deck of the side-wheeler was awash with black soldiers in Union blue, peaked caps with chin straps, canteens and bayonet scabbards hanging from their belts.

It was not a good moment for me. But it soon got worse. For Daken Albert's head suddenly appeared above the gunwale.

He took one look, yelled, "Niggers!" at the top of his lungs, then dropped out of sight.

A huge non-com squatted on his hams next to me. Looking up at his face gave me vertigo, so I looked down at the rest of him. He wore light-blue pants and calf-high boots, a cross-belt over his chest and three gold chevrons on his sleeve. The words THE DEEPER IT GOES THE BETTER IT FEELS were enameled on his belt buckle.

He let out a guffaw of laughter and poked me with his finger.

"He's right, Tully. We're all *niggers* here. We're the Eighth Louisiana Rifles, first *nigger* regiment of the line to take part in a seaborne assault by United States troops, heroes of the Battle of Gomez Gap, freers of slaves and death on white ladies."

I felt a little faint; I shook my head. Black dots exploded in front of my eyeballs. I wished he hadn't said any of it, but especially that last bit about white ladies. What if my microphone were on and the boys in Gomez Gap picked it up? What if Daken Albert heard? The words betrayed a certain suicidal tendency of thought which I did not feel comfortable being within nine or ten miles of.

"You have no idea the shit you're in," I whispered, finally, the small voice of beleaguered sanity.

35

"**I** said turn this fucking boat around!"

I had a tussle with my tote-bag zipper; I was so anxious I couldn't get it to work. I hugged the bag to my chest, feeling the George Dickel through the fabric, and peered about.

"Cato!" I gasped as soon as I got a good look at the sergeant's face.

For an instant, with the drugs and all, I thought I'd only been asleep the last two days, had just awakened in fact, safe in my cell. Cato was about to begin a chorus from *The Student Prince*. A breakfast of steaming hominy grits was on the way.

And then I realized once again I was on the boat heading for Gomez Gap with forty or fifty black men passing witless and inflammatory remarks about white ladies. How Cato French, my old cellmate, came to be there seemed no more incomprehensible on the whole than any in the series of events which had put me on that side-wheeler lolling in the Gulf of Mexico with a cargo of black Yankees. The fresh coincidence only served to confirm my sense of futility, the sense that I was being carried along with a tide.

I glanced down, half expecting to see those underpants with words embroidered on them. But his uniform was standard issue, except for that enameled belt buckle which was in character.

Cato stuck out his hand, palm up for a soul-brother handshake, and I slapped it aside.

"Asshole," I said. "Don't even begin to tell me how this

happened. Not one word."

My former cellmate started to laugh again.

"Tully, I'm the only actor on the boat. Since I've even done stunt work before, they made me ramrod for this bunch. My agent stood me bail for this."

"Turn the boat around!" I snarled. "Gomez Gap has had eight recorded lynchings. That's just the tip of the iceberg. They grow up calling them 'colored' TVs. And you are making jokes about fucking white ladies!"

The ship's steam-engine wheezed; the great, dripping side-wheel began to churn; the deck heaved, almost toppling me once more.

A movie helicopter swung over us, hovering a moment while a cameraman hung out the side hatch on a harness. The soldiers scattered over the deck, suddenly intent on playing cards and cleaning muskets. A half-dozen lounged in a circle singing "Old Black Joe." Two little boys sat cross-legged, hunched over a checkerboard on an upturned snare drum.

"Get your head down, Tully," hissed Cato. "Where the fuck's your uniform anyway? You're ruining the shot!"

I was somewhat nonplussed. The sound of the helicopter rotors got into my head; I felt as if my brains were being beaten up in a bowl. I stood on the deck alone, a white man in a yellow mackinaw with a sword at his waist.

As soon as the helicopter sheared off, the troops crowded in, delighted at my astonishment, with the sensation they had created. They slapped my back, undid my snaps, opened my tote-bag and dusted me off, grinning, innocent as altar boys, shaking hands and making introductions. Over everything hung a heavy greenroom atmosphere of nerves and butterflies.

They were Civil War buffs from a club in Dearborn, Michigan, auto workers, with a couple of farming brothers from Wallaceburg, Ontario, whose ancestors had escaped slavery through the Underground Railroad. They had names like Marvis Shoop and Harnell Whitaker, Hassan Assad and Willis Fekette. Every one of them had taken vacation time to sign on as an extra in Walter's movie.

A clean-cut boy with a brass bugle on a strap over his shoulder pushed an antiquated pair of wire-rim spectacles up the bridge of his nose and said, "Mr French has told us you did time for cutting down a lynch tree."

Cato grinned; I had never seen a man enjoying himself so much.

He said, "That and your duds make you an honorary black man. How do you like that, Tully?"

"It makes me want to puke," I said. "I want a transfer to another boat, one of the ones with white people on it."

As soon as I said the words I regretted them. Cato's face clouded over, huge ridges like plow furrows appeared on his forehead.

An auto worker named Woodis, built like a packing crate with hands like shovels, his sideburns flecked with gray, grounded his musket and said, "Now what's your problem, Stamper? You got something against black extras in the movie?"

"Not me!" I said, despairing of ever getting through to these people. "It's them! They make the Ku Klux Klan look like the NAACP!" I made a futile gesture with my sword toward the beach.

"'Cause it sounds like you want to sabotage *our* movie."

"That's not the point!" I shouted. "I don't want to be in the movie. Never mind putting me on another boat. Just get me off this one. I quit."

"Because we're black, is that it?"

Woodis spoke in a deep bass voice, quiet and resigned. He had sad brown eyes. He looked like he had been born in that Union uniform.

"You see, Tully," he said, "you *are* on the boat. We're all together now. It's right that you should be here because the Negro regiments had white officers. But if you don't get into uniform, if you just stand around and refuse to act your part, you'll mess up every shot we're in."

I looked around. They were all ordinary, decent men with jobs and families and a slightly eccentric yen to run around in Civil War uniforms on weekends. They were too ordinary and decent to understand about lynch trees and hatred. They liked being who they were; they were proud of their little corner of history. The worst thing you could accuse them of was harboring a mania for historical accuracy.

But a crowd of disappointed assembly-line workers was the least of my worries. I had to play along; it was my only chance. A new lie to add to the rest. I was impersonating so many people I couldn't keep track of them all. I slipped out of the mackinaw, rolled down my pantaloons and began to button on the spats, drawing any number of envious comments from the troops who suddenly relaxed and began to banter again.

"You got a great part, Tully," said Cato, brushing off my turban and handing it to me. He spoke kindly—we were buddies; we'd done time together. "You don't need to worry. A white officer in among a regiment of black Yankees is a natural shot. You'll be a star."

"Is that supposed to make me feel better?"

"You're sure to make the final cut."

All at once I started to laugh. It was either that or go for his throat. You can't argue with people who have lost the power of thought. Cato grinned; Woodis shook his head and looked at his feet.

I gazed toward the beach. Not far off now. The giant paddle-wheel went shush-shush, churning steadily in the Gulf. Gulls were zipping and diving in our wake. I caught sight of a crab-trap float; it looked like one of mine. On the beach I could see the fascines and sharpened stakes the property men had put up. From time to time, special-effects explosions threw up waterspouts and geysers of sand and flame.

On the hill beyond, the Col. Bayard Onions Battery of 12-pound Napoleons kept up a steady barrage. Next to us, one of the lighters took what appeared to be a direct hit in the bow. The front end came off in a violent blast, showering us with debris. The troops and sailors had all crowded in the stern, then leaped into the water just before the explosion.

I stared at Cato.

"They're all stunt men," he said, calmly. "We gotta take some hits out here or it doesn't look realistic."

The lighter was on fire to the water-line now, already fifty yards behind. The heads of survivors bobbed in the Gulf like corks. Just under the bow, I caught sight of a half-submerged raft.

"Get your head down, Lieutenant," yelled Cato.

"I'm not your fucking lieutenant," I said.

Just then the raft bulged and shot into the air, breaking into a thousand pieces and showering us with spume. A chunk of board caught me over the eye and I fell backwards into Cato's arms.

"I'm hit," I said. "Get me a doctor!"

"Take a sip of this," said Cato, handing me my George Dickel. "I found it in your bag. I'll pass it around—to inspire martial spirit."

"Not on your life, you overgrown lawn ornament." I snatched the bottle from his hand. "And if you say one more word about white ladies—"

Cato started to laugh, showing twice as many teeth as a white man. He tried to slap me a high five but missed.

"Lick your lips, Tully."

"I'm not going to kiss you."

"Oh, shit. That ain't a proposition. I mean for the camera. That's movie talk for 'Good Luck.'"

36

"Where're you going, Stamper?"

I had a hand and a foot on the gunwale, all set to leap except for the scabbard belt, which had somehow tangled itself around my neck and hampered my movements. It looked bad, I knew, but then I had not had much experience with stunt men and special effects, and I didn't trust Cato to tell me ahead of time when we were in line for demolition. Also I had it in my head that I needed a good start on those black guys, otherwise I would have no chance of going into my Southern-sympathizer routine.

"Charging," I said. "That's what I'm supposed to be doing!"

All at once, we scraped bottom. The side-wheeler ground a couple of feet into the sand, then stopped with a jerk. Cato reached to save me, but grabbed air as I toppled head first into the Gulf.

"Charge!" I shouted, jumping up, brandishing my sword and George Dickel, racing to beat my loyal troops ashore, the Gulf of Mexico dragging at my pantaloons as I ran.

Soldiers in blue spilled over the gunwales like paratroops, their boots churning the water to foam, the sun gleaming off their bayonets. A rebel shell took out a barge. All hands lost. Utter disaster. Corpses bobbed in the surf, their blood staining the water like grape juice. I kicked a body in passing, expecting it to be some kind of dummy, floating on its back like that, all bloated and ugly. The guy lifted his head, spouting water, and glared at me.

I was so surprised I tripped over the scabbard and pitched face down in the shallows.

The fall knocked the wind out of me; I lay there a moment or two, trying to make a plan. I opened the George and had a snort. It was either get completely fucked up or wait ten hours to get sober.

The first wave of Union infantry had hit the beach, attacking in drill formation. Long lines of men formed in the surf, then marched forward, officers and little drummers snapping out the cadence a step or two in front.

The Confederate barricades spewed flame and smoke. Musket volleys cracked like thunderclaps. The strange wild Rebel yell that hadn't been heard in those parts for over a hundred years echoed above the waterfront. Special-effects squibs went up, simulating the impact of bullets. Yankee soldiers died in the dozens, snapped back, disemboweled, blown into the air.

"Nice work, Tully," gasped Cato, giving me a start as he dropped beside me. I looked back; the bugle boy and the rest of the ship's complement had hunkered down, covering my sopping wet flanks.

"You run so fast you could have been in the fucking *O*—lympics." Cato laughed, a deep basso-profundo chortle, and nodded over his shoulder. "The troops just want to be in the shot with you. They know there isn't anybody going to cut the white guy out of the movie."

It was a discouraging moment, as I didn't see how I could desert to the Confederates in the company of four or five dozen black men.

My turban was coming unraveled; I wanted to lie there and be dead. I was just getting my breath back when a skinny black youth, jaunty in corporal's stripes, suddenly leaped out of the Gulf with the regimental colors—a set of slave irons twining like ivy on a blue ground and the motto LIBERTY—and sprinted for the Rebel line. Almost as soon as he stood up, they shot him. He staggered, clutched his chest, went down on his knees, still holding the flag aloft, all ham and heroism.

"Charge!" hollered Cato. Right in my ear. I was nearly deafened.

"Charge!" I screamed. I faked a Minié ball in the leg, collapsed, and lay writhing and kicking in the sand.

"Get up, motherfuck. You can't die yet."

"I can't. I'm wounded. I can't walk. Jesus, I'm going to lose my leg!"

Cato jerked me up by the bolero front. Woodis, Shoop and the rest formed up behind me with fixed bayonets, ready for me to lead the attack.

"Charge!" I yelled, twisting free of Cato's grip. I suddenly realized I had misplaced my sword; I was pointing the way with a whisky bottle, menacing the Confederacy with half a twenty-sixer of George Dickel.

Cato noticed it too. With a frown. But before he could say anything, I took off again, zigzagging to try to throw the troops off my tail.

A squib exploded a half-dozen yards away and I dashed for the dust cloud, passing through it like a dream. I was twenty feet from the Gomez Gap militia; I could see Bubba Driscoll sitting sternly astride that horse while two men held its head. Bubba brandished a saber and, from the looks of things, would take an ear off his mount before the fight was over. I sprinted as fast as I could, screaming with terror.

A dozen Johnny Rebs, former neighbors and drinking cronies, leaped to the sandbag parapet with their muskets poised.

"Don't shoot, for fuck sakes!" I yelled. "It's me, Tully! I'm for the South!"

I just had time to see Bubba's mouth form the order "Fire!" and see the jets of smoke spew from the musket muzzles. I was five yards away. Point blank. And though there were no bullets, the effect of the powder charge was devastating. I dropped with a shriek of dismay and lay deaf and still against the redoubt wall.

I had a little snooze. Thirty seconds, no more. When I woke up my ears were chiming discordantly. Private Woodis was beside me, rolling in the sand and moaning, with his hands in his crotch. His cap had come off; except for the silver sideburns he was bald.

I noted with a pang of alarm that my faithful auto workers were all around, on the offensive, determined to force the wall where I had fallen with such apparent bravery. A squat little private with skin the color of chocolate milk nearly stepped on my head trying to scramble over the sandbags. A musket butt came out of nowhere, catching him in the throat. He subsided with a gurgle next to Woodis.

From the other side of the redoubt wall, I could hear Wheezy Wentzel, Orvis Maberly and Bubba shouting excitedly to one another.

"They're all burrheads!"

"Hey, Rebs, they sent us a nigger army!"

Cato's boots came up (I was lying low, scrunched down with my eyes at sand level). I heard him fire his Colt revolver, then he hissed "Shit!" and ducked, squatting on his heels beside my head.

"Shit," he said. "That asshole nearly poked my fucking eye out." His voice betrayed a mixture of surprise and anger. When I looked up he had a gash along his temple and a drop of blood was snaking down his earlobe.

"What's wrong with these guys?" he asked, pointing to Woodis and the chocolate-milk-colored private.

I tried to say "I told you so." In fact I said it but I had momentarily lost my voice. From fright or just general fucked-up-edness.

I located the George Dickel sticking me in the shoulder blade, with the top off. I took a medicinal sip, straining the sand out with my teeth. My mind was so full of electric cattle prods, flaming crosses, bull whips, tar and feathers, lynch trees, all the painful utensils of irate Southern mobbery that my first, second and third impulses were to get completely unconscious before the next thing happened to me.

Four black privates dashed by with a fifth suspended between them like a sack by his arms and legs, blood dripping from his forehead and nose.

Cato's face suddenly tensed and flattened out like a mask. I think he actually went pale, if you can say that about a black man. Yes, he went pale. He was losing his temper. I couldn't have guessed he was losing his temper except that the next thing I knew he had reached across the redoubt parapet, grabbed Wheezy Wentzel by the shirt collar, dragged him down on our side of the sandbags, and given him such a whack across the nose with the side of his hand that I thought his skull was broken.

Wheezy went limp as a scarecrow. Cato let him fall slowly, and he lay quietly beside Woodis with blood oozing out of his nostrils.

It happened so fast I had no chance to warn Cato, to counsel prudence and caution, to let him know his only chance was to play Uncle Tom, make his apologies and beg forgiveness. He had struck a white man in Gomez Gap; he had laid out Wheezy Wentzel, Purple Heart veteran, survivor of a run-in with a Sherman tank, the closest thing the town had to a hero. This wasn't as bad, mind you, as making that unfortunate remark about white ladies. But it was bad enough.

The rest of the Union troops were still going at it hammer and tongs with Rebels up the beach, but nearby the battle had subsided into a shocked and sullen truce. The bespectacled bugler knelt beside the injured men, ministering to them with water from a canteen. The auto workers stood about in knots, confused, dismayed and cowed, gesturing angrily at the ramparts.

Beyond the sandbags, Orvis Maberly was bouncing on his toes in a frenzy.

"Come on, boys," he yelled, "let's get them knee-grows!"

But most of the Gomez Gap militia had alertly retreat-ed a few steps after losing Wheezy like that. From every direction neighboring Confederate units, sensing an un-even fight, were running to offer help.

A public-address system squealed with feedback, then an anxious voice twanged, "Cut! Cut! Is this thing on? Can they hear me? Extras, please resume the offensive."

I gave Cato's trouser leg a tug, and he bent down.

"What happened, Tully?" he said. "Where'd they get you?"

"Never mind," I said. "Can these men drill?"

"What say?"

"I mean they get together on weekends and pretend they're in the Civil War, right?" I directed the question to the bugler who was squatting within earshot.

He pushed his wire-rim glasses up on his nose and nodded.

Cato said, "So what?" His attention was focused up the beach, where civilians with garden rakes and ball bats were vaulting the sandbag rampart and joining the Confederate mob.

"So make a defense, dummy. Make them stand in a square. Like in the movies."

I pointed with the George Dickel. (It will be noted that I indicated a square with yours truly in the center, hoping for the maximum protective effect. Cowardice, I believe, is one of the prime factors in the long-term survival of the species.)

Cato straightened up.

"Form up!" he shouted.

He grabbed the bugler by his instrument strap, nearly strangling him, and shoved him forward to face the Rebels. He found the corporals and dragged them like-wise into place.

"I don't know the fucking orders. Who knows the fuck-ing orders? Make a square. Wounded inside. Stick your bayonets into any of those rednecks who get too close."

The auto workers, warily eyeing the Confederates, seem-ed to hum and vibrate with indecision. Cato yelled, cajoled, browbeat, raced up and down. First one, then another trooper fell into line, half-reluctant, half-determined, with their muskets at the ready.

In five minutes the whole regiment, fifty men, had joined in, standing two deep and shoulder to shoulder in a hollow square, those twenty-inch Civil War bayonets poking out like porcupine quills, quiet and menacing.

Cato ran along the front, tipping the bayonets up with the barrel of his Colt. Then he grabbed Wheezy who was just coming around and dumped him outside the square with a kick in the pants to get him moving.

Voices, squeaky with bravado, drifted on the warm Gulf breeze.

"I said 'Let's get them knee-grows!'"

"Wait a minute! Wait a minute! Let's wait for Bubba!"

"The hell with Bubba. We ain't got time for him to get a divorce from that horse."

"Tully, you white-trash son of a bitch, what're you doing with all them jigs?"

A fist fight broke out, a little eddy in the mob, between one of Walter's professional stunt men who was trying to herd the Rebel extras back to their positions and a Gap-per, it looked like Orvis Maberly. The stunt man knocked Orvis down, but before he knew what was happening, a dozen Confederates jumped him and dragged him away yelling. At the same moment, Bubba limped through the crowd, hatless, with dust from head to foot. No sign of his horse.

Cato tried to help me up, but there was something wrong with my legs and I fell on my ass.

"How long do you think we'll have to wait for the cops?" he asked.

"Not long," I said. "There's the sheriff now."

I pointed to where Vince, on a lead, was dragging Audie from side to side in restless feints at any human being that came too close.

Cato's eyes swept the Rebel mob, his cheek muscles twitching like tiny hearts. He seemed very calm, so calm I wondered what he was on and if he had any left.

It was an hour past noon. Blood soaked into the sand under the harsh Florida sun. Otto Osterwalder's movie had been forgotten; three hundred years of history resurrected. The entire population of Gomez Gap and maybe half the surrounding county had gathered, driving cars and pickups onto the beach where earlier they had been banned for the duration of the battle. Impromptu tailgate parties started up, booze flowed and little Rebel flags fluttered in the onshore breeze.

37

"What's that?" asked Cato, pointing over the heads of the crowd.

A flare went up, trailing green smoke, dropping like a tear of flame.

Beneath it a little convoy of movie vehicles, an open jeep and a mini-van with a camera crew clinging to the roofrack came speeding along the waterline, splashing in the shallows.

I jumped to my feet, then nearly went down again on account of dizziness.

Walter Hebel, a.k.a. Otto Osterwalder, was standing in the jeep, flare gun in hand, bracing himself against the windshield frame like Patton leading his troops. Lydia sat in the back seat, clutching my daughter's hand, looking pale and anxious under the hot sun. Mother and child wore identical sky-blue jersey dresses; together they looked like a miracle of nature.

"That's my ride," I said. "I'm history. I'm out of here."

Cato frowned. Woodis, his face wrenched into a mask of pain, gazed up at me from the sand where he lay.

"Take my advice," I said. I was babbling, finding it difficult to conceal my relief. "Don't hit anybody, be polite, say 'Yes, suh' and 'No, suh,' and, whatever you do, don't mention white ladies."

Walter's jeep nosed its way through the throng of uniformed Rebels, townspeople and assorted drunks and pulled up in no-man's-land, the dead ground between the mob and the auto workers' bayonets, not a half-dozen paces from where I stood. A quartet of jowly rent-a-cops, pot bellies straining at their shirt-fronts, stepped reluctantly from the mini-van and made as if to guard the director.

Walter squinted about, heedless and arrogant, waiting for the crowd noise to subside. Lydia whispered in Ariel's ear and pointed, and my daughter waved. Little fingers carved in light.

I took it as an invitation. I slipped through the ranks of my former regiment like a ghost. In two steps I had my hand on the door handle. Ariel smiled and scrunched over toward her mother to give me room.

"Let's go! Let's go!" I muttered, slamming the door shut.

I glanced back at the auto workers. Cato gave me a look, a Biblical look, New Testament: "One of you will betray me," it said. I shrugged. He pushed his men aside and started toward the jeep.

I tapped the driver's shoulder with the neck of my George Dickel. He was a dried-up little man with gold chains and a face fried brown as an old shoe.

"Step on it, fathead. You want to get hung from a tree?"

Walter tried to shush me with a wave of his hand.

"Wait a second, Tully. I have a completion-bond company on my tail, ready to come in and take over production on three hours' notice. My star has a week left on his visa. If he stays in this country a minute over, the IRS will cut off his balls for taxes. I gotta clear the set and start shooting again or I'm dead."

As he spoke, the mob bulged and surged, threatening to hem in the jeep. Walter's bodyguards glanced warily at one another, shrugged and started to drift back toward their mini-van.

"Don't listen to him," I said to the driver. "Just give it the juice! Move it!" I turned to Walter. "This is all your fault. You nearly got me killed. Not to mention the fact that you are stark raving mad bringing my wife and child onto the beach like this."

He ignored me. Otto Osterwalder had completely taken over his mind. To my horror, he lifted that monogrammed bullhorn to his mouth and started to make a speech.

"Can I have your attention, please?" he roared. "I want you all to return to your places for the assault. I want you to refrain from further personal violence. I want all the unpaid civilians off this set immediately."

Shouts and laughter drowned his words.

"Hey, Ostermonger, who sent us this nigger army?"

"You know what we do with dead niggers in Gomez Gap?"

"Tell him, Bubba."

"We scoop 'em out and use 'em for wet suits."

Walter's face darkened with irritation; he fiddled with the switch on the bullhorn, got feedback, then tried to speak again.

A brick arched lazily through the air, end over end, like a flare, like a signal, like a bomb, like revenge itself, bouncing off the jeep's hood with a thud.

Walter sat down suddenly. Stunned. Suffering an attack of reality. He passed a hairy hand across his eyes. Lydia shielded Ariel in her arms.

"Tully, you have to help us."

This was Cato, breathing hard at my elbow, keeping a weather eye on the mob. The mini-van spun its tires, then tore away down the beach, scattering Rebel extras like ninepins. Lydia's gaze flitted from that handful of black men standing in a square to the townspeople to Cato to me. She seemed suddenly very alert, but not afraid.

"I already helped you," I said. "I told you not to come here."

"Man, get us some transport, buses or something. These rednecks aren't just going to let us walk away. If we can't bust out somehow, they're going to turn us into little grease spots in the sand."

"Buses," I said. "You got it, Cato. Bye now."

It was fast, very fast.

Broken bricks, stones and chunks of wood, not to mention the odd overripe vegetable, pelted down, most of it falling on the auto workers. I had some egg in my hair, nothing worse so far.

Our driver slammed the jeep into gear. I shut my eyes with relief. I made up a brief prayer of gratitude. Dear Lord, thank you, thank you, thank you.

A little girl sitting next to me reached and touched my wrist, a tiny gesture of support in my time of trial.

"Wait!" cried Lydia, giving the driver's shoulder a poke. "Wait a minute!" She pointed toward the auto workers. "Tully, I think some of those men are hurt."

I shook my head in emphatic denial.

"We got five down," said Cato, startled at being addressed by a director's wife. "Broken bones, concussion and one kicked in the privates."

"We'll take them in the car. Help him, Tully."

My mouth flapped open and closed a couple of times. The whole reborn Confederacy was raging closer than you could spit. Lydia had hunched her body over Ariel; I could see it finally dawning on her, the danger they were in. But her eyes were resolute.

"Otto," she snapped, "get those people away from the car."

Walter just sat there staring through his glasses.

Bubba Driscoll, not five feet away, spoke in a mockery of Southern courtliness, "Ma'am, we don't mean no harm. We figure them niggers din't know it was a whites-only beach. We're just going to give them a little object lesson."

I felt depressed, very depressed, almost insentient. I had an aversion to pain, to conflict, to people disliking me.

Cato had already stepped back inside the defensive square to bring out the injured. I hesitated, waited, hemmed and hawed, then ran after him, very nearly sticking myself on somebody's bayonet by accident. I grabbed old Woodis by the arm and tried to get him up on my shoulder in a fireman's lift. I dropped him twice, having some difficulty with the whisky bottle, but finally got him up securely and struggled back toward the jeep, doing a little duck waddle under all the weight.

Ariel huddled on Lydia's lap. The chocolate-milk private had taken Ariel's place. I squeezed Woodis in where I'd been sitting. Two men supporting each other limped out of the square and sat in front, one on Walter's lap. I tried to get in on top of Woodis but Lydia pointed to where Cato was struggling to drag out the last invalid.

I ran back and took the legs. It was one of the drummer boys, out cold, with a goose egg the size of a tennis ball growing out of his forehead. We laid him on top of Woodis and the private, with his head in Ariel's lap. She started petting him like a cat, playing nurse.

I clapped my hands to my sides and breathed sharply through my nose. I reached for the door.

"Okay, let's go," I said, gripping the handle.

I looked back at the auto workers, forlorn and grim, waiting with their muskets while the crowd capered and surged just out of reach of those bayonets, throwing taunts and brickbats.

White fists reached for the jeep and began rocking it gently.

"Tully, get in. We'll bring help for the others," said Lydia, her tone suddenly softening.

Her eyes sought mine. I read the usual mixed signal, concern and exasperation. Not love or faith or fellow feeling.

My legs trembled to leap into the back seat. A hundred million brain cells counseled flight. But Lydia's eyes prevented me. She had given me back my daughter; now it was my turn to return the favor.

Staying on the beach meant trouble, but I was used to trouble. Suddenly, I just wanted to embrace it.

Hero exits gracefully, stage right, bowing. Gracefully, hero exits with a bow, stage right. Bowing gracefully, hero exits stage right.

It was time to be born like Ariel. It was time for the blood and violence. I felt it in my veins—the great wrench was at hand. But I didn't like it.

I banged my fist on the door panel and shouted, "Get going! Get the fuck out of here!"

The jeep's tires threw up wet rooster tails of sand. But the mob clogged its path. It was a monster with five hundred faces and tongues, a thousand arms and legs and eyes. Something ravaged and cruel that had crawled up on the beach.

Mad, smelly Ted Maberly, the youngest of the Maberly brood, elbowed me in the ribs as he took hold of the drummer boy's leg and started to pull. On impulse, I swatted him across the ear with the whisky bottle and he dropped to his knees with a shout.

"Waste him! Waste him!" hissed Wheezy at the top of his ruined voice.

Others took up the cry; I heard the words; I threw the bottle at Bubba Driscoll's head.

"Give me that!" I shouted, grabbing the flare pistol from the dashboard where Walter had placed it.

Cracking open the breech, I shook the spent shell onto the ground. The black soldier on Walter's lap, evidently a man speedy of thought and insight, banged open the glove compartment with his good hand, found the flares and handed me one.

"Duck!" I yelled, and fired two-handed over the windshield.

The smoke jet zipped by Bubba's ear; it flew toward the Gulf creating a path for itself as it went. The stunned crackers watched the sputtering flame skitter across the waves.

Before they had time to react, I had another flare loaded. I held the smoking muzzle pressed against Ted Maberly's ear.

38

The jeep bearing my wife and child and five bogus Yankees went fishtailing along the shoreline and disappeared into the old fiber-factory site now choked with movie vans, semis and motor homes.

I peeked in the box of flares that private had thrown me; there were three left, plus one in the breech.

Ted shifted uneasily. He wore a Confederate corporal's uniform with chili stains down the front. He had mismatched fishing boots on his feet, one orange, one green; how they had escaped the notice of the wardrobe department, I'll never know.

"A life is a beautiful thing," I said. "If I shoot you, sparks will fly out of your eyeballs."

I had the flare gun in his ear and my arm around this throat; Cato stood next to me; the bayonet square was at our backs. Bubba Driscoll knelt in the sand where the jeep had been, shaken and po-faced.

The crackers, momentarily nonplussed by the sudden reversal of events—Tully armed and ready to make a soufflé out of Ted Maberly's brains—had us all surrounded; the thousand-armed monster grumbled and surged fitfully but gave us a good twenty feet of breathing room all around just in case I should lose control of myself and try to shoot someone.

My enemies shouted my name. I could feel the hot sour breath of their rage, though the sentiments expressed were not remarkable for their wit or elegance.

"You're dead meat, Stamper!"

"Tully, you're an ex-living thing!"

A siren whooped. Sheriff Driscoll's Plymouth, roof lights blazing, shot through a gap in the sandbag defences and cut across the beach on the trail of Walter's jeep.

"Your Hollywood friends ain't going to help you," shouted Bubba, waving his cavalry hat after her. He had split the crotch of his uniform pants ducking my flare. "My mama'll see to that. You watch!"

At every turn I was thwarted, persecuted and reviled. This was my life in a nutshell; no matter how I tried, the desert was my lot. I was a prophet in the wilderness. The great are always at the mercy of small men.

But against all odds my optimism had returned. I had imbibed violence from a bottle. I had absorbed mayhem and dismemberment, rapine and pillage. Not to mention those tiny time-release spansules of Dexedrine which continued to explode like mini-hand-grenades in my stomach.

Cato peered at me anxiously from beneath his dusty eyebrows.

"Don't worry," I said, turning to him with a grin. "I have a plan!"

His Union blue was gray with dirt, dry blood caked the side of his face. Someone had hit him with a tomato; seeds were caught in his hair.

"The last plan you had was for you to get in that jeep and leave us here."

"This is a better plan. Trust me. We'll take the boat."

I pointed toward the Gulf where the tide was rising, lapping at the sand only a few yards away. Admiral Farragut's armada stood offshore, riding at anchor. Exploded hulks, abandoned longboats, broken oars, planks and beams, detritus from the attack, washed lazily in and out with the swell. Smoke drifted inland from the side-wheeler's stack; her crew basked on the wheelhouse roof, eyeing the beach with distant curiosity.

"It's not even floating," objected Cato. "The fucking

boat is stuck on the bottom."

"Listen," I said, "it's a good thing one of us has more than white ladies on the brain. Come high tide, she'll float. What'd I just tell you?"

"Trust me." He frowned. Deep furrows suddenly appeared on his forehead. "But what if it doesn't float?"

"If you wait here, you're going to end up looking like Christmas-tree ornaments. Now lighten up and take some risks."

There was a sudden smash like the sound of a junkyard metal compactor. Audie had parked her Plymouth cross-ways across a neck of beach to block the fiber-factory exit. There had been an altercation. One of those customized motor homes, forty feet long with a double set of wheels at the back, had tried to go over the Plymouth. Audie was crawling out through the back window, her hat gone, her uniform in tatters.

Ted's face made a pathetic wheezing sound.

"Stop laughing, Ted," I muttered. "I'm sick to death of you. I'd just as soon put you out of your misery as spit. Now, do as I say. Don't make a sound. Walk in front of me. Good thing you wore your boots 'cause you're going to get wet."

Audie came limping along the beach toward us, kicking up sand with her police brogans, hefting her riot stick, her gray hair floating about her head like a madwoman's.

"All right, let's take the boat," said Cato.

"Let's haul ass!" I said.

"My ass is already out of here!"

I tried to slap him a high five, but missed. I started to giggle. Purely a reaction to worry and stress. I was amazingly drunk. I was ready to face Death in the eye—if only he'd stop weaving.

"Cato, keep your men in formation," I yelled, shoving Ted ahead of me. "Hang tight and follow close. Don't leave anybody behind. You white guys! Yo, Bubba! Keep your paws off my boys or I'll put a rocket up Ted's ass. You hear?"

The mob was a solid ring down to the shoreline. The boat lay thirty yards offshore. I decided to lay down a barrage to clear our path. I tried to part Bubba's hair with a flare. He saw me aim, squealed and dropped on his face in terror, throwing sand up in the air with his hands.

"Bubba," I said, "you know, you can be such a pussy sometimes."

I reloaded, shot from the hip. A gap you could drive a truck through suddenly opened up. The mob just melted away down to the water, giving us a clear run at the side-wheeler. Reloading, I grabbed Ted by the scruff of the neck and dragged him after me into the Gulf.

Slap, slap, slap. I'd lost my spats in the battle. My turban hung down my back. My pantaloons were some cheap material you could see through when they were wet. Stopping half-way to the boat with the water up to my thighs, I turned to menace the crowd with my gun.

The men from Dearborn did their job like aces. They raised a deep, ragged shout and raced down the beach, jabbing at the edges of the crowd with those bayonets. Slap, slap, slap. Cato dashed by, doing knees-up-Mother-Brown, a huge smile on his face. The black men sprinted straight for the boat, barely giving me a glance. I held my gun high to avoid their splashes.

Closing ranks, the crackers ran down the beach after them, making their own version of slap, slap, slap. I spotted Audie coming my way, smashing friends and strangers aside with that riot stick, an eddy in the mob, a force of nature.

Things happened so fast, I was something confused, not knowing quite what to do with Ted. I started to drag him backward to cover me as far as the side-wheeler; we nearly went down when his boots suddenly filled with water. The ship's steam whistle sounded, making me jump.

Beyond the mob, the sandbags and the cabbage-palms, a column of black smoke rose above the roof of my store, which backed onto the waterfront opposite the break-water and fish restaurants. Flames already licked at the shingles.

"My store!" I screamed. "You fucks set fire to my store!"

"You won't be needin' it no more, Tully," shouted Roy Maberly.

My head began to ache at the thought of that $80,000 painting turned to ash.

"I love the smell of burning faggots!" shouted Wheezy, who shared a belief common in Gomez Gap about the dubious sexuality of artists.

"Kinch!" I gasped.

Shoving Ted aside, I dashed toward shore again. Slap, slap, slap. Wading back from the side-wheeler, Cato tried to stop me by grabbing my arm, but I shook him off. I aimed a wild shot into the center of the crowd. But the flare was a dud and dropped hissing and sputtering at Bubba's feet.

I had some trouble reloading; nervousness mostly. A half-empty beer can came arching lazily out of the mob without so much as a by-your-leave and hit me over the eye hard enough to stun a horse. I went down on my knees in the shallows. As I struggled up, a hundred and fifty or so crackers jumped me with violent intent.

A red-haired youth in a corporal's uniform lunged at my head with a garden spade. I tapped him on the nose; he gushed blood down his front and started to cry.

Ted Maberly came crawling out of the Gulf, dragging his waterlogged boots, yellow-eyed, snarling like a dog. When I tried to kick him, he sank his teeth into my ankle and began to shake it like a rat.

Bubba Driscoll raised the Rebel yell and ran at me swinging a saber.

I struck out blindly, holding my head up like a man in a

life-jacket. Next thing I knew I was on my hands and knees with my eyes stung shut. Something solid hit me on the back of the head and I spun down. A whirlpool the color of India ink opened at my feet. I hesitated an instant, then jumped, holding my breath, diving deep, whirling, swirling, down, down, down.

39

There was a faint, irritating buzz inside my cell. Not inside my cell, inside my skull. But then outside what seemed like a cell and was really my skull. And it was all too dark for words until I opened my eyes and saw the Pole Star blinking like a traffic light through the pine needles.

The sound was a mosquito, the first of the season, and it ceased as soon as I became aware of it and felt the prick of its hypodermic just above my elbow which, on top of everything else, made me want to scream.

The Pole Star winked, a cat's eye in the dusky firmament. My mouth was ragged with thirst; it was full of beach sand. There were indistinct foci of pain distributed fairly evenly over the surface of my body. Moving arms and legs, I discovered even more pains. I felt like a bag of broken china. I was certain some of the damage was irreparable.

I heard someone groan and I passed a few anxious moments trying to locate the source of the groan until I realized it was coming from me.

I supposed, at first, that I lay where I had fallen during the melee on the beach. Left for dead. Lost in the night. I stretched out my arm and palpated the immediate area seeking for traces of my fellow combatants, Ted Maberly perhaps, or the bourbon bottle I had flung away. I found roots, shell fragments, something that might have been a snake but which slithered off quickly, a bed of pine needles and a length of heavy dog chain.

I raised my head warily. I was alone.

All around me the swamp trembled with nightlife. I was perched on a hummock about a dozen feet across, water sucking at the sides, a middle-aged pine tree near the center. To this pine I was attached by a length of chain which wound itself tightly around my ankle like a living thing. I could have been a quarter of a mile from town; or I could have been twenty miles from the nearest other human. It was night, and even in the daylight one piece of swamp looks much the same as any other.

I dragged myself to the tree, and, leaning against its trunk, beat the nearby earth with a dead branch hoping to make my little island uncomfortable for reptiles and unpleasant insect life. The effort raised a sweat and sent blood gushing into my head, forcing awareness upon me like bad news.

I sang a song to keep my spirits up. I rattled my chain. I shouted out to Bubba, Audie and the Maberly brothers, making light of the situation. Perhaps, I thought, they had only just left; perhaps they were spying on me at this very moment from the mangroves, waiting for me to die, sipping Ted Maberly's swamp hooch and smoking dope while I succumbed.

Presently, I lapsed into unconsciousness again, and when I awoke found that I had rolled down to the water's edge, the chain galling my ankle but preventing me from drowning.

As the sun came up, I drank the brackish water from my hand. There was mud in it and tiny things that moved about against the whiteness of my palm. I was naked from the waist up and my shoes were gone. All that remained of my clothes were the ballooning pantaloons of my Zouave uniform, tattered and soiled. The skin of my chest and face was livid and blistered. Such a general conflagration of pain came from those regions that I had not noticed it before. I must have lain in the sun for hours to get like that. Which meant I had been unconscious for a day or more.

I went to sleep, and woke with the sun hot upon me again and the full realization of my terrible position. I sucked more water from my hand, then crawled back to my tree and curled up in its shade. Dozing fitfully. Dreaming.

I dreamed of rescue teams combing the bayous and hummocks. I dreamed Danger Babcox and her daughters sitting up nights, biting their hands, waiting for news of me. I dreamed Ariel sobbing quietly and Lydia berating Walter in my former home. I dreamed of my secret boathouse lover, identity unknown. And then I dreamed of Bubba's silence as he drove through town, of the Maberlys guiding search parties in the wrong direction.

Awake, I tried to recapitulate the events which had led me to this lonely island home. The past seemed nothing short of hallucinatory, a cluttered stage where sea-gulls pecked at the feet of marching Civil War soldiers and beautiful women posed tragically over fallen heroes. Vaguely familiar faces mouthed words of warning which I could not understand. I heard bugle calls and the clattering of caissons and disembodied voices whispering.

I woke in the evening when a light rain began to fall, pocking the surrounded swamp water, washing away the grime of my recent encounters. I lay with my mouth open, savoring the drops as they fell, imagining myself become one with the hummock, with the earth itself. It was pitch-black, no stars in the sky. I sat up and rubbed my fingers through my hair, gingerly tapping the lumps. I was hungry.

Rita Braver's Shrimp-Pot served the best plate of shrimp and hushpuppies in town. I liked to go up there of an evening with Danger when the Gulf was calm and lazy, pelicans balancing on the power lines, the sun going down behind them like a giant sweet potato cut in half. We'd start with oyster crackers and smoked mullet dip, followed by a palm-heart salad with dates and fresh

peaches and lettuce and pistachio. After the shrimp, I'd
lick Danger's fingers, though the other diners sometimes
took exception to this and looked down their beaks at us.
Then we'd feed each other frozen key-lime pie till we
couldn't stop laughing.

But this was of the past. Possibly, I had eaten my last
meal. What was it?

I knew nothing about my father. Next to nothing.
There was a mystery to gnaw your final hours into rags. I
had found one photograph in my mother's underwear
drawer when I was eight. Dad astride a British motorbike,
wearing a worn leather jacket and a rakish grin. Ina
denied that it was him, but I have never been easily fooled
by the lies people tell except once or twice. I knew. When
I was twenty-one, I could have been his twin.

Though there was no hard evidence, save for the
postcards, I imagined that he had wandered the West for
several years on that motorbike, well-liked by strange
solitary women he met in cowboy bars. I believed he kept
birds, gyrfalcons, to be precise. Large carnivorous hunting birds with which he had an instinctive affinity and
which he always let free in their prime to mate in the
wild. In his spare time, he would go overseas for the
government.

In 1971, at the age of thirty-seven, he began to commit
a series of spectacular crimes for which he has never been
caught. The man popularly identified as D. B. Cooper
who hijacked a Boeing 727 over Oregon and parachuted
into the Columbia River, that man was none other than
my father. In Montreal in 1976, he used a 50-millimeter
anti-aircraft gun to rob a Brinks truck in broad daylight
and escaped with $7-million.

It was my father who beat out those wily Texans,
Nelson and Bunker Hunt, when they tried to corner the
world supply of silver.

Subsequently, he had earned billions in complicated

arbitrage maneuvers on the New York Stock Exchange—
all for charity.

At that very moment, while his son lay rotting by a pine
tree in the Florida swamp, he was working secretly to free
hundreds of MIAs held in tiger cages by fiendish Viet
Cong renegades.

My Dad. . .

Clouds going by overhead reminded me of Michelangelo's Rondanini Pieta, which he never finished, never
got out of the studio. Looking at it, he grew dissatisfied,
knocked the head off and recarved it without the head.
Then he did a new top and left off the legs.

Once I thought I saw an ivory-billed woodpecker, one
of those extinct fuckers. But it turned out to be a pileated.
It was hitting the tree with its mouth so hard I thought I
was being shot at.

I examined my chains; they were sound and strong,
with a padlock by my foot and another against the tree,
binding the links. The tree stood thirty feet in the air with
branches starting about eight feet from its roots. An idea
struck me, born of desperation and an impulse not to be
idle during my last hours.

After draping the slack chain over my shoulder, I
slipped the loop that circled the trunk up as high as I
could reach and hooked it over an old knot. I had to
jump three times for the lowest branch, and even then I
barely had the strength to drag myself up to its crotch.
When I'd caught my breath, I drew a coil of the slack over
the branch and began to saw it through.

The wood was tougher than I expected; the chain
threatened to slice my palms. But in less than an hour I
had cut deeply enough to be able to snap the branch with
my hands. Then I slipped the trunk loop over the stump
and set to work on the next branch.

If I could climb the tree like that, I might eventually
slip the chain over the top. But it would take days and my

strength would fail long before I succeeded. My mouth was as dry as a biscuit box, yet I couldn't risk crawling down for a drink for fear of being unable to shinny back up again.

I had sawed through the five thickest branches by morning. Once an owl landed a couple of feet from me during one of my rest periods. We looked at each other up there, he somewhat surprised at the class of bird the tree was attracting.

At daybreak, I saw my first vulture, riding a pendulum of thermals, pretending he hadn't noticed my incipient corpse stuck in a tree fork like a piece of flesh on a spit.

I began to falter as the sun rose. I wasn't even half-way to the top. The trunk was thin enough that I could whip the tip of the tree by swinging my body from side to side, but it was still too thick to cut through. Beneath me the bark was knobbled and scarred with the stumps of branches I had sawn or twisted off. I had no shelter up in the pine, no water or food. I could see most of the sur- rounding swamp, I was that high, but there was no sign of rescue.

I was climbing into the sky it seemed, sawing myself a ladder out of a living tree. The sun rose straight above; I was climbing into its heat. I hallucinated. I saw myself as a bird, fiery orange like a phoenix, drawn into the sun.

I watched the vultures, circling level with me now, their eyes staring inward as they turned round and round my tree.

Afternoon found me resting astride a fork, humming a little ditty, unable to drag myself a foot higher. I clasped a twig a few inches above my head, ruefully aware that twelve hours earlier I could have snapped it in my bare hands. Now it seemed to be made of spring steel. The chain felt like so many lead weights.

I took a little nap to get my strength back, then hoisted myself upright, and stood like a tightrope walker, one foot before the other on a branch that bent and swayed with every move I made. I shaded my eyes like an Indian scout and peered about, searching the lush green jungle of the Florida swamp for a sign or an omen.

Instead, I watched benumbed as a harbinger of another sort, a vulture, glided down, stretching its talons to grip the branch above me, just out of reach.

It ogled me, I swear. It examined, weighed, measured and assessed, all with the greatest good humor, clucking and chomping its beak in anticipation. I screamed; it blinked. I yelled. I gave the tree a shake. That scraggy-necked buzzard just stiffened its grip and ruffled its shoulder plumes.

Suddenly, I wanted to murder that vulture. If it was eat or be eaten, I wanted to eat. If I was going to die in that tree, I wasn't going to let this early bird, this overachiever of a vulture, be the one to strip my bones. I balanced myself on that slippery limb like a sailor on a spar. I gave a little bounce and a jump and grabbed the branch the bird was on.

For an instant, I dangled there by one hand, like a Christmas-tree angel, the branch beginning to sag under my weight, and watched the vulture unfold its sooty wings and flap away. Then, all at once, I slipped free, and fell, hurtling backward, end over end, into the thin blue air.

The chain pulled me up with a snap. The pain of it shot through my leg, exploding in my head like a flash bulb, then dimmed into unconsciousness.

40

I heard the hounds of hell barking a welcome. I heard the demons chanting my name. I was on fire already, turning on Satan's spit, my fingers pointing toward the flames.

There was the barking again, a whole pack of hounds.

"It's him!" someone cried. "It's Tully!"

It sounded like a demon, but a familiar one. The dog was yapping happily beneath my face. I couldn't see it; I couldn't see anything. I'd been dangling upside down so long my head was full of blood and my eyes felt like they were ready to jump out of my skull.

"Tully! Tully! We're here, Tully. Hold on till we get you down."

I couldn't get it out of my head that I was dead already. I was aware of light now, but the world was topsy-turvy and spinning slowly so that I had little opportunity to focus on anything. The only spot that stayed still was directly beneath me and there was something resembling a small wolf there. Or a dog.

I heard the scrape of oarlocks. Then a boat hitting the hummock that had become my home. There were human figures that kept moving slowly in and out of my field of vision, their faces taut and white with concern.

"Is he alive?"

"Please don't let him be dead."

"Tully, can you hear us?"

I tried to smile. It must have looked grisly. I felt someone's hands on my shoulder, lifting me, taking the weight off my chained leg. My face was muffled in hair, someone's long chestnut hair, that smelled of fresh shampoo. The smell cut through my senses like a knife, giving a special pain of its own.

I felt the tree shake above me and other arms take hold of my torso.

"Have you got him?" someone called from above. "I'm going to cut the chain now."

"Hurry," said a sweet voice against my ear. "Tully, love, we'll have you down in a minute. Hold on."

I understood then they were angels and I had gone the other way. They had come to save me. Perhaps after all I had climbed into heaven by way of that tree. I hadn't fallen; I had gone clear over the top.

I felt happy. The pain was gone, I was weightless, still spinning. I was flying over the hummock, over the town, over the Gulf of Mexico. I was free.

41

After that, the first indication I had that I was alive was someone whispering, "I think he's coming around."

Until then I had been floating, pleasantly enough, in a white cloud, one of Kinch's canvases. I felt nothing, neither did I smell, taste, hear or see anything. I imagined myself swathed in a cocoon, asleep but dreaming, altering as I snoozed, changing my life. The changeling.

"Tully." A familiar voice.

"Tully, you tried to run away from me again." The tone was soft and non-accusatory. It was motherly, and I was a wayward child. I enjoyed the mild recrimination. "Tully?"

"Lydia," I whispered. I still hadn't opened my eyes and the whiteness had changed to dark. I could smell her, just beyond my nose, so close I felt her breath when she spoke. "Did you save me?"

"It wasn't me," she said. "I'm here though. I couldn't leave until I knew you were all right."

"Leave?" I whimpered.

"Darling, that was very foolish of you. You saved us from a lynch mob. You rescued all those black men. And when they found you, you had almost escaped from that tree. But it was a very close thing. You could have been killed."

I remembered black men on the beach, voices raised against me, the sound of slap, slap, slap and half-empty beer cans thrown at me in anger. I remembered being chained to a pine tree and the moment when I had flown. I had escaped; I had fled Audie's and Bubba's and the Maberlys' retribution.

I opened my eyes.

The room was hospital white; I was surrounded by faces in a blur of white gauze, hair like flowers. Sunlight streamed through the window; black men watered the lawn outside. Two blond heads, one large, one small, arched toward me.

"Why are you leaving?" I asked.

"Otto has already gone back to L.A." Lydia said. "We've been stuck here a week waiting for you to wake up. He'll be frantic."

"Otto?"

"Oh Tully, don't worry about Otto. He carried it off. He called a press conference at the height of the riot and mooned the newsmen. They thought he had planned the whole thing. The Florida authorities are trying to extradite him."

I summoned all my strength, reached over and touched Ariel's cheek with a finger that was almost a claw. She was Lydia in miniature, a tiny facsimile of her mother. She smiled.

"I'm glad," I whispered. A huge lie told in the spirit of magnanimity. "Is Kinch all right?"

"Here, Tully."

Another face bent toward me. Gentle ravaged eyes.

"Was it you who found me?"

"Nameless, the dog, found you," he said gently.

"That's why it took so long."

"We didn't have anything to go on, Tully. We were hunting blind."

"Who are they?" I asked, blinking at a pair of elfin objects, standing nervously with knots of flowers in their hands.

"It's us, Tully," said Cecily, proferring her bouquet. Her eyes were great with awe. "Danger's outside. She can't bear to see you."

"Neither can I," said Emily. "You look awful."

"Where am I?" I asked.

"Hospital," said Cecily. "They found you—I mean your

dog found you—hangin' from a tree in the swamp. It was Audie and Bubba and them who took you there but they won't own up."

"What hospital?"

"Gainesville," she replied. "Nameless and Oliver and the nigger Cato French and Ruthie, they tracked you in the swamp. They rowed by you three times before Oliver looked up and saw you hangin.'"

"Thanks for the flowers, sweetie," I said.

She suddenly touched my cheek with her lips. As quickly as she had done it she was gone, a ghost in the doorway.

"You broke her heart, Tully," said her sister with a sigh. "I expect from the way she's talkin' she'll be a nun one of these days. After seeing you, she thinks there ain't another man good enough for her. She's just like Danger with Willie Weber."

"That ain't true," said Cecily from the door. "You shut your trap."

"We're movin' again," said Emily. "Danger thinks Gomez Gap ain't a fit place to bring up young 'uns no more. If you ask me, which no one does, I think it's a good thing. We had better chances in the Keys."

I was growing tired by then. There were other faces but they began to turn hazy on me. I grappled with consciousness for a moment or two, then let myself slip back into the cocoon.

"Cato," I said as I went under. "How—?"

"We sailed away, Tully" he said. "They were so busy thumping you they hardly noticed we were going. My man, we thought you were a goner."

"I flew, Cato. I flew. I was up in that tree and then I just flew away."

The next day I sat up in bed and took notice of things. The dog Nameless was curled at my feet, snoring to himself. The room was empty except for a lone watcher seated beside my pillow. She was wearing a T-shirt and her breasts bobbed when she moved. Her eyes were a confusion of care and fear and irritability.

"Ruthie," I said, a mixture of surprise and resignation in my voice.

"So I'm not as beautiful as Lydia," she snapped. "I can't help it. And your friend Danger's skipped town. As soon as her kids saw you weren't going to die, she lit out."

"I didn't say anything," I muttered.

"You didn't have to. You're thinking it."

"Have you always been this easy to get along with?"

"Always the critic, right, Tully? You never let up."

She had little tears in her eyes and she stood up and took off her glasses and let her hair down, combing it a little with her fingers.

"Is that better?" she asked.

"No."

She reached across her belly with both hands and skinned her T-shirt over her head, her breasts, white as egg shells, vibrating in the air. She had hair in her armpits and a deep tanned V coming down from her neck. She lay down beside me and let her head fall against my chest.

"I'm probably pregnant," she said.

"We all have problems."

"If I'm pregnant, you're the father, God damn it!"

"I don't want to hear this."

"What eats me up," she said, "is that you never thought it was me in that boathouse and you never asked me if I rescued you or not."

"Please, I'm a sick man."

"I called Baldossaro and quit my fellowship," she said. "I'm through with vivisection."

We made love then and when I shut my eyes I recognized her. She had a quick small body with amazing sensitivities. I had already learned her habits and we ran together like rivers rushing to the sea. She did not hold herself back this time and when she came I was afraid the nurses would hear us and break in. When we were finished, we lay naked on the sheets and the dog licked the soles of our feet.

Some time, as we lay there, I fell asleep again.

After a week I was better and the doctors discharged me. Cato and Oliver were waiting in Ruthie's car, happy to see me, while Ruthie cast jealous glances at the ward supervisor who had kissed me goodbye on the cheek. I was still weak and lay in the back seat with the dog while they talked.

Kinch had decided he would try living as Horne Tooke again and was heading north where he hoped to live off his reputation as long as possible. Maybe a year or two, he guessed. He had received a polite letter from his ex-wife who said she would put him up.

Cato had a job on the West Coast and had bummed a ride with Ruthie as far as she could take him.

As for us, Ruthie had made up her mind that the thirteen-lined ground squirrel needed watching; she thought there might be a book in it, one with illustrations which I could help her with. We were going to drive to New Mexico in easy stages while I got my health back. And Lydia had said she would bring Ariel out to Santa Fe for a visit once we got settled.

We dropped Kinch at a truck stop off the interstate and watched as he boldly approached a driver and asked for a lift. The driver took him and they disappeared down the road, south, in the wrong direction.

Then we set out ourselves for a fresh start in the West, dawdling along the back roads, stopping every few miles so Ruthie could check out some remarkable example of local animal life or take a pee (her way of reminding me that she carried our future in her belly). I felt like an new

man. Hell, I was a new man. And she was a new woman, at
least that was what she told me (somewhat irritably).

I had spent five years in Gomez Gap. It had been adven-
turous, exciting and emotionally up and down, especially
at the end, but there had also been a tone, a flavor I'll
miss. Ruthie calls it the Gap Curse or Florida Brain-Rot,
the fatal attraction, the insatiable weakness.

For example, I will always remember this: Half-tide. A
pair of ibises hunting in single file in the shallow bayou
behind Danger's house, looking like two old men in white
dinner-jackets, with their hands clasped behind their
backs, pecking at the water. Ring-bills plodding in mud up
to their pin feathers. A single, tall, white crane standing
near a clump of sugar-cane on the bank. Against the
cotton-batting clouds that stand low offshore and obscure
Dog Island and Corrigan's Reef, I can see fishermen
motoring up and down the channel, standing in the sterns
of their open crab boats, looking comic in baggy pants,
Wellington boots and baseball caps. And everywhere there
is the sound of boat engines, birds calling and the gentle
insistent tap-tapping of an oyster hammer.

Or this: I am with Danger's girls, digging Indian relics
in a shell mound on Piney Point. The sun squats and
melts on the horizon as the gloom of night creeps in the
east. A fisherman wades with a cast net in the blood-red
Gulf. A cormorant sleeps on a pole. In the thickets
behind us, a rare Florida panther coughs, then yowls like
a woman moaning. The girls reach for my hands. The
sound gets into my bones. Nothing has ever felt this real.
It hurts, it hurts, but it's touched you.